IRONBORN:

CADMORE'S LIST

By: Kyler Wright

This book is dedicated to
my Mom, the original influencer of my
writing dream.

TABLE OF CONTENTS

Prologue

17th street, West Side Chicago

Illinois, U.S.A,

7:00 p.m.

Abraham

Abraham sat in his chair at the circular table as the heated discussion grew louder. With the city at war, none of his fellow leaders could stay calm. Not even his normally quiet son Darius.

Abraham listened to the useless yelling for a few moments before standing up from his chair. "Silence!"

Everyone paused and turned towards him.

"Silence."

The eight leaders all slowly sat back into their seats, still throwing glares at some of the others.

"The news of the Revenant's recent events in Atlanta are alarming, but nothing we did not anticipate," Abraham said. "Although we may not currently agree on how we should react, we must decide now. If Atlanta falls, it may be too late to make a decision."

"The Navys cannot be trusted!" one other leader said, slamming his fist on the table. "The Red Army has held their own in Chicago for many years now without the help of the Navys. We must do this ourselves."

"Father Abraham," another spoke up. "Two separate capital cities have now fallen due to the Revenant's power, both of which were of equal strength to our own. With our city divided, we will not be able to defend against the threat he poses!"

"So we will get aid from somewhere else," another said.

"But where?" the second asked. "Atlanta is the only city that has enough Reds, and they are currently facing the same threat."

"Which is exactly why we must only rely on ourselves!" the first said.The room again began to break into chaos but Abraham held up a hand.

"No."

As the room quieted, he spoke. "As the General of the Red Army, I care deeply about our pride, and about our conflict with the Navys. However, I care much more about our lives. I have decided that the best course of action will be to discuss with the Navys and try to come to an agreement. If that does not succeed, then we will look for new paths." He nodded. "Meeting dismissed."

The room once again broke into chaos and Abraham turned to look at the only quiet person in the room. Leech, who was wearing his white plastic mask as usual, was sitting silently. Leech was very trustworthy but his powers made everyone wary of him. Being one of the only Ironborn in the Red Army, people had a natural hate for him, as being an Ironborn was typically what defined their main rivals, the Navys. Though even for an Ironborn, Leech was very powerful. He was a man capable of miracles.

Looking at his most trusted leaders now falling into chaos around him, Abraham was worried that a miracle might be their only option.

PART I

CALL FOR HELP

1- A Sign Of Loyalty

Torman High School, Sacramento
California, U.S.A,

2:00 p.m.

Flynn

Flynn bit his lip, trying to remember what he had learned in class last week while he had studied for the test. Today was finals day for the first term. After looking at the problem for a few seconds, he made his best guess and turned his paper over, having finished the test.

He leaned back in his chair and took a deep breath. This test meant a lot. He would get in big trouble if he didn't have all A's this term. Not from his parents obviously as they hadn't been around for years, but from Bi.

Even though it had been nearly three months now since they had been removed from the IPA, Bi was still constantly checking in on them, making sure they were keeping up on their schoolwork. It felt odd for Flynn to be able to fully focus on school, not having to worry about fighting or learning that another IPA compound was under attack. Now he and the others in his old squad were worried about things like homework.

School seemed to be exceptionally hard for Ryan yet somehow exceptionally easy for Zane. It wasn't that Ryan

14

wasn't smart, it was just that he didn't want to do his work. The twins and Tarff had previously gone to different schools throughout Sacramento to research Projects they were assigned to but now that they didn't have to worry about that, they were transferred and the five boys all went to school together.

No one had seen Blackeye since the separation, but Bi had told them that she had packed away her suit and was now living a more normal life. She, of course, had always gone to school in normal clothes, but had lived at the warehouse with her suit on.

Bi, being in her mid twenties, had most likely picked up a job, but they hadn't heard much about what she was up to.

Cago was the only one that hadn't seemed to change. All he had ever wanted was a family. A family that didn't fight, didn't separate. Didn't die. And now he felt as if he had failed again. Flynn had been helping him try to get rid of the depression by including him more in everything the group did, but it never seemed to help much. Flynn would have actually found himself down right now, but he had a reason to be happy.

Flynn felt someone grab his hand. He looked to Emily, who was sitting next to him. She smiled at him, knowing he was nervous about this test. She, of course, had finished a while ago, and was probably going to get one-hundred percent. Again.

She squeezed his hand in reassurance as the teacher came by and picked up their papers. All of the grading was done electronically, so they would get their scores back in a few minutes.

Life with Emily was much easier now that he had more freedom, and she'd come hang out at the bakery quite often.

Ryan, Zane, and Tarff had gotten pretty accustomed to their new living spaces at the bakery as well. The twins slept in the room on the third floor and Tarff across the hall from Flynn. He had set up his room like the one at the warehouse. Nothing but his wicker sleeping mat. Flynn guessed it probably reminded him of home, wherever that was. There was another bedroom, but Cago liked sleeping on the couch in the living room upstairs.

No one had gone back into the office since the first day. He had shown them the office, and told them everything that had happened that night when his parents died. It had been locked ever since.

Flynn thought of these things as the teacher scanned in the tests, trying to get his mind off the fact that Emily was holding his hand. Despite all of the times she had done it in the past three months since the Blood Squad attack, he had never gotten used to it. He didn't think he ever would. She could always somehow make him just as happy as ever.

Flynn had made a full recovery from his injuries, although his leg still had occasional stabs of pain from where it had been shattered, and then later shot, by Shark.

For a brief moment, he remembered how Shark had gotten away. The only member of the Blood Squad left. He wondered what Cadmore Industries was using Shark for now.

Flynn looked up to see that the teacher had finished scanning the tests. The rowdy classroom quieted down. The teacher handed back the scores as the class waited in silence.

Not only were his grades important to Bi, but also held great value to him. At Flynn's high school, you had to have an eighty percent or higher to go to activities, which mostly consisted of dances. The first dance of the year was this Friday, in four days, the end of the first term. In this class, the final test could change someone's entire grade. Flynn currently had a B in this class, his only grade that would hold him back from going. He would have to get a ninety percent or higher on the test in order to go to the dance.

The teacher walked up and down the aisles, handing people small slips of paper with their scores written on them. The classmates began talking to each other, some excited because they had passed, and others disappointed because they had not.

The teacher walked down Emily's row. She smiled at the piece of paper when she picked it up. One-hundred percent, as always.

Flynn looked up as the teacher placed a slip on his desk. He flipped it over, nervousness rising inside of him.

Ninety-three percent.

He sighed in relief and saw Emily smiling at the numbers on his paper. The bell rang and they both stood up. Emily hesitated for a second before releasing Flynn's hand.

He shouldered his backpack and walked out of the room with her. "I can't believe that I actually got a good grade."

"Oh, come on," she said. "It's not like you're not smart."

He shrugged. "Some days my brain will do really stupid things. I'm just glad today wasn't one of those days." He saw his friend Dom approaching from down the hall along with Cago and Mia, who had been dating ever since Flynn and the others had been removed from the IPA in the aftermath of the Blood Squad.

Dom man-hugged Flynn, pounding him on the back. The groups joined together and began walking down the hall.

"Did you pass?" Dom asked Flynn as the others separated themselves into a different conversation.

He nodded.

Dom looked over at Emily, who was talking to Mia. "So...are you going to ask her?"

Flynn's brow creased. "Planning on it."

"How are you gonna do it?"

Flynn shrugged,."Don't know yet."

"Don't tell me you're still too nervous to ask!" Dom said. Flynn looked at the ground. "Ah, come on man! You guys have done so much together! You've known her for more than a year now. We both know that you wouldn't feel comfortable with anyone else."

Flynn shrugged again. "I guess you're right."

Dom leaned in to whisper to him. "And by the sound of it, you might have done a little more with her than you are letting on." He puckered his lips and moved his arms through the air, pretending to kiss an invisible person.

Flynn looked at him like he was crazy. "You really think that I would do that? I'm the one who can't even ask her to the dance."

"I don't know, man," Dom said in mock hesitancy. "I think I saw some lipstick still left around your mouth the other day."

"Dom," Flynn said. "Emily doesn't wear lipstick."

Dom's eyes grew wide. "Oh, Flynn got multiple girls going now!"

Flynn punched him on the arm. "Shut up."

Dom started laughing. "Whatever, man."

They got to the end of the hallway and walked outside. The air was warm and the ground was coated with orange and brown leaves. Dom looked toward the front of the school. "Looks like Jackson might be asking Jessica to the dance," he chuckled. "I am going to want to see this. See you later Flynn." Then he added, "You better do it." He ran off.

Mia and Cago, who had been lost in their own conversation for some time now, walked off, leaving Flynn and Emily alone. They reached the edge of the school's front property, the place where Flynn and Emily separated each day. Flynn going to the truck, and Emily going to the bus. His least favorite place on the planet. He was going to change that today.

He stopped and turned to her. "Hey, Emily." She turned toward him, her eyes bright, full of curiosity. She looked so pretty when she was curious. Flynn pushed the thought out of his mind.

"I was wondering if, um..." She looked at him expectantly. He forced himself to finish the sentence, speaking quickly. "I was wondering if you wanted to go to the dance with me."

"Oh my gosh, yes!" She hugged him with excitement. He sighed with relief. She pulled away from him. "Would you want to go with a group?"

"I was thinking Cago and Mia could," Flynn said.

"Cago asked Mia already?" Emily asked.

"Well, if he hasn't yet then he probably will."

She laughed. "You're probably right." She looked over to where the two of them were talking. Cago looked scared out of his mind. He hadn't asked her yet. "Those two are so cute together. They have to come with us." She paused. "We could invite Abby and some of her friends too."

"That sounds fine." He scratched his head. "I don't know if Tarff or the twins are coming but they might be able to go with us if they are." As he said this, the truck pulled up. Ryan and Zane had added a bunch of modifications to it including twice the amount of engine power, bulletproof body panels, two shiny steel tower-shaped exhaust pipes and jacked-up suspension, finished off with orange flames on a silver and purple paint job. The new truck had already been big in the first place, but now it was huge.

The window rolled down to reveal Ryan sitting in the front seat, wearing a leather jacket and aviator sunglasses. "Flynn, stop talking to your girlfriend and get in the truck! You were supposed to meet us twenty minutes ago." Flynn glanced at Emily when Ryan said "girlfriend." She didn't seem to notice.

Zane's head poked out from the passenger seat. "Well, technically, it was only two minutes ago, but Ryan got really bored and-"

"Yeah yeah, whatever," Ryan said. "Just get in."

Flynn looked back at Emily. She kissed him on the cheek.

"See you," he said.

She smiled. "See you."

Tarff opened the door for him and he pulled himself up into the backseat of the truck, which was multiple feet off the ground. He looked back at her as they drove off.

Zane turned to face him. "Your ambitious strategic arrangements seem to be working on the primary female."

"What?" Flynn asked.

"He means that was a nice move," Ryan said over his shoulder.

Flynn shook his head. Zane was too complex, and Ryan's speech was way too simple for Flynn to understand anything.

Tarff leaned over to him and whispered in his ear. "I think they are telling you good job with Emily."

"Oh," Flynn said. "Thanks." They stopped and picked up Cago, who was in front of the school. He got in the truck.

"How did it go?" Flynn asked.

"How did what go?"

"Asking Mia?" Flynn said.

"Oh." Cago looked at the ground. "Well, we were walking in front of the school and I was in the middle of asking her when I tripped. Most embarrassing moment of my life." He shook his head. "Surprisingly, she still said yes."

"Well that's good," Flynn said. He turned to the others. "Hey, do you guys have the grades you need?"

"Oh yeah!" Ryan said. "4.0 baby!"

Flynn smiled. "I thought you had an F. How did you do that?"

Ryan shrugged. "It may have taken some hard work."

Zane looked back at Flynn. "Well, it was more like he-"

"I used my epic brains?" Ryan said quickly. "Yes, good description Zane. How did you do Tarff?"

The Tongan shrugged. "I did alright. I was keeping up all term so I wasn't worried."

"So are we all going?" Flynn asked. There was no need to ask Zane about his grades.

"I'm not," Tarff said. "I don't want to. My mom would pound me into mush if I went on a date with a girl outside of our tribe." Flynn wondered if there was anyone in the world that could pound his large friend into mush. Tarff must have seen his expression because he added. "And I have one strong mama."

Flynn chuckled. "Do you guys already have a group you're going with?" he asked the twins.

They shook their heads.

"Well, my group is always open. Cago is coming with us."

"I am?" Cago asked.

"You are now."

Cago shrugged. "Ok."

24

Ryan looked at Zane. "Well, I still need to ask someone out, but if she doesn't have a group then I'll go with you."

"Do you have someone, Zane?" Flynn asked.

Zane looked at the ground. He appeared uncomfortable. For a moment Flynn thought it was because of Blackeye. He wasn't going to let her ruin his high school dances was he?

He took a deep breath. "Yeah, I asked someone."

"Really?" Ryan asked. "Who?"

"Doesn't matter," Zane mumbled.

"You can tell us," Ryan prompted.

"She said no," Zane relented.

"Oh." Ryan looked out the front window as the car went silent.

"I'm sure you can find someone else to ask," Flynn assured him.

Zane smiled lightly. "I guess."

The truck pulled up in front of the bakery and came to a stop. They all piled out and walked inside.

"I'm going to make a smoothie," Tarff said.

Flynn chuckled. Tarff always wanted a smoothie. He loved the fact that the kitchen was so big, and he used it all of the time.

The other four boys all walked up stairs.

"*Kingdom Mayhem* anyone?" Ryan asked.

"Sure," Flynn responded. With term finals done, they didn't have anything else to do.

The group walked to the third floor and went into Cago's room, which was also used as a gaming cave. Ryan and Zane had set it up with multiple consoles and what they called their "Gaming Setup."

"Proxy, turn on Xbox," Ryan said as they sat on the couch.

"Ok," Proxy said. Ryan and Zane had installed Proxy into the house's system. They had to turn it off if guests came over.

Zane passed out remotes. Choosing Flynn's character was easy for him. They had bought a premium pass that let them customize their own soldier. Flynn had given his character the closest things he could find to a mataka and hiveblade, along with light metal armor etched with glyphs, and long, flowing robes. If he was ever in the IPA again, he would have Zane make this suit for him. It looked way cooler than his old one.

Flynn was on Ryan's team, fighting against Cago and Zane. If the twins were put together, they would win every time. It was a fighting game that took place before modern technology, with knights, assassins and kings.

Flynn thought it was funny how unrealistic the fighting was in the video game. It was far from real life.

After a few minutes, Tarff came upstairs, having finished his smoothie. Flynn offered to trade places with him, and went downstairs to his room.

He laid down on his bed and looked up at the ceiling, hearing shouts of joy and frustration from his friends playing the game upstairs. He sighed. As fun as this life was, he sometimes wondered whether or not it was better than before. It wasn't that he liked war, he just hated sitting around and doing nothing while he knew other Ironborn were suffering and dying.

Flynn felt a vibration in his pocket and pulled out his cell phone. He had gotten the phone from Bi for his sixteenth birthday two weeks ago. He checked the screen. It was a text from Emily.

What should I wear to the dance? it read.

Flynn started typing back. *It doesn't matter. Anything will look amazing.* He sent it and waited for a minute before a response came back.

You know, I was thinking about wearing my Grandma's old dress that she wore in high school. She sent a picture. The dress was a heavy brownish red color, and had white lace on the neck and sleeves. It looked like a rug.

Flynn laughed. *As long as it's on you, it will look fine.*

I was joking. she replied. *I was thinking light blue?* She sent another picture, this time not of a full dress, but just of a small section.

Fine with me. Flynn responded.

What should we do for our date? she asked.

It's a dance.

Would you rather have me call it that? she replied.

He smiled. *No.*

You know, I could just call you. she responded. *It would be easier to plan stuff.*

We'll probably just end up talking for hours.

She took a while to respond. *And?* He went to her contact and pressed the call button. She answered a few seconds later.

"Hey Flynn." He could tell by the sound of her voice that she was smiling, and he found himself doing the same. "Do you have any ideas for the date?"

"Well you know, I was thinking I could go pick up some microwave dinners," Flynn joked. "Throw them in the freezer and pull them out when you come over."

"Stop." She started laughing. "What are we actually going to do?"

"Well, if it's fine with you, Tarff isn't going to the dance," Flynn said. "He could make something for us. He's an excellent cook."

"That's fine with me," she replied. "What do you want?"

"Well I shouldn't be deciding that," Flynn said. "This stuff should all be your choice."

She paused for a moment. "I honestly don't know. Just have him make something. Let it be a surprise. It's a guy's ask date anyways, so you can plan the stuff."

"Alright, just don't be surprised when he makes us pineapple smoothies."

She laughed again. "What are you doing right now?"

"You mean other than talking to the most amazing girl in the world?" he asked. "Laying on my bed. You?"

She chuckled. "Well, I was reading before but I got bored."

Flynn whistled. "Emily is getting bored of reading! That doesn't happen everyday."

"Well, I don't get asked out on a date by you everyday," she said. "I couldn't focus."

Flynn laughed. "Neither could I, and I was just playing video games."

"I couldn't imagine me distracting you that much," she said.

"Oh, you would be surprised," he said. "Up until today, I was just stressing about whether or not you would say yes."

"Flynn," she said. "I would never say no to you."

Flynn took another bite of his lasagna, savoring it in his mouth. He had ended up talking to Emily for nearly three hours before being called to dinner. "Hey Tarff!"

"Yeah?" he called from the back of the kitchen. Everyone except him was seated around the table. He had gone back to the kitchen to get something.

"Would you mind cooking for our date?" Flynn asked.

"Sure." Tarff walked out with a pan of garlic bread and set it on the table before sitting down. "What do you want?"

"I want you to surprise us."

"Shouldn't you ask Emily?" he asked.

"Emily wants you to surprise us," he informed him. "Plus me Cago and Zane couldn't decide on anything."

"I still need a date," Zane pointed out.

"Well it's not that hard to ask someone," Ryan said.

"Oh yeah?" Zane challenged. "I'd like to see you try! Right here, right now."

Ryan looked up at him for a second. "Deal. But if I ask whoever you want me to, you have to ask Jessica."

A tension surrounded the table. Jessica was the most popular and, according to Ryan, the hottest girl in the grade. She had already turned down Jackson. Zane took a deep breath. "Deal," he said. A cheer went up from the others. "You're asking Mary."

"Alright." Ryan pulled out his phone and exited the room. Mary was another decently popular girl from their grade.

"Five bucks says he fails," Cago said to Flynn.

"I'll raise you. Ten he succeeds," Flynn countered.

"Deal," Cago said.

After a few minutes, Ryan walked back in. "Done."

"Are you kidding me?" Zane exclaimed. "There's no way you did it!"

Ryan smiled. "Yes. I. Did." He said each word like its own sentence.

"No. I refuse to believe it."

"See for yourself." Ryan handed him the phone.

Zane looked at him. "You did it over text?"

Ryan shrugged.

Zane handed him back the phone, his face paling. "I am so dead."

"Don't worry Zane," Flynn said. "It'll be fine."

Zane said nothing, and his stressful look did not fade. Maybe this was another reason that Flynn liked Emily so much. She was kind. Simple. Undramatic.

Flynn finished his dinner and cleared the table. As he walked back to the stairs, he thought about how different life was now than it used to be. It was strange to see how he could live without fighting. His life almost felt empty and meaningless.

But, through all this, it was nice to know that their group was still together. They would always be together somehow. The sign of loyalty. They would never be far apart.

He was about to go inside his room when Cago came down the stairs in front of him, ten dollars in his hand. He gave it to him. "Five bucks says Zane fails."

Flynn smiled. "Ten bucks says he succeeds."

"Deal."

2- Dancing In The Moonlight

The Bakery, Sacramento
California, U.S.A,
8:00 a.m.
Flynn

When Flynn woke up early on Friday morning, he was surprised to see Zane up early as well, cooking breakfast in the bakery kitchen. There had been three days of break off from school and the dance was tonight. Flynn couldn't wait.

"Why are you up so early?" he asked.

"Hmm?" Zane asked, looking up from the pan he was using to cook bacon. "Oh, I'm just in a good mood today."

Flynn smiled. "Is there a reason?"

"Does there have to be?"

"So there isn't a reason."

"I didn't say that." He flipped over a strip of bacon.

"So what is it?"

Zane took a deep breath and bit his lip. "Don't tell Ryan this but... Jessica said yes."

"Really?" Flynn asked. "Dude, that's great!"

"I know right?" Zane smiled. "I still can't believe it. Just don't tell him because I want to break the news." He paused for a second. "Oh, also, I hope you don't mind if I'm not with you guys. Jessica already has her own group."

"That's fine," Flynn said. He stood up and began setting the table. After a few minutes, the others came downstairs. Tarff looked confused as to why Zane had made breakfast, but did not say anything.

The group sat down at the breakfast table and started eating. Zane finished quickly before standing up. The other boys stopped their conversations.

"I have an announcement to make," Zane said. "Last night, I asked Jessica to the dance." He looked at Ryan. "And she said yes."

Ryan nearly choked on his bacon. "Impossible."

Zane smiled smugly.

Ryan stared at him for multiple seconds before he stood up and left. Flynn knew that Ryan would have preferred to go with a girl like Jessica himself and would now be extremely jealous.

"How has she not already been asked?" Cago asked.

Zane shrugged, still smiling. "Guess I'm just lucky."

Flynn leaned over to Cago. "I think you owe me another ten dollars."

Emily walked back into the bathroom for the thirtieth time. She looked at her reflection in the mirror. Her hair was done in a French braid. It weaved around the back of her head, and she had placed the lower half of it in front of her left shoulder so it flowed nicely down onto her blue dress. The dress itself was very comfortable and it had a nice spread at the bottom, but the top half was a little tight. She had never worn a dress like this before. She was always worried that her body would look bad or too childish. It was nice to know that Flynn would not care, but she still wanted to look nice.

This was also the first time in a while that she had put makeup on. Her little brother Carter would have probably made fun of her for caring so much about Flynn. The reminder that he was gone made her sad so she pushed it out of her mind.

She checked her watch. Ten minutes until Flynn would come to pick her up. She felt a buzz from her pocket and pulled out her phone. It was a text from Flynn. She smiled.

I'm on my way over. This morning has been filled with cleaning up the bakery so it doesn't look like a dump. There are definitely not a bunch of things shoved in my room right now.

36

She smiled wider and sent a heart emoji. *I'm excited.* She walked into the front room of her house. They had gotten a new house after the last one was destroyed. Part of it was paid for by insurance, and part was paid under the table from the IPA. This house was much larger than the last one, and her parents did not have to pay anything for it since, after speaking with Clan Vilo Leaders about how Enforcement was the cause of their son's death, they understood the whole situation and opted to be silent.

After a few minutes, she heard a car pulling up. She ran back up the stairs and into her room. "Mom! Flynn is here! Pretend I haven't been waiting at the door for ten minutes!"

She heard a knock on the door and her mom went to answer it. She heard the door open.

"Hello Mrs. Sharp." It was Flynn's voice. She found herself smiling. "Is there any chance that Emily might be home?"

"I think she is, let me go check." Emily heard her mom come up the stairs. She debated checking in the mirror one last time before her mom appeared in her doorway. "He's here."

Emily walked out of her room and paused at the top of the stairs, where the doorway was out of view. She took a deep breath, excitement filling her. "Please don't trip," she mumbled to herself. Then she began walking down the stairs.

When he came into view, she saw Flynn was standing at the front door, his black hair combed nicely, wearing a black suit and a light blue tie. An exact match for her dress.

She looked into his eyes and almost tripped. *Just keep walking,* she told herself.

"Hey Flynn," she said when she got to the bottom of the stairs.

"Hey Emily." He seemed curious about something. Emily didn't know what he was thinking about.

"What is it?" she asked.

He blinked multiple times. "Nothing, it's just...you look better than I expected." Emily hoped the fact that she was blushing wasn't showing too much. He looked at the ground for a moment. She loved the fact that his confidence waned sometimes when he was around her. "Well, I have a surprise for you," he said.

"Really?"

"Yeah, I had to pull some strings with Bi but-" He opened the front door.

"No way." Sitting at the end of the front walkway, parked on the side of the road, was the yellow custom Lamborghini. She had seen it in the garage before they left to save Flynn in the Rizen. It had been gray at the time. Apparently they had gotten a new paint job.

"Oh my gosh Flynn!" She hugged him. "You shouldn't have. How did you even get this?"

"Well I have no idea how Bi convinced the IPA to let her keep it, but she was willing to lend it to me for one night. Besides, I couldn't take you on a date in the truck," he said, taking her hand and leading her to the car. "It's way too messy." He opened the passenger door for her and motioned his hand toward the vehicle. "Your Highness."

She laughed.

"What?"

She shook her head. "Nothing." She grabbed the skirt of her dress, being careful not to let it get caught on anything, and stepped into the front seat. The car's interior was extremely nice and the seat was super soft.

Flynn hopped into the driver's side. Even though he had gotten his license a month ago, it was weird to see him driving. He was one of the most mature sophomores at the high school, and probably the only one with a car. He put the key into the ignition and revved the engine.

She felt the wind on her face as the car pulled away from the house and sped down the road but she still tried to keep her hair nice. She knew Flynn could go much faster than this. She smiled at the idea of him being careful around her. She looked over at him, and was surprised to see that he was wearing sunglasses.

She laughed. "Flynn, why are you wearing those?"

He turned toward her for a second. "The sunglasses?" He looked back at the road. "Ryan gave them to me. He said if I was going to drive the Lambo then I needed to wear sunglasses."

She crossed her arms jokingly. "Well I disagree. You should take them off."

He paused for a second before removing the sunglasses and placing them on the dashboard. "Why?"

She smiled. "I like to see your eyes." Despite the wind, it was actually an exceptionally warm night, probably one of the only ones they would have for the rest of the year.

They stopped at an intersection, waiting for the light to turn green. Flynn stopped a long distance from the car in front of them just to be careful, despite the fact that Zane said the Lamborghini was custom-made to be bulletproof.

She looked around at the drivers of other cars. They looked very surprised to see two teenagers driving such an expensive car. One man just shook his head.

After a few minutes, they pulled up at the bakery. Emily had been here a few times. While here, she had become good friends with everyone except Blackeye, who she had not seen since the incident with the Blood Squad.

They all had told her about their experiences in the IPA and specialties they were assigned, without giving any information that may be useful to an enemy.

Emily watched as Flynn got out of the car and opened her door for her. She smiled up at him and wondered what he was thinking right now. His eyes were perceptive, and had a piercing feel to them. They were so warm and comforting that she could-

She quickly ended her train of thought and got out of the car, grabbing Flynn's hand as they walked up to the front of the house.

She was surprised when she saw the inside. The bakery seating had been decorated nicely, almost like the old restaurant it had been all those years ago. Strings of lights hung from the ceiling, and music played lightly. A few couples from their group that Emily knew sat on the various circular tables. She recognized Cago with Mia, Ryan with Mary, Jackson with Abby, and Dom with Jenna. They all sat talking at their tables, but none had food yet.

Flynn led her to the one that was right next to the window that overlooked the street outside. He pulled back her chair and stayed standing until she had sat down. He pulled his chair over so he could sit closer to her. She smiled to herself.

She heard heavy footsteps and watched as Tarff emerged from the kitchen, wearing a white button-up shirt and his typical blue lavalava. His hair was combed nicely.

He walked in front of the bakery counter and cleared his throat. "Welcome!" he said as the talking and music quieted down. She again found herself startled by his surprisingly low voice. He would be a great bass singer. "I am so glad that you guys have all come. Now, I have some menus for you guys. Please tell me if there is anything else you want, I will make special orders." He paused for a second. "I guess that's it. I hope you guys have a wonderful night." He walked to Cago's table, handing them a few menus before conversing for a moment. The music turned back on.

"This is really nice," Emily said.

"Yeah, it is," Flynn said. "Tarff is really excited to be able to make food for all of us." He paused. "He's kind of nervous too."

"I'm sure it will be great," Emily said.

Tarff walked up to their table and handed them menus. "Anything to drink?" he asked.

"Root beer for both of us," Emily said quickly.

"Sounds good." He walked away.

"Why did you do that?" Flynn asked.

She shrugged. "I knew that you would be too polite to ask for anything except water while I'm here, and I wanted some root beer." She opened up her menu.

"I guess that makes sense," he responded.

Emily was surprised by how many items there were. After a few minutes, Tarff returned with their drinks. "What can I get started for you this evening?"

Emily looked back over the menu and ordered a dish she had never heard of. Flynn ordered a steak.

"A steak?" she asked him as Tarff walked away.

"What?" he asked innocently. "It goes with the root beer!" She laughed and shook her head. Flynn took a sip of his drink. "I can say that I have never seen Cago quite so happy." Emily looked over at the table where he was sitting. He and Mia were talking and laughing their heads off. "He's got to make his move."

"Make his move?" Emily asked curiously.

"Yeah," Flynn said. "You know, you've got to take these opportunities to do something. To go out of your comfort zone. Subtly of course," he added.

She again looked over at Cago. He was sitting pretty close to Mia. If he wanted to he could-

She felt something touch her hand. She hadn't even noticed Flynn move.

"See?" he asked. "Like that."

She looked into his eyes, and could tell he was still nervous. How could he be nervous after all this time? At least he wasn't over-confident. Sometimes she wondered if she came across as shy as well. "You know, the first time you did something crazy, I don't remember it being so subtle," she stated.

"Well, that time I thought I was going to my death," Flynn justified.

She rolled her eyes jokingly. "As if that's an excuse," she chuckled. It had been so confusing for her at the time. She wished he would have told her sooner. He had pretended to be a human supporter for so long that she believed it was true. Sometimes she wondered what other things he might be keeping from her. She silently prayed that there was nothing.

Emily let the water cascade down and over her hands. After finishing dinner, the group had gone to a park to take pictures and then headed off to the dance, which was in the school gymnasium. Emily had gone to the restroom when they got there.

She looked in the mirror, and again didn't understand what Flynn saw in her. She looked so nerdy.

She sniffed her hair to make sure it still smelled good. She straightened her posture. After double-checking everything again, she exited the restroom and walked into the gym.

It was dark and crowded with people, tables, and chairs, yet she spotted Flynn instantly. He was all the way across the room. Somehow she had an aptitude for doing that. She wondered whether or not he could do the same.

She went back out into the hallway and walked around the gym to the other side. She entered through the doors and walked up behind him. He was talking to Zane.

"-found out that the only reason she said yes to me was because Trevor couldn't come because of his grades," Zane was saying. "He snuck into the dance somehow and she disappeared."

He looked so down. Emily felt bad for him. "I'll dance with you," she interjected.

"Really?" He looked up at her.

"Sure."

He looked at Flynn. "I don't really know if-"

"Oh, come on!" She grabbed his arm and ran into the crowd. She turned around to look at Flynn's face. She couldn't understand his expression. Concern? Jealousy? Both? She winked at him and watched as his expression faded into a blush. She saw him look at the ground before he disappeared as she entered the crowd.

She turned to face Zane.

"I-I don't really know how to dance," he said.

She smiled at him. "It's not that hard." She began teaching him some steps that would fit to the rhythm of the song and they started dancing. It was a bit fast, but still worked for partners. She noticed him constantly looking in Flynn's direction.

"Flynn will be alright," she assured him. "I'm going to dance with him later. You didn't think you would have me all night, did you?"

His eyes grew wide. "Oh, no, I didn't mean-"

"I was joking." She smiled at him. "Just loosen up a little."

She saw him relax slightly. He began to relax more as he got used to the dancing. "This is almost easier than programming a dancing robot!" he said.

She chuckled. "Well I sure hope it is!"

He laughed too. After a few minutes the song was over, and they went back over to where Flynn was now seated on a foldable chair.

He stood as she approached. "You know, you caused me a lot of trouble," he joked. "There were probably twenty girls that asked me to dance while you were gone, and I had to turn them all down. They were devastated."

"Oh shut up," she said. She turned to Zane. "Are you going to be alright?"

"Yeah, I'll be fine," he said. "Go have fun." He walked off. She turned back to Flynn.

"You want to dance?" he asked.

She smiled. "I'd love to."

They walked out onto the floor. The first two songs were fast-paced, and so they stayed separate, but next to each other, as they did some freestyle dancing. Flynn put his sunglasses on.

"Those again?" she asked. She almost had to yell because it was so loud.

"They help me get my moves on," he said.

She laughed and shook her head, but she couldn't deny it. He was pretty good at dancing. "You know, you could have gone to get something to eat at the snack table while Zane and I were gone."

"I didn't want my breath to smell bad," he explained.

She rolled her eyes. "For what?"

Flynn was about to say something when the DJ cut him off. "Hey guys, we're gonna have a slow song!" A cheer went up from the crowd.

Flynn turned toward her and answered, "For this." He put one of his hands on her waist and grabbed her hand with the other one. The music started, and they began

47

dancing slowly around the floor. It was a good song. One of Emily's favorites.

She looked into Flynn's eyes. He looked so handsome standing there in the dark. His eyes glinted as the small string lights that were hung across the walls shone into them. She felt a hair fall in front of her face. He moved his hand up and tucked it behind her ear. She felt a shudder of excited nervousness flow through her as his hand went back to her hip.

She looked up at him. His hair was combed but still had a spot in the back where it was messy. She reached up and ruffled the rest of his hair.

"What was that for?" he asked.

"I like it better that way," she said. They danced in silence for a moment. "Do you think getting the grade was worth it?" she asked.

"Are you kidding?" Flynn asked. "It was beyond worth it before you even got into the car." He smiled. "I guess the question is, will you go on another one with me?"

She tilted her head. "Our date hasn't even ended yet and you're asking me to another one?"

"All I know is that I want to do this forever," he said.

She smiled. "Then I guess the answer is yes."

"Friday?" he asked.

"Friday." To be honest, she wanted it to be sooner. She pulled him closer and leaned her head into his chest. He put his arms around her as they swayed back and forth. She felt so secure. He felt so strong. *I guess training in an army for three years pays off on your abs,* she thought to herself. She sighed. She was glad he did not have to fight anymore. Even though she never knew he was in the first place, she knew she would have been worried.

"Vanilla," he said quietly. From this close, she could hear him whispering.

She looked up at him. "What?"

"You smell like vanilla."

She blushed. She had been wondering if he would notice.

"I like it," he said.

She felt her insides melting as she realized how close the two of them were. Their faces were inches apart.

She found it hard not to look into his eyes. They were so mesmerizing and deep. They were warm. She wanted to be swallowed into them.

The music stopped but they didn't move. He smiled at her and she tried to fight the urge to kiss him. It didn't work.

She found herself slowly closing the space between them. His forehead pressed against hers, and she felt her nervousness rise. "I love you Emily," he whispered softly. She could feel the words he spoke as his lips brushed against hers. She closed her eyes. Despite what Flynn always said about her having a lot of confidence, she got nervous kissing him.

"Scorpius!"

Flynn's head darted to the side. Apparently all of his training in the war hadn't faded after all.

Emily turned to see Zane running toward them. The few people around her that had noticed him yell turned back to what they were doing. For a second she was worried that he hadn't wanted her to kiss him. Zane wouldn't do that, right?

"Flynn," his breathing was heavy. "It's Cago. Something has happened."

Emily saw fear flash across Flynn's eyes. She had only seen that fear once. On the rooftop of the bakery.

He grabbed Emily's hand and the three of them darted out of the gym. Zane led them outside, to the side of the school, where the property met with a neighborhood. They approached a fence that led into someone's backyard. A figure lay sprawled on the ground in front of it. Emily ran to her.

"Mia!" she cried out. "What happened?"

"Emily." Mia looked up at her. Emily could see blood glinting in the dark. "I don't really know. We were talking for a while and everything was going normal. We came to this fence and he grabbed my hand. I started to get excited-" She started coughing for a second. "He leaned in for a second and I thought he was going to kiss me when he paused. He looked over my shoulder and his eyes began to turn white. Then he attacked me and took off."

Flynn looked in the direction that Cago would have been facing. A full moon poked out through the clouds. "Oh no," he mumbled. Cago must've been too distracted with Mia to notice. Flynn turned to Mia. "Where did he go?"

She pointed to the fence, where a hole had been torn through. Flynn began to walk toward it.

Emily stood and grabbed his hand. "Wait." She couldn't let him get in danger again. She had heard what happened with the Werewolf effect last time.

"I need to get to Cago before he gets himself killed," he said.

"Flynn," she said.

He continued talking, turning his attention to Zane. "Call Bi. We need to get Blackeye over here to help Mia."

"Flynn," she said again.

He ignored her and turned to Zane. His battle instincts were kicking in. "Tarff as well. If this is anything like last time, we may need his strength."

"Flynn." He got so serious in dangerous situations that it scared her.

"Contact Ryan and put him on standby."

"Flynn!"

He finally seemed to notice she was there. The look in his eyes told her there was no stopping him from going after Cago. She wondered if that was the way he had looked when he had gone to save her. Pure determination.

"Be safe," she said quietly.

He nodded. "I will." He pressed a button on his watch and a suit spread over his body. His backup suit that had been designed by Zane and Ryan. At least he had that.

He turned to Zane, who was also suited up. His distorted voice sounded much deeper. Nothing like the Flynn she knew. "Let's move."

Flynn dashed from house to house, diving above fences and hurtling over objects. Zane, who had taken a moment to contact the others, was falling behind but Flynn didn't care. He needed to get to Cago as fast as he could.

He briefly regretted what he had just done. Not because the night was spoiled, but because he had left Emily so fast. Hopefully he could make up for that.

The adrenaline he had felt being around Emily now empowered him as he ran. He wondered if she had been as nervous as he was. If she had been, she hadn't shown it.

Flynn used his suit's night vision to follow Cago's tracks down a road and onto a street lined with stores, each one old-looking and multiple stories tall. He was in the area near the bakery. Flynn had just run three miles. In ten minutes.

He slowed as he entered an alleyway between buildings. He searched the shadows but saw nothing. He saw the tracks going up a ladder. He climbed to the roof.

He saw Cago sitting on the edge, and memories came back to him. He disengaged his helmet. "What happened, Cago?"

Cago didn't move. "I didn't even use my powers this time, Flynn," he said. "I saw the moon and just blacked out." He paused, taking deep breaths. When he spoke next, he was nearly yelling. "I didn't even do anything!" He slammed his hand against the roof. He lowered his voice to a whisper. "Every single person I love." Cago moved his hand slightly and Flynn saw what was next to him on the roof.

A gun. And six empty bullet shells.

3- Vilo

The Bakery, Sacramento
California, U.S.A,
1:00 p.m.
Flynn

Cago picked at a string that was fraying off of his jacket. He wanted to pull out his knife and just cut it off, but it gave him something to be distracted with.

"Well, that *is* her right." Cago looked up at Flynn, who was laying back on his bed, his cell phone up to his ear. He was talking to Emily. Yesterday, she had spoken to Mia about the situation at the party. Because of Mia's care for Cago, along with some convincing from Emily, she had not spoken to anyone about the incident, but she also had not spoken to him since it happened. That had been nearly a week ago.

Every time that Cago thought about her a spike of pain shot through him. He hated people seeing him that way. He had done nothing wrong, and yet they treated him like he had a disease. He proved what the government was saying about the Ironborn. That they were evil.

Cago tried to get himself to think positive. Today was a Wednesday. Every week on Wednesday, the boys went to the outdoor court to play basketball. He was not good at it, but he enjoyed the game. Maybe playing with them today could get his mind off of the events of last week.

Cago leaned back into the chair and ran his hand across his forehead. Mia had been another light in the darkness in his mind. Now that she was gone, he could feel it creeping closer.

"Ok," Flynn was saying. "I'll try to figure it out." He hung up and turned to Cago. "Emily found out a lot while talking to Mia. Emily explained to her how you went unconscious, and that you weren't trying to hurt her in any way. Mia said she wanted to still be with you but..." he sighed. "She is nervous about it happening again."

Cago looked down at the ground. He wished he could promise her that it would never happen again but he couldn't. It wasn't his choice. At least she still wanted to talk to him.

"Just give it some time Cago. Things like this can heal."

Cago nodded his head. "I'll try."

A knock came at the door. "We're going to play basketball." Cago couldn't tell if it was Ryan or Zane.

Flynn stood up. "Are you ready to get schooled?"

Cago smiled. "You wish."

"Alright," Zane said. The conversations died down. They were standing on the red and white court, its chainlink hoops reflecting the setting sun. It may not have been the best court in town, but it still worked. "Me and Ryan will be captains."

It was only ever fair for Zane and Ryan to be captains. They were super coordinated with each other, and if you put them on the same team they would always win.

The twins flipped a coin. Zane got to choose first. Flynn looked around him, measuring the other players. Along with themselves, they had crammed Jackson, Dom, and Dom's little brother Marcus into the back of the truck.

"Dom," Zane said.

"Jackson," Ryan said.

"Are you kidding?" Zane said. "You're going to get schooled. Flynn!"

Flynn walked over to Zane's side and fist-bumped Dom. The two of them together were nearly as good as the twins. Nearly.

"Tarff."

"Marcus."

"Cago," Ryan said. The teams walked onto their halves of the court. Ryan, being second to choose, got the side with his offense facing away from the sun. He also got to start with the ball.

Ryan walked to the far edge of the court and passed the ball to Marcus. Marcus was much shorter than Flynn but he still managed to speed down the court, his legs moving at an alarming speed.

Dom went to guard him, and he slowed his pace. Zane side-shuffled over to Ryan, and Flynn took on Jackson, with Cago on Tarff.

Marcus passed it to Ryan, who pivoted around multiple times, his head turning back and forth. He looked up and his eyes focused on something. Flynn turned and saw it. Tarff had gotten right next to the hoop.

Flynn bolted in his direction and jumped, catching the ball in mid-air as Ryan passed it to the massive man, preventing a very possible dunk.

Flynn dribbled the ball around Ryan and sped down toward the opposite hoop, letting the other players fall behind.

Flynn got into the key and jumped, leading the ball toward the backboard. The chainmail net jangled as the ball fell through, and Flynn got high-fives from his teammates as he backpedaled back to the other side of the court.

The game continued on for a while until finally Flynn's team won twenty-one to fifteen. They always played games to twenty-one.

After playing a few games, they decided to switch teams. Flynn was now with Marcus and Ryan, but still stayed with Cago.

Flynn was again running down the court, ball dribbling against the ground. He got near the hoop and planted his feet, jumping forward and using his powers to let him fly higher just slightly, so no one would notice. As he jumped in the air, he noticed someone sitting on a bench a few yards away. She had not been there before. He recognized something in her cold, confident eyes, and it startled him so much that he lost focus and missed his dunk, falling to the ground and scraping his knees.

His teammates ran to him. Ryan lifted him to his feet. "Are you alright?"

"I'm fine." He looked over at the woman on the bench. "You know what? You guys play without me. I need to go do something."

Ryan looked confused for a second as Flynn walked off of the court, but he must have seen the woman because he simply shrugged and went back to the game.

Flynn approached the person on the bench. He would guess that she was probably in her early thirties. She had black, straight hair that went past her shoulders. She had pale skin, and wore a blue windbreaker. He sat down next to her.

When she spoke, her voice was confident and metallic, as if it was resonating through a metal room. "Using your powers in public can be dangerous, even if done subtly," she said.

He swallowed uncomfortably. She had seen him influence his jump. "Who are you?"

"My name is Janet," she replied. "I have come with a message." She revealed a shiny piece of metal, and Flynn recognized it as a Den Commander badge. It had two blue lines at the top, signifying Clan Vilo.

He blinked multiple times. There was only one female Den Commander. Commander Sorelet, notorious for being a skilled gunner who, like Sergeant Bi, wielded dual pistols. "A message?"

"Yes," she replied. "A message that could put my authority at risk if I give it to you." She turned toward him. Her dark eyes pierced into him. "A few hours after Sergeant Bi's squad left our organization, researchers in Clan Troy discovered something."

"What was it?"

"A trail," she answered. "A trail to the Redstone. You see, before now, the IPA had been wandering in the dark, searching randomly, trying to find any clue as to where the headquarters were. This search started a few months after the war began, when we found a message from David Cadmore telling us that the base was the weakness for the entire army, and that he had left clues for someone to find it, were the need ever to arise." She chuckled sadly. "The need definitely did arise. Unfortunately, after following the first few clues on Cadmore's List, we found ourselves in a stalemate. The last clue told us that we needed to take down The Spire. Clan Troy, which was the squadron that had been trying to find the clues all this time, had spent two full years trying to overtake the Industry's forces at The Spire. But recently, after attempting to do so for so many years, we have a way to move forward."

"We finally took it down?" he asked.

"No," she said. "Clan Captain Dax and his elite squad had obtained a file during a recent mission, which they sent in while they were heading back to their base. The research half of Clan Troy decoded it and found a message. That message led us to a very important detail that we had overlooked while reviewing a previous clue. We were wandering in the dark before, but now we had found a rope. The series of clues that will lead us to Cadmore Industries is again in our grasp."

Flynn took a deep breath, trying to absorb the information. "Why are you telling me this?" he asked.

She sighed. "This 'rope' is very sensitive. If our enemies find out that we have discovered it, they will cut the rope, and our chance of finding the headquarters will be severed. And that is where we have our problem. Only a few hours after receiving the data from Captain Dax's group, Enforcement raided one of our compounds and stole a very important file. The records. The records held the names, ages, and DNA codes of every soldier currently in the IPA, and their information is now in their records." She shook her head. "Ever since the Industry got a hold of that file, our forces have been less effective. They have installed new scanners, previously developed by David Cadmore of course, that can scan an area for DNA codes that are put into their programming. Because of this, anytime one of our soldiers goes within the radius of one of these scanners, our mission will essentially be lost, and the soldier as good as dead."

She took a deep breath. "So, with the mission of discovering the rest of Cadmore's List being so delicate and important, we couldn't risk sending any of our soldiers, even our best ones, to accomplish the task. We found ourselves in a new stalemate. This was, of course, until we realized something. There was one squad who was taken off of the data files before they were stolen, therefore putting them in a very small group of soldiers that are, as we now refer to them as 'Cleared.'" She looked him in the eyes. "The squad of Sergeant Bi."

Flynn's eyes widened. "You want us back?"

She nodded.

"Would Bi become a sergeant again?"

"Among other things, yes," she replied. "That is, if she decides to join you." She paused. "Do you think you can get the group back together?"

Flynn knew that they would all come back. They had talked about how they felt like they should be helping, wishing they could still fight.

He looked up at where they were playing basketball, and an idea came into his mind. He rubbed his chin, as if contemplating her question. "Do you think we could get the Rizen back?"

She raised her eyebrows. "I believe I could get something arranged."

Flynn smiled. "Then you've got yourself a deal."

She stood up. "Thank you Flynn."

"Well, don't thank me yet. We still have a mission to accomplish," he said. "Besides, I'm not sure how happy Captain Vilo is going to be about this."

The girl's coat blew slightly in the wind and Flynn saw something he hadn't noticed before about the badge that was attached to her belt. There was a third blue line at the top instead of two. She was a clan captain.

She turned back toward him and smiled. "Somehow I have a feeling Vilo will be just fine."

4- Welcome Back

Talia walked briskly down the hallway in the office building. She had been contacted to meet here a few hours ago, and afterwards, Flynn had told her about his encounter at the basketball court. Like she had suspected, the IPA had come to a time when their squad was needed. And she would come back to them willingly.

The movements were almost automatic now. She walked down the hallway to the seventh door on the right, Blackeye following behind her. When they entered, the rest of her squad was seated in their suits around the table, and they looked up as she entered. She nodded to them and sat down.

Blackeye pulled her sniper rifle off her shoulder and set it down on the ground, leaning it against the chair as she sat down.

Talia looked around the room. Flynn had his normal confident, but slightly unsure posture. Zane had his back perfectly straight, like usual, but Flynn noticed that he kept glancing over at Blackeye. Ryan was leaning back with his feet propped up on the shiny black table. Tarff was sitting cross-legged on the ground but looked the same height as all the others.

The only other person in the room was Captain Vilo. She sat with her forearms on the table, her fingertips pressed together, a mask covering her face. "Welcome." Everyone perked up. "We don't have lots of time so I'll skip the pleasantries." She pulled a small, black, card-shaped object out of her belt and slid it into a slot in the table. "Captain Dax and his elite squad recovered this file from an Enforcement base a few weeks ago."

A hologram projection appeared in the middle of the table. It showed the shoulders and head of a middle-aged man with short black hair that had a few signs of gray. He had a kind face, showing small wrinkles of laughter and concern. It was a face that everyone in the room, but especially Talia, knew well.

"Greetings." He smiled kindly. "If you are watching this message then the Iron Warrior was probably correct with his predictions, the Industry has been corrupted, and I am most likely dead. Well, I have some good news for you." His concerned eyes differed from the smile on his face. "I, David Cadmore, have left a trail. A trail to the destruction of the army that I currently have named Enforcement. If you have found this message, I assume that you have already gotten the first three previous clues. If not, you are currently in the middle of the trail.

Congratulations." He scratched at his neck beneath his collar and Talia saw a glint near his hand.

"Wait," she said.

Vilo gazed over at her in curiosity.

Talia reached for a button on the small control panel on the table in front of her. She rewinded the video and paused it. "Look." She pointed to his neck. There was a small piece of metal on the inside of his collar.

Vilo stood, leaning closer to get a better look. "Of course," she said. "The previous clue mentioned something about metal. We thought it had to do with The Spire."

"You were planning on sending us to The Spire?" Talia exclaimed. "That's in the center of the Industry's territory in Florida. Not even Troy can get in there."

"No one ever said this was going to be easy." Vilo said firmly. "Besides, it seems we have a change of plans." She looked closer at Talia. "And there are many things Troy can't do."

Talia felt memories from the past fill her mind and could feel anger rising. She held Vilo's gaze for multiple seconds before silence was broken.

"Would you look at that?" Zane said, standing up. "This guy was a genius." He pointed to the metal chip. "This has a decoding inscription on it. Any machine that would try to read this would have its circuit completely destroyed! This quality of an inscription is nearly-" He finally seemed to see Vilo and Talia looking at him. He swallowed. "Sorry."

Vilo pressed a few buttons and enlarged the size of the chip. She then used a tool to single it out from the rest of the image and spun it around, looking at it from all angles. "Well, looks like we're in luck," she said. "We're going to the catacombs."

Talia saw Flynn shift slightly in his chair. "The catacombs?" she exclaimed. "That place is insanely hard to navigate, even for the hundreds of robots that used to guard it. This is almost worse than The Spire."

"Do you not think your squad is up to the task?" Vilo sounded like she was smiling.

Talia swallowed. "We are perfectly capable. What are we going to do about Duo? The catacombs are in her territory."

Vilo hesitated. Then she regained her confidence. "You're going to work on her terms."

Talia folded her arms. "Clan Duo's tactics can hardly be counted as terms."

"But they are effective nonetheless," Vilo said. "Duo's tendencies may be hostile but they have held against their enemies on their own for three years. That has to mean something." She turned back to the inscription. She studied it for multiple seconds in silence, occasionally looking down at a small screen on the table. "This inscription is the shortest clue we have had." She sat back down in her chair, and Talia did the same. "Its instructions are clear. In the vault of the catacombs, there will be some kind of encoded file. Something that only our best supercomputers will be able to dissect. You'll need to get that file and bring it back to the main Duo headquarters."

"That's it?" Ryan asked.

Vilo nodded. "But there are more complications outside of your own mission." She paused. "As far as we can tell, the Industry is expanding its last troops. After David Cadmore died, Dr. Griffin had no way to make any more robots, and he had to use the ones he had left sparingly. It seems now he is using the rest of his supply to kill all of our forces at the same time. He is trying to overwhelm us. And he is succeeding." She looked around at the others in the room. "There is a possibility that we may be able to win this part of the war, and the Industry will be utterly defenseless, but until that outcome becomes certain, which it is far from being now, your mission is our greatest hope." She turned to Talia. "Their forces are getting stronger every day. If we don't move swiftly, we may run out of time."

"When do we leave?" Talia asked.

"Tonight," Vilo said.

Flynn's head flicked up in surprise.

"Do you have a problem with that, soldier?" Vilo asked.

He leaned back again. "Of course not, captain. It's just," he paused. "I had a date."

Flynn sat staring at his phone. He had been sitting on his bed for nearly thirty minutes now, Emily's contact pulled up on his phone. He knew how much she hated him fighting. How on earth was he supposed to tell her he was going back to war? Especially when he was practically going on a suicide mission?

He knew what had to be done. There was no way around this. He had to tell her the truth. He had to tell her exactly what was going on.

Taking a deep breath, he pressed the call button. It rang a few times before he heard her pick up.

"Hey Flynn." He smiled at the sound of her voice. For a second he forgot why he was calling, and that everything was just like it had been over the past few months, talking to Emily over the phone for hours a day, and thinking about her whenever he wasn't.

He blinked multiple times and laid back in his bed. "Hey Emily. How are you doing?"

"Good. You didn't respond to any of my texts," she said. "I missed you."

Flynn felt pain rack his mind. How could he leave her like this? "I missed you too."

"Well I bet I missed you more," she said. She paused, waiting for him to say what he always did. He missed her most. When it didn't happen she knew something was wrong. "What's going on Flynn?"

Flynn ran his hand across his forehead and took a deep breath. "They want us back, Emily. They asked us to come back to the IPA again."

There was a long silence. "I assume you agreed?"

The sadness in her voice nearly shattered Flynn into pieces. "Yeah." He couldn't trust his voice to say anything more than that. There was another pause. "There's something else Emily. We're leaving tonight." The date was tomorrow night. With their last one ending as it had, Flynn knew she had been looking forward to one without any interference. She had wanted tomorrow to just be the two of them tomorrow. Together. He paused, not feeling ready for her reply.

"I'm coming with you," she said.

"What?" Flynn asked, surprised.

"I can't stop you from going, but I can go with you," she said.

Flynn sighed. "Emily you can't-"

"Yes I can," she said. "I don't care if I don't have powers. Didn't you say last week that you were impressed by my fighting abilities?"

Flynn had been teaching her over the past few months to protect herself. Her skills had improved by a substantial amount. He must have said that during one of her training sessions.

"Besides, who knows what could happen while you're gone? I could be dating someone else by the time you come back. With your squad, my options are a lot more limited."

Flynn chuckled lightly but what she said stuck with him. She had said when he came back. She was so confident that he would. He wondered why he didn't.

He paused for a while, thinking it through. Emily had gotten good enough that she could hold up on her own, so she wouldn't be weighing down the rest of the group. And he could protect her more.

"I might have to pull some more strings with Bi," he said finally. "And you better not pass out as soon as you see a gun."

"Hey!" she said. "I'm not that much of a wimp! You know me better than that!"

Flynn chuckled. "I'm serious Emily," he said. "It takes practice not to freeze up when there is a gun pointed at your face. Or at mine."

She was silent for a second. "I know what it's like to see you on the brink of death, Flynn. I think I can handle it."

He sighed. "What about our date?"

"Seriously, Flynn?" she asked. "We're going to war and the only thing you can think about is our date?"

"Hey," he said. "I want to at least go on one date with you before I go marching to my death. It's not like our last one really counted."

She laughed. "Yeah, I guess not." She paused. "You'll get your date, Flynn. Once this is all over. We'll be able to go on one with no interruptions, nothing to run away from."

"Promise?" he asked.

"Promise."

"I'm not surprised," Bi said. Flynn had told her about his conversation with Emily. "She really cares about you, Flynn. And she cares about our cause. She wants to help."

Flynn was currently sitting in a chair in the warehouse kitchen. It felt good to be back. It felt more like home. "Do you think she can come with us?"

"Which would you prefer?" she asked.

Flynn ran a hand through his hair. What did he want? Would he rather have Emily be safe, or have her not be so worried? Would she even be safer if he left her here? Would she be any less worried if she went with him?

He sighed. "I want whatever she chooses."

"I expected as much," Bi smiled. "Then I guess she is the newest member of The Scorpion Squad. She isn't on the IPA's records, afterall."

"The Scorpion Squad?" Flynn asked in confusion.

Bi shrugged. "We needed a name."

Flynn laughed. "Was this Ryan's idea?"

"It was mine actually," Flynn heard a voice say behind him. He turned to see Emily standing in the kitchen behind him. She already had a fitted suit and two black pistols hooked to her utility belt.

"Emily?" he asked, surprised.

"I had her come over and get ready a while ago," Bi explained. "I already knew what choice you were going to make." Flynn shook his head. Bi seemed to know everything.

Emily walked over to the table and looked toward Flynn. "So, what do you think?"

"About what?" he asked. She motioned to her suit. "Oh." It looked more like a sniper-class suit, like Blackeye's. It fit her body's accents perfectly. He had to convince himself not to look toward her hips. "Looks good," he said.

"Good enough to pass as a ruthless soldier?" She engaged her helmet and pulled out both of her pistols, aiming them at the wall. She actually did look quite intimidating.

Flynn laughed. "Yep. Do you think you're ready?"

She holstered her guns. "I don't think I'll ever fully be ready."

The door opened and the other five members walked in, Blackeye with them. She wore her suit like always.

"Hey Flynn," Zane said as they walked in.

"We have something for you," Ryan said.

"We've been building it over the past few weeks while you weren't around," Zane explained.

Ryan reached out his hand to Flynn. "Let me see your suit."

Flynn pulled the box that held his suit off of his belt and handed it to Ryan, who pulled a smaller box out of his pocket. He slid his extension box onto the side, attaching it into place and handing it back to Flynn.

"Well," Zane said. "Try it out."

Flynn attached the box to his belt, pressed the button on the extension box, and watched as it expanded. It, at first, looked just like his regular suit, but instead of fitting tightly to his body, it hung more loosely than his suit did.

Flynn looked down at what it had created in surprise. He was now wearing black jeans and a leather jacket. "A fashion savvy suit?" he asked.

Ryan chuckled. "I guess that is what you could call it."

"Both the leather and denim are infused with dragonsteel," Zane said.

"It gives for a more natural appearance, but is still just as safe."

"And your entire normal suit can go on under or on top of it," Zane finished. "Pretty cool huh?"

"Really cool," Flynn smiled. "Thanks guys."

"Well, I guess we have everyone," Bi said. She stood up, and Flynn followed. "Our plan is to get to Duo's territory by the end of tonight. Mr. Z doesn't want us to waste any time."

"If we take the Rizen at cruising speed, we still have a few hours to get ready if we want to get to Hawaii before midnight," Zane said.

"To Hawaii, yes," Bi said. "But we need to get to Captain Duo's base. That means a lot of the way will be on foot. If we don't want to be shot by the night patrols, we need to leave now."

Everyone looked at each other.

"Well, I guess there isn't a point in waiting around," Tarff said.

"Proxy?" Bi asked.

"Everything is ready," the artificial voice said.

She turned to the others. "Well, let's go get the next clue."

5- Clan Duo

Ryan stood at the top of the ramp leading out of the Rizen. The flight had been short this time, just over an hour. The Rizen could go much faster of course, but they had to go slow if they didn't want to show up on military scanners.

The Rizen had landed in a small clearing in the middle of a dense forest. The trees stretched on for miles in all directions. Vines and moss weaved up the sides of the tall trees and ferns and bushes littered the ground. The foliage was so thick that Ryan could only see a few feet outside of the clearing.

He engaged his helmet and began walking down the ramp with the others. The vast amount of small creatures in the forest made his thermal scanner go fuzzy so he turned it off.

He looked back and watched as the ramp closed. The group then entered the thick forest, the sun setting in the distance ahead.

"Careful," Bi's voice came over his comm. "This forest is a middle-ground between the Enforcement and Duo bases. Be cautious."

Ryan pulled out his rifle and held it level at chest height, scanning the forest as he did. The others did the same. Ryan felt secure in the surroundings of his squad. He looked to Flynn who, as normal, was taking point, his staff drawn. How could he do it? If Ryan was in front, he would start to get edgy, like he knew something was about to happen but he wouldn't be able to react fast enough when it did.

Ryan watched as Flynn held up a hand. He stopped and looked around, scanning the area around them.

He heard a rustle to his left and spun toward it. Nothing.

He heard another rustle and spun again. He turned his thermal scanner on again but still couldn't distinguish anything. There was too much.

Ryan heard another noise, and when he turned this time, he did see something. An Enforcement soldier. With his gun raised at Ryan's chest.

The soldier's head exploded in a shower of sparks as Blackeye shot it from her kneeling position on the ground.

The group looked at the fallen soldier for a second in silence. That was when the chaos started.

Robots flooded in from all directions, firing wildly at the now seemingly small group of soldiers. Ryan drew his gun and started firing into the wall of black that now surrounded the group, not feeling like he was making much progress.

He saw Flynn mowing through the lines of soldiers, being the fighting machine he always was, but even he couldn't stop them all.

The robots began to close in, filling the only space between them and their enemies with gunfire. Ryan threw a grenade at the soldiers but not even that seemed to help. They were outnumbered.

Ryan felt a skeletal hand grab his arm. He struggled against it but more hands grabbed him and he got shoved to the ground. He watched his comrades getting caught in similar ways around him.

Flynn and Tarff were soon the only ones standing. Flynn used his powers to ram soldiers together, throw them to the ground to be trampled by the flood, and pull them into him to bash them into his shield or impale them with the end of his staff. He cut down every new soldier that rose up against him, every enemy reduced to scraps.

Ryan watched as Flynn's staff got knocked out of his hand. He pulled his Mataka off of his head and slammed it into a robot's head and it went flying off. Ryan saw a soldier ram a pole into the back of Flynn's knee. Flynn collapsed onto his knees, but continued fighting even after soldiers grabbed his arms.

Tarff was still standing strong, smashing the robots with all four of his muscular arms, but not even he could stay up forever. Robots began to climb up the trees, jumping onto the giant of a soldier. Eventually he was completely out of view, covered in soldiers, and he collapsed to the ground.

An officer stepped out from behind the rest of the robots. Three red stripes marked his left shoulder. He walked up to where Bi was kneeling on the ground, her arms held in place by two soldiers.

"Not so strong now, are you?" he asked. His face held a crazed expression, his eyes empty. "How do you think you'll fare in The Rift? Do you think you'll be able to stand against Vrazda?" He asked the questions as if Bi would have the answers. Then he laughed. "Of course not," he spat. "You're too weak."

The man looked up to the trees and his eyes began to twitch. His voice lowered to a whisper. "They come for us."

A figure dropped out of the tree, falling nearly twenty feet before driving a knife into the officer's chest with the momentum of its fall before hitting the ground.

Dozens of other figures began dropping out of the trees from above, dropping enemy soldiers as they did, slashing through the enemy soldiers rapidly until they had all collapsed to the ground like their officer.

The figures gathered around the group, and Ryan was surprised to see that there were only eleven of them. There had seemed to be hundreds before.

They all wore very sparse amounts of camouflage clothing, each holding a set of two knives. None had guns or suits. And they were all female. Ryan had always heard that Dax and Duo had gender specificities but had never confirmed either theory.

The leader stepped forward as Bi stood up. She had dark, flowing hair. She was the only one without knives, and was instead holding two katana-like swords, which she placed in sheaths on her back. "Sergeant Bi. Vilo said you were coming."

"Captain Vilo," Bi said. "Her rank should be addressed."

She chuckled. "We don't address ranks here *sergeant*," she said, enunciating the last word. "Duo is a much different group than the rest of the IPA. The sooner you understand that, the sooner you will fit in." She looked at the dead body of the officer that sat on the ground in front of her. "We better get moving. Duo is waiting."

6- Eliza

Duo Compound, Kauai
Hawaii, U.S.A,
7:30 p.m.
Emily

Emily wasn't able to see the base until they nearly ran into it. It was a large concrete building that was covered with vines and pressed close to the trees.

The past few hours had been filled with walking through the forest, now with their own personal guard surrounding them. The soldiers at Duo seemed to be more like animals than people. Every once in a while, they would find a dropped Enforcement soldier that had been taken out by the scouts that Cara, their squad leader, had sent out. Emily would occasionally even look up to see disassembled parts of robots hanging from the trees as trophies. There was one that had been a human officer instead of a robot. She had kept her eyes on the ground after that.

Cara led them to a solid metal door on the side of the building. She began pressing some buttons on the door's control panel.

"You think they would keep guards," she whispered to Zane, who was standing next to her.

She felt a nudge on her shoulder and turned to see Blackeye, who was pointing upwards. She looked up and saw two wooden platforms attached to the trees above them, each holding two sniper rifles, their guns trained on the newcomers.

"Very welcoming," Zane joked.

The door opened in front of them and the group began to walk through. She looked back over her shoulder at Blackeye.

Emily had wondered what she thought of her. Would she be against Emily because she was another girl in the group? Or welcoming of it? She guessed that she would just have to find out. Hopefully that didn't include getting a bullet in the back of her head.

The inside of the building looked surprisingly like the outside. The ground and walls were made of cement, and everything was slightly damp, as if it had just barely rained. A few bits of moss climbed up the walls and clung to the fluorescent light strips attached to the ceiling.

As they were led farther into the base, the conditions got slightly nicer, but not by much. The Duo soldiers walked with complete confidence, their knives still drawn.

A door in front of them opened and they were led into a large room with a domed ceiling. This room was much nicer than the rest of the base that Emily had seen, and had a few furnishings. The thing that stood out from the rest of the room however, upholstered on a large pedestal, was a throne. And sitting on the throne, was a young girl with the fiercest eyes that Emily had ever seen. They reminded her of Flynn's eyes that night on the roof. She pushed the thought out of her mind.

The Duo soldiers stepped forward and dropped to one knee in front of the throne, sheathing their knives in the process.

"Rise," the girl on the throne said. Her voice sounded older than her face did.

Bi stepped forward and gave a small bow. "Captain Duo."

This is Duo? Emily thought. *She looks younger than I do!*

"Sergeant Bi," Duo said. "Vilo told me you were coming but couldn't tell me why over a long distance message in case it got intercepted."

"That is correct," Bi said. "Our mission is of extreme importance." She looked around at the other soldiers in the room.

"They are fine," Duo assured her.

Bi took a deep breath. "Me and my squad are following a trail. More specifically, Cadmore's List. A set of clues that, according to Mr. Z, is allegedly supposed to lead to the location of the Industry's headquarters."

Duo leaned forward in her chair. "So one of the pieces of this trail is near our location?"

"Yes," Bi said. "In the catacombs."

The Duo soldiers drew in a quick breath. "The catacombs are dangerous," Duo said. "And the way there may cause even more peril. I assume you will have to go into the catacombs alone?"

"That is our best bet," Bi said. "Our squad isn't back onto IPA records yet. To the Enforcement army, all of us are supposed to be dead. We're Cleared."

Duo scratched her chin. "Well it is a good thing you came when you did. The war is getting worse each day, and it will take a while to prepare for a voyage to the catacombs. You and your team will have to get accustomed to how we do things around here because we have some things to get done before we will be ready to attack. You can start by removing your helmets and suits. We don't like any kind of deception here."

Bi disengaged her helmet and motioned for the others to do the same. Emily felt a rush of cold air on her face as her suit collapsed into the box attached to her hip.

"I wish to speak with Bi alone. Cara will show the rest of you around the facility," Duo said, motioning her hand.

The group left, leaving just Bi and Duo behind.

They entered a hallway that was, to Emily's relief, just as nice as the room they had exited. At least the entire base didn't look like an abandoned sewer drain."She seems nice," Emily said to Zane as they exited the room.

"She looks like she's twelve," Zane said.

"That doesn't mean she can't rip your throat out," Emily said back to him.

"I like this girl," Emily heard a voice say next to her. She turned and saw a girl walking next to her. She had navy blue hair that went down to just above her shoulders, contrasting well with her pale skin. "My name's Genny." She extended her hand. "It's nice to meet you."

"You too." Emily shook her hand back. She looked up at Flynn, who was walking a few yards in front of her. She watched as one of the Duo girls moved over and started talking to him. She absentmindedly started to eavesdrop.

"Hey, that was some pretty good fighting back there in the forest," she said. "I was watching from the trees," she explained.

"Oh yeah?" Flynn asked.

Emily studied his face in surprise. Was he... flattered?

"Yeah," the girl went on. "You are easily the best in your squad. You fought like Troy."

"As if I didn't notice that," Emily mumbled to herself.

Flynn chuckled. "I guess training pays off. But for the record, Tarff was the last one standing."

"And, for the record," she said. "Mr. Giant back there is a twenty-foot tank of solid muscle. Not to say that you don't have some muscle yourself." She nudged him on the arm.

The girl turned to the side partially and Emily got a good look at her face. She had long, bright orange hair, bright blue eyes, playful eyebrows and high cheekbones. Emily also couldn't help but notice the fact that her body was more defined and looked much older than Emily's. She was very pretty. Much more than Emily could ever be.

Emily felt strange and realized that for the first time in her life, she was jealous. This girl didn't even know Flynn! *She* should feel jealous. Emily calmed down slightly. She was just talking to him. Unless she did something, everything was fine.

"And it sounds like you guys have a pretty important mission going on," she said. "You must be pretty good fighters if they asked for your help."

Flynn shrugged. "We have some experience."

"I can tell," the girl said. "I have a decent amount of experience myself. Been through quite a few battles." She smiled at him. "Sometimes my teammates say I'm a bit too fiery."

"Oh yeah?" Flynn asked. The tone in his voice suggested that he was either casual or trying to act like he was. Emily prayed it was the first one.

Cara led them to a hallway. "These are your rooms. I'll let you guys figure out arrangements and get settled before I continue to show you around." She turned to her soldiers. "You are dismissed to your quarters." The soldiers dispersed and the girl began to walk away.

"Hey," Flynn said. "I never got your name."

The girl turned back around and smiled. "Eliza."

7- Stingray

The Duo base was much larger than any that Flynn had ever seen. He was surprised to learn that, unlike Clan Vilo, Pris or Dax, who had a base like the warehouse for each individual squad, Duo only had this one base for their entire army.

They had finished their introduction a while ago, and Flynn had now gotten accustomed to his room, so he was feeling bored. According to Bi, it would take another three days until Clan Duo would be ready.

Flynn looked down at the leather jacket and jeans. They looked and felt normal, but when he looked closely, he could see the small strands of dragonsteel weaving through the fabric.

He was glad to have the jacket. It was cold in the Enforcement base, and the jacket had a built-in heating system. It was much better than the plain white short-sleeved training shirt that he was wearing underneath.

88

Flynn walked down the hallway where the rooms were, ending up in front of Emily's. She had taken a room by herself.

Flynn knocked.

"Come in," he heard a voice say from inside.

He opened the door. "Hey, Emily, they have some really cool training rooms here, and I was thinking, considering the terrain we're going to be fighting on over the next few..."

His voice trailed off as he saw her. She was sitting on the edge of her bed, her hands in her lap, looking at the ground.

"Hey." He walked over and sat down next to her. "What's wrong?"

She took a deep breath. "I don't know. I guess...I guess it's just been a crazy day."

Flynn smiled. "Yeah, it has been." He noticed that there were goosebumps on her arms, which were bare now that her suit wasn't on. He quickly pulled his jacket off. "Here." He offered it to her. "It has a heating system built in."

"Thanks." She smiled lightly as he put it around her. She sighed and rested her head on his shoulder. They sat in silence for a while.

Flynn studied her face. Her eyes were closed, half in concentration, half in peace. Her forehead was wrinkled slightly, and the corners of her mouth turned down. He wished that he could get rid of her problem, to see her smile again. See her bright, curious eyes looking into his. He wished he could be there on the dance floor again, with them so close and-

Stop, he told himself. *We're fighting in a war. We don't have time to wish.*

He could tell that she was hiding something from him. Something was bothering her. "Is there anything wrong?" he asked her.

She drew in a deep breath. "I think I just need some rest."

"Ok," he said.

She handed the jacket back to Flynn. "Thanks."

"Anytime," he said. "If there's ever anything you need, I'll always be here."

Emily lay back on her bed, the last words that Flynn had said ringing out in her mind.

I'll always be here.

She wished she could know it was true.

Zane heard a knock at the door. "Come in," he said.

The door opened and Cara walked in. "Ryan, Zane, we were wondering if you could help us with something."

Zane looked over at Ryan, who shrugged. "Sure."

The twins stood up and followed Cara out of the room. "We have something that we captured from the Enforcement army a few weeks ago. None of us have much experience with machinery, so we were wondering if you would look at it." She led them down multiple hallways, eventually making their way into the less accommodating section of the base, and entering a large garage.

A few soldiers wandered around inside, weaving between various Enforcement vehicles. Zane noticed that a D-12, like the Rizen, was not among them.

Cara led them around the vehicles and to the back of the room. "We've been studying everything else in this room for a while but when this first came in, we couldn't even figure out what it was."

A unique vehicle came into view. It was treaded and low to the ground and, like all Enforcement tanks, had no spot for a driver. The tank was a robot itself.The surprising part of the vehicle was on top. Where there would typically be a gun barrel, there was instead a long piece of metal protruding from the front with a claw shape at the end.

"What the heck is that?" Ryan asked. He walked up to the tank, hopping onto the side and inspecting the cannon. Or whatever the rod of metal was.

He pulled a screwdriver out of his utility belt and began unscrewing a plate on the side of the rod. When it popped off, it revealed a mesh of wiring beneath.

"Zane," Ryan called.

Zane hopped up onto the side and inspected the panel closely. "This is crazy," he thought out loud. He turned to Cara. "This paneling has a vortex sequence with varying differentiators. That would be impossible unless..." Cara looked at him with a blank face as the gears began to turn in his head.

Using the pole to steady himself, Zane moved toward the back of the cannon, where it connected to the vehicle. "Screwdriver." He held out his hand to Ryan, who handed one to him. He unscrewed another panel on the top of the small dome that was at the base of the strange-looking pole. He pulled off the panel to find a small cylinder inside, surrounded by more wires.

"Ryan." Zane moved out of the way as Ryan came over to look at it.

"This is some hardcore engineering," Ryan said. He engaged his helmet and turned one of his scanners on. "No way," he breathed.

"What?" Zane asked.

"They figured out how to make a dragonsteel reactor."

"No," Zane said.

"You have a scanner," Ryan said. "See for yourself." Zane engaged his helmet and turned the scanner on. "See that?" Ryan pointed to a sphere on the inside of the cylinder.

Zane leaned closer to find that he was right. The sphere was made of small interlocking pieces of dragonsteel, and on the inside, a hexagonal sequence of the same material. Zane didn't know exactly what the hexagonal sequence would do, but he guessed that it was what Ryan called the reactor.

The Xion engineers had always wondered what would happen if they got David Cadmore's dragonsteel and combined it with his other invention-metal reactors. He guessed they were about to find out.

"If David figured out how to do this before, then why did he only make one invention with it?" Zane asked.

"Maybe he only made a few before he died, and now that they are trying to do their 'Final Push' they are using them," Ryan said.

Zane turned to Cara. "Do you guys know what this thing does?"

She pulled out a medium-sized digital pad and handed it up to him. "We got one video of it in action."

Zane watched the screen. It was shown from a soldier's perspective. She looked around her and gave a signal to the others to move forward.

They drew their knives, moving forward hesitantly. They crept through the trees, searching the area for enemy soldiers.

A noise came from the trees in front of them and they paused. The leader gave a signal to them to fan out, and they moved into a semi-circle pattern.

They looked forward expectantly, waiting for something to come into view. Zane guessed that they were expecting Raptors, considering those were forest terrain vehicles. And they were surprised when the strange tank came right on top of them.

It weaved through the trees, maneuvering expertly. The soldiers, unsure what to do, turned to their leader.

"Fall back!" she said.

The soldiers turned and ran in the opposite direction. Zane was surprised at their speed. Flynn was the only person he had seen run faster. For a second he thought they were safe. And then the cannon turned on.

It started as a low-pitched hum, but grew to a loud whirring noise. The soldiers looked back in confusion as

94

the tank stopped in the middle of the forest nearly a hundred yards behind them. In the dense forest, a normal tank wouldn't even be able to reach them from that distance.

The leader held up her hand to stop them. They turned, thinking they were being led into some kind of trap, and searched the area. The leader herself looked at the cannon, where the humming was now growing extremely loud.

A large flash of light filled the screen, bright enough that it hurt Zane's eyes. He squinted them to find that the blast had come from the cannon of the tank. It was a plasma stream. It blazed its way through the foliage for multiple seconds, incinerating trees and disoriented soldiers alike until it stopped, and the humming started again.

"Three out of the twenty in that platoon returned," Cara said. "These machines are more devastating than any that the Industry had used before. Ground attacks are going to be much more difficult from now on for our armies."

Zane looked up from the screen. "Does anyone have any idea how many of these the Industry has?"

"I do," Ryan said from behind him, who was still looking at the cylinder.

Zane turned to see him pointing at a small golden plate on the side of the metal. He read it slowly.

Stingray-174

8- Incineration

Duo Compound, Kauai
Hawaii, U.S.A,
4:30 p.m.
Emily

Emily laid back on her bed. It was now day three of their stay. They would go to the catacombs tonight. The new vehicle that Ryan and Zane had researched had gotten everyone to start being nervous. Even Flynn. Emily got scared when Flynn was nervous about something.

The last three days had mainly just been training, small planning meetings, and sitting in her room. She had not spent much time with Flynn. It wasn't that he ignored her, in fact, he checked on her every once in a while, but she always said she was just tired. She wasn't sure why.

She heard a knock on her door. "Come in," she said.

The door opened and Bi walked in and she felt something drop inside of her. Why was she hoping it would be Flynn? She knew she would just end up turning him away.

"How are you feeling?" Bi asked.

"A bit nervous I guess," Emily said.

"Well you have a good reason," Bi chuckled. "The catacombs aren't exactly the most ideal first mission."

Emily smiled lightly. "I guess that's true."

"But you have something else on your mind, don't you?" Bi said. "You're worried about Flynn."

Emily looked up at her. How did she always know everything?

"Now, of course, you have good reason to be worried about him too, after seeing the extent of the Stingray's abilities," Bi continued. "But that isn't what you're worried about is it?" She looked at Emily with a small glint in her eye. "You're worried, for some reason, that even when he does survive, he might not care about you." She paused and then nodded, as if confirming to herself that it was true. "Why?"

Emily sighed. "I guess he just seemed... distant lately."

Bi smiled. "You're just seeing another side of him. This is the way he is at war. Always training, always trying to protect others. It's just what he does. You'll get used to it."

"I'll try," Emily said.

Bi took a deep breath. "Well, everyone is getting ready to go."

Emily stood up. "I guess there's no point in staying in my room. It's not like I'm going to miss it."

The two of them walked out of the room and walked down the corridors, making their way to the large garage that the soldiers at Duo had been using to prepare the past few days. Zane and Ryan had even been helping some soldiers learn how to pilot the captured Enforcement vehicles.

Bi walked over and began talking to Tarff. Emily looked around, searching for Flynn. She wanted to talk to him. Not just a small, "How are you doing?" but an actual conversation.

She walked around the garage, trying to find him, but he was nowhere to be found. She walked over to Ryan, who was talking to Zane. "Have either of you guys seen Flynn?"

Ryan turned toward her. "Not in the past little while."

"The last time I saw him was this morning," Zane said.

"I think he was here a few hours ago."

"But he must have gone somewhere because we haven't seen him."

"Thanks," Emily said. She walked out of the garage and into the hallway. She began wandering around, not knowing where she was going. She made her way past the bedrooms, past the room with the throne, and back into the damp tunnels that they had entered through. It wasn't until she got here that something caught her attention. A metal door was attached to the concrete wall on her left. These doors were all throughout the base periodically, so the door itself wasn't out of place, but this door was cracked open, as if someone had gone in and forgotten to close it.

Curiously, Emily crept over to the door, opening it slowly. A spiral staircase led upward from the entrance. Looking around to make sure no one was watching, she started up the stairs, closing the door behind her as quietly as possible.

She made her way up the stairs carefully, going until she reached a door. She walked up to it and was about to turn the handle when she heard voices on the other side of the door.

"I'm worried," a girl's voice said. "Your shield might be strong but those Stingrays can blast right through nearly anything."

Emily leaned forward and peeked through the crack between the door and the doorframe. Two people stood on an observation balcony. Emily guessed that it was used to look out over the forest to scan enemy movements. She also guessed that this wasn't what these two people were using it for.

"I'll be fine," Flynn remarked. "I won't be using my shield to protect myself anyways. It's just a last resort. My first option is to just take out the enemy before they can fire."

"I've seen you do that before," Eliza said. Emily couldn't help but notice how close they were to each other. She had her head on his shoulder, and had one of her hands on his arm. At least Flynn was just looking out over the forest instead of staring at her like she was him. "You really are a good fighter."

Flynn shrugged. "Fighting is a big part of my life. I try to be good but I still need to get better."

"You know, I never realized how humble guys were," Eliza said. "We don't have many of them around here." She nudged him jokingly.

"Yeah I guess you don't," Flynn said.

"Do you guys have many girls down there in California?" she asked.

Emily held her breath. What was Flynn going to say? "Just like everywhere else in the world," he said.

"Huh," Eliza said. "I haven't left this place in three years, and you guys are the first visitors we've had that I've been able to talk to. I haven't talked to a boy since I was twelve."

"That must have really sucked," Flynn said sarcastically. "Guys are *really* great."

"I'm finding that out," Eliza said, ignoring his sarcasm.

"Oh really?"

"I know one," she said, She leaned closer to him and Emily was glad that she had left her pistols back in the garage. "And he's a great fighter and really strong..."

"Well, I can always be better." Flynn noted.

She moved so she was standing in front of him. "So you're saying you give in easily?" She raised her eyebrows.

"That isn't exactly what I-" She grabbed the front of his shirt and pulled him into her, kissing him.

Emily grabbed the handle to the door but it was locked. Apparently Eliza had checked this door.

Eilza kept kissing him for much longer and deeper than Emily ever had. She watched them for a couple of seconds before looking away. She sat down on the top step of the staircase. Emily glared at the ground. How could Flynn do this?

It seemed like forever before Eliza finally pulled away. She heard Flynn take a deep breath from the other side of the door. "Eliza, I-"

A loud explosion filled Emily's ears, and she felt a wave of heat blast against her back from the direction of the door. She ducked down as the door flew over her head, banging against the wall in front of her.

She spun around, horror filling her as she saw the observation deck. Or, at least, where it used to be.

In the place where Flynn had been, there was a massive hole, like a crater had hit the building. There was a pile of concrete rubble on the ground beneath where Emily now stood on the edge of a fifty-foot cliff. And in front of that rubble were a dozen Enforcement tanks, multiple platoons of soldiers, and a Stingray, with its cannon pointed straight at Emily.

She heard footsteps coming up the stairs behind her. She barely even felt the arms grab her. She barely heard the voices telling her that they were under attack, barely heard the alarms going off. She was in a daze. She couldn't think.

A pair of soldiers carried her down the stairs and to the garage. People were rushing around, grabbing weapons and hopping into the vehicles they had prepared. Bi walked up to them.

"She was right near the explosion," one soldier said. "I think she's in some kind of shock."

Emily slowly began to gain her consciousness back, and began to understand what was going on. She shook the soldier's arms off of her. "I'm fine," she told them, and they backed off. "Flynn got hit by the blast. He didn't even have his suit with him."

Bi looked at the ground. "We can't go out there to find out if he is alive. Duo will have to do that. We must get to the catacombs. They are prepared to leave."

Emily was about to object before she realized she was right. There was no way anyone could survive out there if Flynn couldn't even last with one tank attacking him. Why did she want to search for him anyways? Would she be happier if she found out he was alive? And if he was alive, would Eliza be as well?

Emily followed Bi to a heavily-armored vehicle and hopped inside, her vision still blurry. She found the rest of the squad inside, everyone suited up. The troop carriers began moving out of the garage, surrounded by an entourage of other vehicles.

"What happened to Flynn?" Zane asked Emily.

Emily didn't think she could answer that without either yelling or crying. Bi saved her. "He got hit by the blast we heard, and Cago has gone missing during the commotion. We'll have to go on without them."

"What?" Ryan exclaimed. "A mission without someone like Cago would be difficult, but we won't stand a chance without Flynn. Especially with Tarff not being able to reach full size in the catacombs."

"We'll have to continue on for now. Who knows what condition they might be in but we have no other options until we get back from our assignment," Bi stated. "We will pull through, as we always have."

"In case you haven't noticed, we've always had Flynn with us," Zane said. "Remember Flynn? The guy who took out the entire Blood Squad by himself?"

Emily remembered Flynn. She wished she couldn't.

"I'm not saying I don't wish he was here," Bi said. "I'm just saying there isn't anything we can do about it. We have to continue."

The group fell silent as the vehicle rolled across the ground. Emily tried to picture what was going on outside the vehicle, her mind trying to think about anything but what had just happened.. She tried to picture the armored carrier rolling along the ground on its ten tires, smashing anything it came in contact with. She felt safe.

She then remembered the video of the Stingray burning through the same trees they were currently driving through like they were nothing. She shuddered.

"The catacombs," Bi said. "As we have already discussed, it is a series of underground tunnels that used to serve as a research facility for Cadmore Industries until it suddenly went dark a few months ago. Since then, no one who has ever gone inside has ever returned. I assume that we are most likely looking for a vault as vaults are common in research facilities such as this. The main difference about this base in comparison to others is that it is built like a maze. The vault with whatever our clue is will most likely be at the bottom of the base, so if you have the choice, always choose to go down." She paused. "Now, we might have to make some group adjustments now that Flynn is gone. Zane, Ryan and Tarff will go together. Blackeye and Emily will go with me. And remember, no one outside of our group can go with us. They are still on the grid, and therefore have a much higher chance of being recorded on any scanners that the vault may have, and that will end any chance we have of continuing the mission. Understood?"

The group members nodded.

The latch in the front of the vehicle opened and the co-pilot looked back at them. "The Enforcement army has been alerted about a group of soldiers leaving the base. Be prepared for anything."

Emily looked down at the ground, the blurriness finally beginning to fade from her vision. She almost got lost entirely in her absence of thought but she felt someone nudge her on her shoulder.

Turning to the side, she was surprised to see Genny sitting beside her. Emily had never even noticed her sit down.

"Are you doing alright?" Genny asked. Her hair, unlike yesterday's navy blue, was now a bright orange.

Emily paused for a moment before nodding. "I'm fine."

Genny raised her eyebrows sarcastically. "Clearly."

Emily sat back, looking over at her recently- met comrade, "And what might you mean by that?"

"You haven't moved in nearly ten minutes and you weren't responding either," Genny replied.

Emily blinked. Had it really been that long? It had seemed like only a moment. "I'm just disoriented," she said, brushing it off.

Genny seemed to think for a moment before deciding not to mention it anymore. "I know I won't be able to go into the catacombs with you, so good luck," she said,

"Thanks," Emily said. Her voice sounded so dull. She felt like she should say something else but didn't know what.

Genny exhaled. "Hopefully the-"

Suddenly the entire carrier got thrown end-over-end as the back exploded. Emily rolled roughly as the carrier stopped moving and the noise of a battle began around her. She was slightly shaken but having her suit on had cushioned her fall.

She felt Tarff's large hand lift her out of the wreckage of the now-burning wreckage of the troop carrier. He set her down gently beside some of the others as the surviving soldiers began to gather in a group. Emily looked around to see that one of the other five carriers had also been destroyed as the army of Enforcement soldiers caught up behind them and the rest of the vehicles were swiftly turning around to fire back as the enemy tanks moved in.

Explosions and bullets rained through the air as sergeant Bi, alongside one of the Clan Duo sergeants, began to quickly direct the soldiers further into the dense forest.

Emily began to run with the rest of the soldiers, looking back to see Tarff grab the broken husk of their troop carrier and throw it toward the line of approaching Enforcement tanks, destroying a few and momentarily halting their charge before lumbering behind the others.

Emily gasped as a stray blast from one of the Stingray tanks vaporized a pair of soldiers off to her left. With everything happening around her, she had almost forgotten about what had just happened to Flynn. Almost.

The sounds of the battling vehicles slowly faded away as the group headed deeper into the forest, continuing in the direction of the compound. When she looked forward, she saw an Enforcement patrol in the forest ahead. A pair of soldiers, looking away from the incoming group.

The Duo soldiers moved silently up to them, plunging knives into their backs before they even knew what hit them. One of the soldiers laid the robot down gently with mock respect before pressing her boot firmly against its throat, disconnecting its head from its body.

Emily shook her head. Even for murderous robots this seemed brutal.

She had once wondered why blades were so common in the IPA when they could use powerful guns, but she had been told that because a robot doesn't bleed out, taking off a limb with a precise attack from a sword paired with the added strength of an IPA suit could be effective if you could just get close enough as an attacker could be much more precise, cutting the robot's cords using chinks in it's armor.

It was Flynn that had explained that to her on the flight here. He was so worried about her knowing everything that might be able to keep her safe. And now he was-

Not gone. He was Flynn. He would survive.

She pushed thoughts of him out of her mind and watched as the soldiers moved through the forest in a wide arc, weaving through the trees. It reminded Emily of what she had learned about velociraptors in science class. Moving silently upon their unexpecting prey before tearing them into shreds.

They passed multiple patrols before the forest narrowed into a ravine and the trees gave way to large boulders.

Cara turned to Bi. "This is where the catacombs begin. We must leave you here. May whatever luck that might be left in that horrific place be with you."

Emily watched as the Duo soldiers disappeared into the forest, vanishing from sight, most likely setting up to ambush the Enforcement tanks that would inevitably arrive. She turned and began walking down the ravine with the others. The ravine itself was broad and had large, gray stone walls that rose high up into the air.

The group moved along the boulders for a while before Bi held up a hand. "We have arrived."

To Emily's surprise, she pointed down. Emily peered over the edge of the boulder at where Bi was pointing.

About twenty feet beneath them, at ground level, there was a gap between two boulders where it looked like there had once been a metal door that had now long since been bashed in. All that was beyond was darkness.

The group moved down the boulders and to the ground. Emily began to feel claustrophobic as she realized how quickly these boulders could shift and crush her into bits.

They stood for a moment, looking at the foreboding hole in the ground before hearing a noise from the forest behind them. Gunfire.

Bi motioned them forward. "Let's find this clue."

9- Catacombs

As soon as the group entered the cave, the temperature seemed to drop to near freezing. The entrance led down a steep staircase until it became a damp metal hallway. Emily saw the others turn on their suit's thermal scanners and night vision as the light from the entrance began to thin. She struggled for a moment to figure out how to turn her own on before finding the controls and looking around.

The inside looked like a zombified version of an Enforcement base, metal walls warped and cracked as vines seeped their ways down the corridors.

Emily shivered as she saw a skeleton dressed in a Cadmore Industries uniform lying on the ground, its empty eye sockets seeming to stare up at her.

"A scientist," Bi said. "Like most of the workers here."

The tunnel came to a split. "Tarff, your group will go left. We'll go right."

Tarff nodded silently and headed down his path, disappearing out of sight as Emily followed Bi. Their path winded downward quickly, the walls becoming more broken as they continued, the air dampening with each step.

"Bi should we-" Blackeye stopped. Emily was surprised to hear her voice out loud and, by the looks of it, so was Blackeye. It was still her altered metallic voice, but it was coming through her helmet, not through the comms.

"Tarff, do you copy?" Bi asked. "Shoot. They must have devices in place to block our communications. I can't even send a comm to you from this close. This is going to make things difficult."

As they continued, slower than before, Emily saw more fallen workers, but even more common were broken Enforcement robots, their cords mangled and their bodies dismembered.

Bi leaned down and inspected one curiously.

"I don't like this," Bi said, thinking out loud. "According to Duo, dozens of soldiers on either side have gone missing down here, but there isn't any immediate identifiable danger in sight." She turned to Blackeye. "Anything?"

Blackeye shook her head.

Bi exhaled. "Then we must continue on and hope we are prepared for what awaits."

"This way," Bi finally decided, leading her group down the corridor to the right. Emily felt like they had been going through the catacombs for hours, and yet nothing had happened yet. No threats, no sudden attacks, nothing to shoot at, not even a single noise besides the three soldier's footsteps. It could have been peaceful to some but to Emily it just made her more tense. She couldn't even imagine how Flynn could get used to this.

Flynn. She would never be able to forget about him. He was buried too deep into her mind, and she couldn't get him out.

"I wonder how Tarff is doing," Emily said. trying to think of other things.

Bi sighed. "We won't know until we get out."

Emily looked down as they passed one of the skeletons littering the ground and shivered.

If we get out, her mind seemed to tell her.

As they turned a corner, the group slowed as a new scene was laid out before them. Unlike the skeletons that they had seen scattered occasionally around the rest of the base, the floor in this hallway was covered in fallen scientists, and they seemed only half-decayed, as if they had just barely died.

Bi stepped forward, leaning down and inspecting one of the scientists closely. She then carefully stepped over the body, slowly inspecting the hallway as Blackeye and Emily followed cautiously behind.

A low groaning noise sounded suddenly through the hallway and everyone froze. The silence rang out for a moment and Emily looked around. The loud groan turned into a crashing sound and Emily spun to see the hallway they had just come from collapsing. A wall of dust swept down the hallway, fuzzing Emily's night vision scanners for a brief moment.

"Well that limits our options," Bi noted as the dust cleared. She looked down at the ground. "I just can't make any sense of this. The bodies down here should not be preserved like this. The lack of decay makes it look like they died only hours ago but they aren't radiating any heat. Not to mention the fact that no one has been down here in months."

"How did they die?" Emily asked.

"They were stabbed," Bi said. "But the wounds are bloodless."

Emily felt an odd feeling run through her body and she continued to make her way closer to Bi, who had nearly made it to the end of the hallway. They had just barely stepped over the last couple of bodies when Blackeye suddenly drew her sniper rifle off of her shoulder and shot down the hall behind them.

Bi and Emily spun to look at her in confusion.

Blackeye seemed hesitant to speak out loud but pointed at where she had shot. "That one moved its hand."

"What?" Emily asked, but her confusion quickly turned to surprise as the bodies on the floor began to shift, rising to their feet.

"Go!" Bi yelled as the three soldiers ran down the hallway.

"What are those things?" Emily yelled as they ran away from what was now a mob of half-dead Enforcements scientists.

"I don't know," Bi said back. Wasting no time, she pulled a canister from her belt and stabbed it into a hole in the metal wall. A few moments later the wall exploded, collapsing the hallway behind them.

"Did those things just come back from the dead?" Emily exclaimed breathlessly as they slowed down.

Bi looked behind them to confirm that the threat was gone for the moment. "Not exactly."

"What was that then?" Emily asked.

"My best guess?" Bi said, who still seemed mostly unfazed. "Whatever killed all of the people down here was an Ironborn. Specifically one with a hypnosis ability."

"Ironborn can control people?" Emily asked. No matter what Bi said she still had more questions.

"I've heard of some that could in the past but never like that," Bi said. "Unless..."

"What?" Emily inquired.

"No, that's impossible," Bi reassured herself, ignoring Emily's question. "We need to keep moving. And be wary of dead people."

Tarff lumbered down the damp tunnel, his massive sword drawn. The sword had been a gift that Zane and Ryan had designed for him a few years ago. It was made of dragonsteel and, like Flynn's hiveblade, it had a shocking ability that worked very effectively against robots, especially in close spaces.

"We've lost comms," Zane said.

Tarff cursed. "Now we won't even know if they've found it. We'll have to just search as best as we can." They continued down their tunnel for a while before it split again.

"Now what do we do?" Zane asked.

"We'll have to guess." Tarff began looking at the entrance to one of the tunnels, investigating it for any clues.

"Hey, check this out," Ryan said. The other two turned toward where he was crouching near the other entrance. Ryan looked up at where a small black dome stuck out of the ceiling, "Video camera." He pulled out his gun and shot it. "This is our tunnel."

Tarff shrugged and started down it, the other two following behind him.

"How does it feel to be leading?" Ryan asked.

Tarff shrugged. "A bit strange. If we have two groups, Bi and Flynn are normally the ones to take point and make decisions. It has a bit more stress I guess."

"I'm just glad all of that stress is on you buddy," Ryan said sarcastically. "This is practically a vacation for me."

"Look." Zane shot his gun at a small inlet in the ceiling, where another camera exploded in a shower of sparks. "We're on the right track."

"Or we're heading toward a grouping of tunnels full of Enforcement soldiers," Ryan said.

Tarff glanced back at him. "Don't jinx us."

Ryan shrugged. "We can probably take them."

Zane looked over at him. "Let's say by chance that we do run into a group of soldiers..."

"Ten."

"Deal," Zane said. "Remember, Flynn isn't with us this time."

"Are you betting on whether or not we lose?" Tarff asked.

"Why not?" Zane asked.

"That way, even if we die, Zane still owes me ten bucks!" Ryan said. "He will be eternally in my debt."

Tarff shook his head. "You guys are crazy."

The group exited the tunnel and entered a large cavern, its ceiling rising about twenty or so feet above them. There were four tunnels leading out of the room, including the one they had just come through. Tarff decided to go to the door directly across from them.

The group started across the cavern. They were about halfway across when Ryan stopped. "Did you guys hear that?"

"Hear what?" Tarff asked, pausing.

"It sounded like..." He trailed off as the sound became clearer. "Feet."

Not a moment later, three of the four hallways around them began flooding with hundreds of humans, causing the three boys to run the only way they could. Forward, deeper into the catacombs.

Tarff looked back over his shoulder, trying to figure out what it was that was chasing them. The longer he looked, the more confused he became. The horde looked like a scramble of bloody Enforcement officers and broken IPA soldiers, each one with pale, dry skin and glazed-over eyes.

"Are those zombies?" Zane asked with a panicked tone as he tried to shoot backward at them with his gun.

Ryan pressed a button on his wrist and spun around, spewing flames out of an attachment on his suit. The horde slowed slightly but pushed the burning bodies to the side with surprising carelessness and efficiency.

Ryan cursed. "It's like they all share a single mind."

Up ahead the hallway split and the Tarff decided to lead them to the left. They seemed to be gaining a slight lead on the swarm for now but, unlike their enemies, Tarff knew the twins would get tired at some point. They needed a way out of this.

The metal wall beside them began to creak as if under immense pressure before a massive hole suddenly opened, dead soldiers pouring out as if they had burrowed through solid dirt to intercept their target. Luckily for the twins, they had a tank to protect them.

Tarff quickly crushed the zombies that stood in their way as they passed the opening in the wall, but more holes opened in front of them, and soon the hallway was flooding with bodies from all sides.

As they turned around another corner, Tarff heard a grunt and spun to see that in an attempt to use his wrist-mounted flamethrower again, Ryan had tripped and was quickly being swarmed by the wave of zombies chasing them.

Tarff quickly dove backward, smashing through the ball of bloody bodies around Ryan before grabbing him and slinging him over his shoulder. Although he had only been vulnerable for a few moments, Ryan's suit had multiple tears and he did not move as Tarff ran with him alongside Zane.

As the amount of zombies continued to thicken, Zane was forced to run directly behind Tarff, using him as a human plow.

The next turn came up ahead and Tarff began to feel more and more fear as he realized just how large this base was. They could barely survive in this place, let alone find a file that was designed to be hidden. As he turned the next corner, however, that fear turned into dread.

Down the hallway was a dead end. The hallway in front of them had collapsed, sealing them in.

Tarff heard heavy breathing behind him and turned around to check on Zane. He could tell his friend was slowing down. Despite being able to outrun the zombies for most of the time, he was bleeding badly from one of his legs, making it very difficult to run.

As hope began to seem entirely lost, Tarff noticed the screen inside of his helmet change. He was back online.

"Proxy!" Tarff said desperately.

"Sir," the robotic voice responded. "Suit battery life is-"

"I don't care," Tarff said quickly as the end of the hallway began to get closer. He could now see a small, mostly unrendered map in the corner of the helmet's screen, and it gave him an idea. "How high up are we?"

"We are currently at 1,758 feet above sea level sir," Proxy responded.

Tarff tried to think back to every turn they had made. The entrance to the catacombs was a little ways up an incline, so if his calculations were correct, they weren't actually entirely underground yet, just inside a mountain.

"Let's hope it's enough," Tarff mumbled. Turning around, he scooped up Zane with his upper right arm, holding the twins over his shoulders while shoving the zombies out of the way with his two lower arms.

Plowing through the last few layers of zombies, Tarff smashed into the end of the tunnel and, just as he had guessed, the hallway wasn't actually collapsed, the builders just hadn't realized the exact limits of where they could build and had to stop suddenly when they had hit open air. The same open air that Tarff was was now falling through.

Tarff felt his whole body tense up as he looked down, but managed to tuck himself into a ball, protecting the twins like a ball of human armor.

"Why am I the one who always has to deal with the heights?" Tarff asked as his body slammed against the forest floor like a meteorite, downing a few dozen trees as he rolled.

Tarff groaned as he blinked the blurriness out of his eyes. He looked down to see that the twins, although both unconscious, were still alive. He then looked up to see that they had just fallen directly into the center of the battle between Clan Duo and Cadmore Industries. They were now behind enemy lines.

"Suit is now in critical condition sir," Proxy said.

Out of the pan and straight into the fire.

Blackeye stabbed every dead body in each new hallway that they turned into, although Emily wondered if a bullet would even be able to kill something that was already dead.

"I see something," Blackeye said as they came across a division between the hallways.

"Which way?" Bi asked.

Blackeye pointed to the left and after about a hundred feet they came across a group of doors. They had passed many doors on their journey through the catacombs but this time the doors' control panels were lit up.

"These rooms are running on an independent power system," Bi noted. "This is our vault." She pulled out a card that she had swiped off of the body of a dead scientist and scanned it across the door panel.

The door slid open to reveal a room full of control panels and monitors.

"Blackeye," Bi instructed. "See what you can find."

Blackeye nodded, walking over to one of the monitors and beginning to search its contents. After a few moments she looked up at the doorway. Emily froze, and realized she could hear a light rumbling noise in the distance.

"Try to hurry," Bi said as Blackeye turned back to her screen and Emily followed the sergeant back out into the hallway. The two stood back-to-back, looking either way down the hall. Emily had always felt safe around Bi but she felt vulnerable now as she realized that she might not be able to see an enemy sneaking up on them considering they gave off zero heat signature.

She held her gun ready as the first undead Enforcement scientist came around the corner, firing multiple shots into his abdomen. It did nothing.

The scientist ran much quicker than Emily would have imagined he could based on how ragged he looked. Understanding the danger, Bi jumped in front of Emily, drawing a long blade from her belt and kicking the scientist in the stomach, slashing deep into his chest and shoving him into the wall.

Emily looked down at the body, making sure it wasn't going to move again. She then looked back up at Bi, who was turning to address two more undead. Emily had always known her to be an intelligent leader, but had nearly forgotten how good of a soldier she was by herself.

Bi drew a knife in her other hand, easily dispatching the two enemies before looking back out in the darkness. "More are coming." She turned to Emily, handing her the knife. "Use this. They will only stop if they are unable to properly fight."

Emily was shaking as she took the knife and turned around to see an undead scientist rushing down the hall toward her. She jabbed the knife forward as her opponent reached her, but the scientist trampled right through her weak defense and she fell to the ground. The scientist grabbed the knife by the blade, carelessly cutting his fingers and he wrenched it out of her hand to jab it toward her abdomen.

Attacking out of pure instinct, Emily punched the scientist in the face. She was surprised to hear a snap as her enemy got thrown to the side, his jawbone broken by the added power of her suit.

Grabbing the knife again, she turned just in time to thrust upward into a new opponent, dodging to the side and trying to cut the scientist's arm off at the forearm before kicking him into the ground. Despite the added strength of her suit, she felt like she was somehow still barely surviving.

"Get back inside!" Bi said as more undead shuffled into the hallway.

How are there so many of them? Emily wondered as she retreated back to the doorway. Bi followed, finishing off the two injured soldiers Emily had been fighting.

Bi paused when they reached the doorway. "Go talk to Blackeye. She might have a plan."

Emily ran into the control room, and ran over to where Blackeye was waiting for her.

Looking over at the monitor where Blackeye had been working, Emily realized that she had found something. On the screen were two files. The inside of her helmet informed her that it had scanned the computer screen, and found that the symbol that took up half of the screen was an encoded message, and the other half was a map. It didn't take Emily long to realize that it was a map of the catacombs.

"Bi!" Emily yelled. "Blackeye found the clue and a way for us to get out of here! There's an elevator to the surface just on the other side of this room!"

Bi glanced over her shoulder for only a moment, but Emily knew instantly what she was thinking. The hallway was now swarming with enemies that, although dead, were still intelligent enough to use their cards to open a door.

Emily didn't even have time to object as Bi closed the door with herself still outside.

10- The Next Clue

Emily ran through the forest with Blackeye, using her suit's built-in tracking system to find her way back to the Clan Duo compound. After letting her suit's technology scan over the strange encoded symbol that Emily had seen on Blackeye's screen, she had quickly run to the marked location that Blackeye had left on the map and located an elevator that had taken her to the surface. The sounds of war rang out through the air as soon as she left the small metal building that the elevator had brought her to on the surface and Emily knew that she had to move quickly.

An explosion went off in the distance as Emily and Blackeye ran side by side. The enemy was getting closer. They didn't know where she was, but if the fight happened to be between her and the compound, she would never make it, and the information would be lost.

Suddenly, a thought came into her head. The comms. They had been disabled in the catacombs but now that she was back on the surface they might be working again.

"Can anyone hear me?" she asked into her helmet. "This is Emily! I have a very important piece of information that needs to get back to the compound immediately."

She heard a scratching sound from the speakers in her helmet. They were busted. She had no idea if anyone was responding.

As the two girls ran, an Enforcement soldier came into view ahead of them. Blackeye shot him down instantly, but as they neared the fallen robot, Emily saw that it was simply a scout. The scouts were often positioned at the edge of an Enforcement army, and their death would alert the rest of the soldiers exactly where the enemy was.

It didn't take Enforcement very long to find them.

Within a matter of minutes, robots were beginning to show up from every side, the attacks becoming more frequent as they went along.

They were only about halfway back to Clan Duo headquarters when they got fully surrounded by robots. This time, instead of simply shooting and running, Blackeye stopped and held a defensive position, drawing a knife in each hand.

She locked eyes with Emily. "Go."

Emily followed her direction without hesitation and ran. Blackeye clearly knew that leaving Emily behind would be fruitless as she would barely slow down a squad of soldiers. It was better to let her run and hope she could get back.

As Blackeye disappeared from view, Emily once again tried to reach out on the comms, once again hearing simply static in response.

She decided she would just keep trying.

"I've made it back out of the catacombs!" she said, hoping someone on the other side was listening. "There was an encoded message in their database that I now-" She paused as she heard a rumbling noise in the trees in front of her.

She heard the crunch of trees being pushed over by a giant object that was rapidly heading her way. She had to dive to avoid getting crushed as the trees in front of her fell and knew she was doomed as she looked up to see that it was not an IPA tank to bring her back to safety.

It was a Stingray. Followed by a platoon of Enforcement soldiers.

Emily had no time to react as the energy cannon had already charged up and was facing toward her. They must have traced her signal as soon as she had crossed into enemy lines and used the comms.

She couldn't even brace herself as the blast shot toward her. But she didn't need to.

A figure jumped out of the forest in front of Emily, holding a circular shield up to block the cannon as it fired. They dug their feet into the ground as the force of the blast pushed the figure back. Emily watched as the beam from the Stingray hit the shield, the collision causing sparks to spray out in all directions along with small bits of liquified metal.

The blast stopped, and the robots looked startled to see that the figure was still alive. And so was Emily.

The man straightened, holding the shield at his side as he drew a slender, bladed staff from off of his back. He turned his head to the side slightly, his penetrating eyes looking at the Enforcement soldiers around him in pure concentration.

Flynn.

The enemy robots opened fire but it was no use. They were all dead in seconds, their smoking bodies littering the ground as Flynn shredded through them with his hiveblade.

The Stingray charged up another blast but Flynn ran forward, sliding under the vehicle as he pulled a grenade from his belt. He attached the explosive to the underside of the vehicle like he had done it hundreds of times. The Stingray exploded, sending pieces of metal flying through the air. Emily watched, half dreaming, as Flynn appeared through the flames of the explosion, a grin on his face.

Emily ran to him. She didn't know why, but she did. She embraced him. "You're alive." She felt so secure in his arms. His living arms.

"I had my jacket on," he explained. "It saved my life."

She looked up at him and realized she hadn't seen the left side of his face. It was burnt, bleeding and covered in blisters. It looked like his skin had been ripped off of his face, leaving nothing but blood and muscle. "Flynn," she gasped. "Your face."

She reached up to touch it but he stopped her. "Please don't. You have no idea how much it hurts to have exposed nerves touched." She let her hand fall. "The Stingray was shooting from far away, so my casual suit saved most of me. My face got a bad blow, but it will heal. My chest is worse. Wearing my jacket without zipping it up was not a good idea."

She didn't even want to know what this kind of pain was like. "And Eliza?"

"What about her?"

"Is she alive?"

He shook his head. "She incinerated into thin air. After I fell two stories to the ground, I lost consciousness. When I came to, I saw the troop carriers leaving and ran after you." He chuckled. "Seems like I caught up right in time."

"You didn't even check to see if she was alive?"

"No. You guys are much more important," Flynn said. Then he paused. "Wait. How did you know she was with me?"

"I..." Emily swallowed. "I went looking for you. I found a door cracked open and followed it up a staircase. I went to the door at the top and heard you guys talking and...I was watching you guys." Now that she was saying it, what she did sounded so stupid. "I'm sorry. I should have just walked away." Why was her voice cracking? She couldn't cry. Not here. Not in front of Flynn.

"Don't be sorry." He reached his hand up and stroked her hair gently. "It was stupid what Eliza did, especially after she found out about the two of us being together. She told me she was going up there to show me some places that Cara had told her to warn me about in the forest. She did at first of course but then..." He took a deep breath. "I'm the one that should be sorry."

"So you didn't enjoy it?" Emily asked.

"Not at all," Flynn said. "When it comes to someone kissing me, I have very specific expectations."

"Really?" she asked. "And what might those expectations be?"

"Well, for starters, there's only one girl who's allowed to do it," he said.

"And after that?"

He smiled. "After that it doesn't matter."

"Oh really?" She looked back up at him, and for a second, she didn't care that he was covered in blood. She felt herself leaning closer. She wanted to-

"Actually," Flynn said, making her pause. "There is one more thing. I won't do it in the middle of a battlefield." He released her. "Anyone who breaks those two rules has a high chance of getting vaporized by a tank." He turned back to the forest, the smile on his face fading. He was back to serious again. "We need to get back to the base."

Emily grabbed his hand as they ran through the forest. She knew that it was a lot slower, but she couldn't let go. She couldn't lose him again.

Flynn tried to hold perfectly still as the arms of the machine worked away at the left side of his face, the small metal prongs removing pieces of shrapnel from the tissue.

"With the active help of a healer, your face should make a full recovery," the nurse in the room said as the robotic arms rose away from him, the chair sitting him up automatically. "Your chest, on the other hand, will be much different. The blast caused major nerve damage to parts of

134

your spinal cord as well, and could affect movement in your entire body."

Flynn looked down at his chest, which was still blackened and made the veins in his midsection look much darker, spreading out in a spider-like pattern before returning to their normal color. The pain had been so excruciating that he could barely stand before, but the healer had given him medication to help numb the pain. "So...I won't be able to fight?"

The nurse looked at him. "Not nearly as effectively as you used to, at least for the time being." She opened the door to the small room. "The others are waiting for you in the library."

"Thank you." Flynn stood up and exited the room. His entire body felt sore, and his face ached with every movement. He walked past a mirror and paused to look at his face. The burnt section spread from across the left side of his face, starting about an inch away from his eye and stretching all the way to the back of his neck. There were small strips of metal that curved along the area that were supposed to help his skin grow back into the shape it was before. Luckily the blast had been a bit low so his ear hadn't been entirely incinerated. He thought of how Eliza had just disappeared, vaporizing in front of his eyes. Those weren't things he would forget.

He made his way to the library, where a group was gathered around the table. There was Cara's squad,

Captain Duo, Emily, a few other Duo soldiers, and Cago, who had been rescued from the collapsed part of the base after the others had left. It took Flynn a second to realize that these few were the only uninjured soldiers in the attack squad that were still alive after the ambush. And they were waiting for him.

He walked up to the group, who was gathered around a large circular table behind the throne. Flynn sat next to Emily, placing his arm around her shoulder. She stared at his face for a moment before turning to Captain Duo, who stood across the table.

"All of you fought bravely," Duo said. "We would like to recognize those who fell during the attack. Jane Turner, Namio Yogel, Hazel Maria..." She named off about five more people before reaching the end of the list. "Eliza Garside. May these soldiers rest in peace." The soldiers around the table nodded in agreement. "Now, we have some information for our friends from Clan Vilo."

The eyes around the table turned to one side, where Flynn sat alongside his two comrades.

"Cago and Flynn are still healing but will recover eventually, due to our healers," Duo said. "As for the other five members of their team..." She sighed, "All were captured, along with many of the others from our attack force. They are now well out of our territory.

"We sent out scouts but couldn't find any signs of them anywhere," Duo said. "Flynn, by order of the IPA regulations, you are now the standing leader of squad V-9. You now have the rank of Sergeant Scorpius. Your position will be held until Bi returns or is confirmed as dead."

Flynn felt a small shiver shoot through him and took a deep breath. The leader of the squad. "Thank you Captain. I will be honored to hold this position until Bi returns."

Duo looked as if she was about to remind him that she might not return before deciding against it and turning to the next point of interest. "Luckily for us, this mission was not a failure. Emily, you managed to come across the encoded message on Cadmore's List that we needed from the catacombs."

"Do we know what it said?" Emily asked.

Duo nodded, "It was an identification patch for a person named Jakar along with his residence in Atlanta. Searching for this 'Jakar' in Atlanta could lead to the end of this trail of clues. Atlanta is one of the many capital cities that have been established since the Ironborn came into existence, which means that it is under the jurisdiction of a group of powerful Ironborn leaders. As such, this means that Enforcement will have no power there, but you will not be able to receive help from the IPA. Your remaining squad members must go in alone."

Emily and Cago seemed to shoot a nervous glance to Flynn but he simply nodded. "Understood."

"There is another piece of news that I thought you, Flynn, might find..." she hesitated, "interesting. In their missions in Florida, Clan Troy recently recovered this recording of David Cadmore explaining the programming of his elite guard."

She pressed another button and a projection of David Cadmore appeared, again just showing his head and shoulders. However this time it looked like he was talking to someone else, unaware of whatever camera was filming him.

"The Blood Squad restriction is a safety precaution I made," he said. "Some people have asked, why have you only made five super soldiers in the Blood Squad? Why not make more?" He regarded the invisible person across from him knowingly. "The answer is simple. More than five will be too powerful. If the industry falls, and the wrong hands take it, having an army of Blood Squad soldiers would be catastrophic. Then again, having only five could also be disadvantageous if someone with good intent gains control, considering they could not rebuild any that were destroyed. Well, I have a simple answer for that as well. Each member of the Blood Squad can regenerate or heal, very quickly, without being organic. Likewise, there are hundreds of small 'eggs' in classified locations with a miniature super soldier inside that has the ability to grow quickly into a full-sized soldier. Now, some might ask, couldn't the eggs just be hatched, still creating the army that was feared? The answer is no. Each soldier also contains a small chip." He held up a piece of metal. "This chip lets the Blood sSquad's soldier's minds be connected, allowing them to think with supernatural speed. This chip is also how they know where each other are. If the chip senses that there is a sixth soldier with its chip active, then it will destroy said sixth chip, and the soldier along with it. The same will happen with any amount of soldiers. This ensures that there are always five super soldiers, no more and no less."

Flynn stared at the space above the table as the image disappeared. "So it was all for nothing?" he asked. "There are just new Blood Squad members to replace the old ones?"

Duo nodded slowly. "Apparently Dr.Griffin did not think it necessary to use the super soldiers until now, which makes sense considering this is his final push in the war. As far as we know, there is now a new Blood Squad."

Flynn cursed and slammed his fist against the table. Emily put a hand on his shoulder, reassuring him. "You still defeated them," she said. "Not even Troy could do that. That didn't change."

Flynn swallowed and nodded. "So what's next?"

"The three of you will go to Atlanta immediately," Duo said.

Flynn looked up, surprised. "We aren't prepared. I can't even fight yet, and I need a healer."

"You don't have time to wait here. The war is already becoming too desperate as it stands," Duo said. "I will send Genny with you." She motioned to a girl sitting next to her. She was small and slim, with blonde hair that was buzzed on one side. The top and other side was dyed a dark blue and fell down a few inches above her shoulder, partially covering her eye. "Genny was only admitted to the IPA a few weeks ago, and wasn't yet on the records when they were stolen. She is one of our best healers." Genny nodded toward them. "As for being ready, I believe you have proved yourself in combat enough to show that you are ready. The three of you are very resourceful. I believe in you. *Our species* believes in you."

Flynn nodded. "I won't let you down."

Blackeye awoke with a start, fogginess clouding her mind. The last thing she remembered was attacking the parasites in the Catacombs. Where was she now?

Her senses kicked in. She could feel cold metal beneath her. She could see the cuffs holding her hands in place. She could tell there was a blindfold on her but that didn't matter. She could see anyways.

She looked around without moving her eyes. They were in a van. By the looks of the other figures tied in the back of the van with her, the only ones not present were Flynn, Cago and Emily.

She could see the four Enforcement guards standing in the corners of the van, along with the two in the front. She desperately wished that she had her sniper rifle so she could blast their heads into bits.

But there was no way to fight back. She was stuck. And based on how fast the van was speeding along the road, she and the others were being taken somewhere.

INTERLUDE

11- Havoc

Easton could feel his muscles straining as he tightened the bolt on the underside of a lander. After it felt secure, he got out from underneath the vehicle, walking around it so he could assure himself that everything was fixed.

He glanced around the garage for a moment. This base was part of Clan Neo, specifically district 5, in Goblin Valley, Utah. Because of the immense amount of sandstone in the surrounding area, the base itself was built directly into a mountainside. This kept it hidden well, but also caused lots of dust to get everywhere, making more maintenance work for Easton.

"Hey 1357!" someone called from across the garage. Easton turned to see Havoc walking toward him. "You almost got that thing fixed? I don't want it falling apart on me on my next mission."

"I think it's good now," Easton said as Havoc approached. Havoc was a few inches taller than Easton, and was much more thin. With his black hair and serious

146

complexion, he looked more like a politician than the flaming menace Easton knew him to be.

"Good," he said. He walked beside Easton and looked at the lander. "I wonder when they will put us out again."

"Soon, probably," Easton replied. Every few months each squad from Clan Adila would be deployed onto the battlefield, fighting for a couple of months in the long plains and massive deserts before coming back to the base with a truck full of injured soldiers.

Havoc sniffed. "Our squad will be ready. We have doubled our training."

"And the Enforcement have doubled their strength," Easton reminded him. "We need to be careful. We can't lose you, or our district will be lost. Besides, you don't do too bad here."

"Here?" Havoc asked. "You mean defending the base from the raids? You guys could do that without me. I'd be much more valuable on the field."

Easton shook his head. Havoc was the only soldier he knew that enjoyed the war. Maybe that's what made him such a killing machine. Or maybe it was just his powers.

An alarm began blaring through the garage. "Let's see if you're right," Easton said. "I bet Commander Gideon will give you some notice if you do good in this raid."

Havoc chuckled darkly, the closest thing to humor he ever showed. "Yeah right. Like Gideon has ever given me any notice before."

Easton made his way across the garage and grabbed his rifle. He was so used to the raid alarm going off that he hardly even heard it.

The other members of Easton's squad came into the garage and hopped into the lander, filling the benches in the back. Easton sat down with them as the truck pulled out of the garage and into the desert, speeding along the dusty orange land with the sun blazing in the cloudless sky overhead.

The only color outside the base was orange. Orange rocks, orange mountains, orange pillars of stone. The area of Goblin Valley around their base was riddled with hoodoos, filling the land by the hundreds, making it impossible to see more than thirty or so feet in any direction.

The jeep drove for a while before stopping, allowing the soldiers to get out. "Soldiers, split up!" Gideon yelled. "We can't allow the raid to get to the base. Use dragon formation."

The soldiers spread out, moving around the hoodoos and pillars of rock. Easton held his gun at chest height, ready to shoot any enemy that came in sight.

He turned his scanner on and searched the area. With the rocks in the way, the scanner was ineffective from a distance, but Easton could see an enemy making its way through the rocks. He ran towards it, pressing his back against a rock as the soldier approached.

As soon as the robot came into view, Easton shot, and the soldier dropped to the ground.

He stepped over the soldier, following in its footsteps. They weaved through the rocks, heading away from the base.

As Easton followed the tracks, the rock in front of him exploded, sending bits of rock and orange dust flying through the air.

Easton spun and spotted the robot, laying on a rock pillar in a prone position, his sniper rifle aimed at Easton.

He blasted the bot off of its perch before continuing farther away from the base. More enemies came into view but he eliminated them quickly. The key with these raids was to kill as many enemies as you could. Once their forces had been reduced enough, they would back away, calling off the attack.

Easton didn't know why the raids even happened. They didn't do very much, and only one base had ever been greatly affected by it, but the robots continued doing them, about one every day.

After going for a while without finding another enemy, Easton climbed atop one of the rocks, searching the area. His attention was instantly captured as he watched a scene play out about fifty yards away from his position.

Multiple explosions went off, blasting bits of rock through the air as enemy soldiers all fired at a single target.

A figure rose into the sky above the black robots, contrasting their dark silhouettes with the intense light it emitted. He had the shape of a human with an aura of fiery skin, spreading its flaming wings like a phoenix as it glared down at its opponents. Somewhere beneath all that, Easton knew that there was a face with dark, piercing eyes with matching hair and a wicked, crazed smile.

"Havoc." Easton shook his head. "Always stealing all of the attention."

The flaming soldier blazed down toward his enemies, incinerating everything in his path as flames erupted from all around him. He spun and dove, soaring in between the pillars of orange rock, leaving the robots with no chance of survival.

The dragon formation. The soldiers fanned out in two directions, like the wings of a dragon, with Havoc in the middle as the fire-breathing head. Easton spotted another area where more of his teammates were fighting and ran over to the action.

The soldiers fought together for a while, dropping any troops that appeared in their little clearing in the rocks. A group of three soldiers came into view in front of Easton. He raised his gun and shot, dropping two before the last one dove behind the cover of a rock.

Easton kept his gun trained on where the soldier would come back into view but, to his surprise, it never came.

All of the soldiers looked around in confusion as the robots began dispersing, disappearing into the rocks.

Commander Gideon turned to one of his soldiers. "Kai, where are they going?"

Kai ran and jumped high into the air, spinning before landing down on one of the pillars. "I can't see them."

Gideon cursed. "We need to follow them."

"There is no need." Havoc appeared in the clearing, seeming to materialize out of nowhere. "They are retreating."

"Retreating?" Gideon asked, confused. "These are raid soldiers. They never retreat this quickly."

"And yet they are," Havoc replied. He lifted a few feet in the air and looked in the distance. "They're not even in sight now."

"This is different from anything they have done before. Something is coming." Gideon looked off in the direction where their enemies had fled. "Something bad."

PART II

THE HUNT

12- Welcome to Atlanta

"What does this one do again?" Emily asked.

Flynn looked to where she was pointing. "That's the release switch," he said. "When the Rizen is flying over cities, we don't want people to see us, which is why we have the camouflaging underside of the ship, but we also don't want them to hear us. While the release switch is down, the Rizen can't go above the speed that will let us be visible."

Emily nodded and leaned back in the co-pilot chair. With Zane and Ryan being gone, Flynn had taken their place as pilot, and had begun teaching Emily all the things he could remember about the ship's controls.

The door in the back of the cockpit opened and Genny poked her head through. Her hair was a dark red color today and her feet were bare, like usual. "Flynn, it's time."

Flynn nodded and stood up, following her into one of the rooms. Genny had set up a medical area in one of the

156

unused bedrooms, which was now full of many tools and small machines that Flynn did not recognize.

"Lie down," Genny said, motioning to the table in the middle of the room. Her voice was light and optimistic, but also had a bit of a spunk to it. Flynn did what she said, feeling the cold metal through his thin shirt.

Genny pulled out a few tools and inspected the side of his face, jotting down notes and making observations as she went. She then moved to his chest, studying where it was damaged.

"Everything seems to be recovering well," Genny said. "If you continue healing at this rate, you might be able to fight without any restriction in about..." She looked down at the screen in her hand. "Eight months."

Flynn ran a hand through his hair. He didn't care if he was injured. He would help his species survive. No matter what.

Flynn and Genny walked back out into the hallway and to the front cockpit where Cago and Emily were talking in the two piloting seats.

"Hey!" Genny called to them. "Can you two come back here?"

They walked to the back section of the cockpit and stood around the table.

"What do you guys know about Atlanta?" Genny asked them.

"It's a capital city," Flynn said. "And even that doesn't mean much to me."

Genny nodded. "Not many know much about them unless they live there," she said. "Luckily, I have done a fair share of research on various capital cities. In a capital city, Enforcement will have little to no control. This is because each capital city is owned by a very powerful Ironborn, and usually a group of his or her followers. Some of these powerful Ironborn may have the ability to disable robots or create near infinite amounts of destruction on its enemies. These Ironborn have been confronted by the Industry many times, but still they stand strong. Atlanta is run by two major gangs, the Reds and the Navys. Our target, Jakar, is probably a member of one of these gangs."

"Reds and Navys?" Cago asked.

Genny nodded. "In these cities, the human populations make up the Red Army and the Ironborn make up the smaller group of Navys. Each group has their own leaders that help dictate the city... 'together.' Despite the protection from the outside world, these places are far from safe. There's a reason that even Cadmore Industries avoids these cities. We need to be cautious."

Flynn nodded. "I'll look into it more before we arrive."

"What are we supposed to do once we find this guy?" Cago asked Genny.

"Don't look at me." Genny turned to Flynn. "I'm not in charge. I just know about the city." She had pulled one of her knives out from somewhere and had begun fiddling with it.

"Well," Flynn looked at Cago. "We'll have to see whether or not he'll help us or if we will need to..." Flynn paused. "Convince him."

Genny smiled, still twirling her knife. "I like this 'convincing' idea."

Flynn looked toward her. "We will only do that if necessary." Genny pouted but said nothing. "We don't fully know what exact problems we might face here. I think we should get to the city first, then discuss our plan."

Some glances were shared around the table. "Sounds fine with me," Emily said.

"Proxy, how much time do we have until we reach Atlanta?" Flynn asked.

"Twenty eight minutes," the voice said.

"Alright." Flynn turned to the others. "Let's go get ready."

Flynn went back into his room and started to get all of his equipment ready, setting his hiveblade, mataka, and gun out in the hallway. He put his leather jacket on and slid a backpack over his shoulder before walking back out into the cockpit. Emily stood with her backpack, frowning slightly.

"What's wrong?" Flynn asked her.

She sighed. "I just feel like I'm forgetting something. In Hawaii, it was like all of my training had vanished. Once I entered the actual battle, everything you had taught me was gone."

Flynn nodded. "That's how I was for a long time, but I got used to it. Besides," he continued, "I'll be with you this time."

She smiled. "That will be nice."

Flynn smiled in return. "How are you feeling after your first fight?"

She looked down at the ground. "It's a bit scary, but this is what I want to do. I want to help the world be more equal."

Flynn wished he could help her feel safe. He wished he could make it so that she wouldn't have to worry. The problem was, he didn't know if he would even be around to save her.

Genny walked in and looked at the two talking. "My apologies for intruding." She smiled jokingly and walked to the front of the cockpit. Her tone turned darker. "Hey guy, we are approaching our destination, but our scanners aren't reading very many life forms. I suggest you bring this thing below the clouds."

Flynn walked to the front and sat down in the pilot's seat. Cago walked in and sat next to him a few seconds later.

Reaching forward, Flynn pulled a handle down slowly as they dropped through the layer of peaceful whiteness. And beneath, chaos.

The city of Atlanta was in flames, the high rising buildings crumbling and collapsing to the ground below. Surrounding the city was the cause of the destruction. Hundreds of Cadmore Industry airships cast a shadow over the dozens of Enforcement tanks and platoons on the ground.

For a second, Flynn and his crew watched the chaos in silence, staring as destruction rained over the city. Genny was the first to break the silence by using a word Bi would have criticized Flynn for saying.

As the reality of his situation fell upon him, Flynn tried to think of a way out.

"There!" Emily pointed out the front window at a ship attempting to escape the city. "Follow it! Enforcement will think we're one of them."

Flynn turned and looked at Emily.

"What?"

"That's just..." Flynn blinked. "That's a great idea."

Moving quickly, he spun the Rizen around and followed the escaping ship, trying to mimic Enforcement maneuvers.

As they got closer, two guns on the rear of the ship began firing back at them. "Cago!" Flynn said quickly. "Hail them!"

Cago fumbled with the buttons for a second before pressing the right one. "Air cruiser!" he said into the comm. "Stop firing! We're from the IPA!"

Flynn flashed him a look. "Just because they're running for their lives doesn't mean they like the IPA."

Cago shrugged.

The guns stopped firing but stayed trained on their ship. "How do we know that you aren't enemies?" a voice said back through the comms.

"Wouldn't we have shot you down by now?" Cago asked.

"Good point," the voice responded.

"You're from the capital city, right?" Cago asked, "We're Ironborn, like you probably are."

"All of us in here are. However," the man said, "not all Ironborn are good. None of them helped us escape from the flesh guard."

"What's the flesh guard?" Cago asked.

"The flesh guard?" the voice asked. "They are the reason all of this started. The reason that Revenant and his followers have run to Chicago. The reason for everything you see behind you."

Flynn pulled up next to the other ship so he could see the pilot. He was a middle-aged man with a bald head and a long beard. Beside him sat a few others. His family.

"But what are they?" Cago asked.

The man seemed about to respond when his ship exploded into a ball of flames, pieces of shrapnel falling out of the sky as another Enforcement ship flew past them.

Genny used her favorite word again.

"No!" Emily exclaimed. Her face turned from surprise to anger. "He had a family! They might've not even been Ironborn!"

Flynn drew in a deep breath. "That's the way that Enforcement works. They don't ask questions, they just kill."

Genny said what they were all thinking. "Let's get out of here."

13- Interrogation

A jet flies above a breathtaking mountain landscape, speeding across the sky as fast as it can. The pilot, his helmet obscuring his concerned face, says something to the co-pilot seated behind him.

As the jet goes over the next ridge, black ships begin to appear, coming out of the obscurity of the trees below, rising up around the jet from all directions.

The pilot looks from side to side, his eyes studying his surroundings. As the enemy planes begin to fire, he swerves and dodges every shot and weaves through the small shield of enemies in front of him. The ships follow behind as he bolts away and more enemies begin to rise from the ground.

The other pilot grabs the ship's gun and begins firing back but, despite his deadly accuracy, it is nearly ineffective as more ships begin rising up, swarming around them.

In front of the jet, the enemies create a wall of pure metal out of their ships, blocking the way. The pilot swerves quickly, trying to find another escape, but it is in vain. The pure number of ships is too much. They are surrounded.

The two pilots watch as the sky around them begins to turn black, and the wall of planes spreads in a full ring around them, trapping them in. Even then, more enemy ships begin swarming around the small aircraft.

The pilot continues to swerve and dodge, not letting a single enemy hit its target. His reactions are better than any other soldier. They seem impossible. They seem... inhuman.

The wall begins to close in, and the ships swarm around the two pilots like a massive flock of starving, carnivorous birds, creating a tornado of metal.

The pilot turns the nose of the jet to the only place that still has any light. The top of the tornado.

With determination, he grits his teeth and begins weaving toward it. As he flies upward, the swarm begins to disperse but the hole begins to close in, the space darkening more.

As he analyzes the swarm, the pilot realizes he won't make it out before the hole closes off. He turns to the pilot behind him and hands him a small data chip.

The other pilot stares at it for a second. "No! Don't-"

The pilot in front presses a button and the gunner gets ejected from the jet, falling past the swarm unnoticed.

The hole closes off and plunges the area into darkness, the only light is the engines of the thousands of planes.

The jet spins toward the ground, spiraling through the swarm, blasting enemy ships apart by the dozens before disappearing from view as enemy ships cover it. A few moments later, a blast of light bursts through the darkness. The ship is destroyed.

As the pieces of metal fall, a single piece of burning cloth still clings to a metal badge. A pilot captain badge, marked with gray.

The highest ranking pilot of Clan Troy, the best pilot in the world, was now dead.

"Ryan, wake up!" Ryan heard a voice pierce through his mind.

He slowly opened his drowsy eyes to see Tarff's familiar face looking down at him. "What's going on?" He sat up and looked around. "Where are we?"

He was currently in an entirely metal room, the only thing other than himself being Tarff. Both of them were in solid black jumpsuits. Both of their IPA suits were gone.

"They transferred us from the truck to this cell," the Tongan replied. "I don't know our exact location."

"Where are the others?" Ryan asked.

Tarff sighed. "I wish I knew. I only woke up a few seconds ago. Maybe they kept you and Zane separate because they knew of your similar powers."

Ryan nodded. "That would make sense. I wonder if he is near us."

Tarff furrowed his brow. "I guess there's no way to know."

Tarff looked around at the cell surrounding them. "These walls are too strong to break through. I already tried. I think our best bet is for you to try to get in contact with Zane. Who knows? Maybe Blackeye can even see us."

"I could see them earlier," Blackeye said.

"Can you see them now?" Zane asked. He himself could see nothing. Their cell was pitch black.

Blackeye shook her head. "They have toxins running into our cells to lessen our abilities by dampening our brain power."

Now that Zane paused to think, he realized that he did feel quite tired despite being unconscious for multiple hours, and felt less in touch with his powers.

Zane had always compared using powers to running a race. A runner can not run forever, and the faster he runs, the faster he runs out of energy. With an Ironborn's powers, the more you used your powers, the quicker your reservoir would deplete. But, after the race is over, the runner can regenerate his energy, and can run again after a little break. The same goes for Ironborn abilities. If they had them captured in a cell, they could keep their energy spent forever using a controlled amount of numbing toxins.

"I wasn't able to find Bi," Blackeye said.

"Maybe she got away," Zane said.

Blackeye did not respond.

Zane looked over at her. She had actually begun to talk to Zane regularly ever since they woke up in the cell about half an hour ago. She always had a rather annoyed tone in her voice but at least it was something.

"I can see two forms approaching our cell." She said to him. "Get up. They're almost here."

The sound of footsteps could be heard, but they still seemed far away. Zane decided to stand up anyways. The footsteps stopped and a few clanking noises were heard and the latches to the door were undone.

A hissing noise filled the air as the door's vacuum seal discharged and the door swung open. A dozen Enforcement soldiers stood outside, along with one low-ranking officer.

"You're coming with us," the officer said.

A few guards stepped forward and grabbed Zane, pulling him out of the room. The group of robots pulled Zane down the hall where they stepped into an elevator.

"So where are we going?" Zane asked jokingly. "Am I getting a room upgrade?"

The officer continued looking forward, unamused. "Not quite."

"Well if you could maybe put a word in for me to whoever's in charge here that would be nice," Zane said as the doors to the elevator opened. The Enforcement soldiers led him down the hall where they stopped and a door opened.

"Let me tell you," Zane said. "Our room is not the brightest, it's all dark and..." He trailed off as he saw the room in front of him. Like the rest of the prison, it was made of dull gray metal but with shelves lining the walls. In the center of the room was a large metal chair.

Zane was beginning to think that his cell wasn't so bad after all.

The robots forced him into the chair where his arms and legs were clamped in place. The four soldiers stepped back to the edges of the room as the officer held up a digital control pad in his hand. He pressed a button and Zane felt two pieces of metal beside his head compress closer. He hadn't seen it before but now he noticed each one had a half-dozen sharp probes.

"Not so jovial anymore, are you?" the officer sneered as the probes sparked with electricity.

Zane smiled. "I'm doing just fine actua-"

The probes quickly pressed into the sides of Zane's skull, and he groaned as the pain caused his body to tense up.

The probes released themselves and Zane took a deep breath.

The officer smiled maliciously. "That was only the lowest level of this machine." He looked at Zane as if trying to read him.

Zane smiled in return.

"Your smile will fade soon enough," the officer said scornfully. "You and the rest of the rebels that were captured in Hawaii could be carrying valuable information."

"What makes you think we're going to tell you anything?" Zane asked

"Oh, trust me," the officer said. "Pain can be very convincing." He pressed a button on his control pad and the metal plates pressed themselves into the sides of Zane's head again.

The shock this time was even more surprising than last time, and the pain had doubled, causing Zane to jerk to the side. When the pain subsided, the smile on Zane's face stayed the same but he could feel his energy dropping, as if the machine was physically draining him.

"Tell me," the officer said. "What was it that your squad was looking for in the catacombs?"

Zane took a few deep breaths. "A sandwich."

The probes shocked him again with the same power as last time.

The officer gave a knowing look that made Zane want to punch him. He doubted he would even have the ability to do so.

"What would be so important that four soldiers sacrificed themselves to assure its security?" he asked.

Zane's smile was barely detectable now. He felt like he had just run a marathon but he hadn't moved. His entire body felt sore, and his mind was weak. "A sandwich."

This time the probes' power had leveled up again and Zane heard an involuntary scream leave his mouth as the probes moved away.

"Still comfortable?" the officer asked. "Good. Now remind me." The officer pressed a button on his control panel and Zane could now hear the probes buzzing beside his head. "What was it again that you were searching for?"

Zane stayed silent, not wanting the pain to return. He could hear the probes moving closer to the sides of his skull. The officer stared at him, now emotionless.

The buzzing got louder and Zane felt his hands begin to shake, as if they were trying to force themselves out of the chair.

"A file!" Zane didn't even feel like he had said it. It was like his brain had forced him to speak. "We were looking for a file."

Zane heaved a sigh of relief as the probes moved a few inches further away from his head, not enough for him to be out of danger yet, but enough to calm him down slightly.

The officer smiled, knowing he had broken through. "What kind of file?"

"I don't know," Zane said. The probes were still only inches from his head.

They then shot inward, digging into the sides of his skull. Zane felt a scream burst out of his mouth as he felt like electricity was coursing through his veins. He then heard a loud crack, and he opened his eyes to see something astonishing. Arcs of lightning were shooting across the room, exploding outward from his chest and dissipating into the floor and walls.

The probes turned off, and Zane took a couple shuddering breaths. He felt like he now knew what it was like to be on the verge of death. Every bit of energy inside him was gone.

The officer looked around the room, still astonished at what he had just seen. He then looked back at Zane. "Interesting." He jotted down a few notes on the electronic pad in his hand. "Have any answers for me now?"

Zane didn't even know if he had the ability to speak.

The officer shrugged. "No matter. There are three more who went with you. I will find out from them."

Ryan smiled at the officer as he was tied down to the chair.

"Your brother has the same smile," the officer said. "It wasn't there by the time I finished with him."

"Zane?" Ryan asked. "He's weak."

"Well then," the officer said, "Let's see how much stronger you really are."

Ryan felt pain stab into the sides of his skull as the torture began.

"Your brother mentioned a file," the officer said. "What was on this file?"

"I don't know," Ryan said snidely.

"Well at least it's not a sandwich," the officer mumbled. He looked deep into Ryan's eyes. "The IPA sent you on a mission to retrieve a file and you went in without even knowing what you were looking for?"

"They told me it would hurt people like you," Ryan said, still smiling. "That was enough for me."

He felt the probes stab into him again.

"You have no idea the amount of pain I can inflict on you," the officer said, walking up to his chair. "All you need to do is tell me what you know."

Ryan looked up at his enemy. If he hadn't been tied down, he could probably reach up and knock the guy out. He felt his hand close into a fist. One of the robots on the edge of the room saw the movement and stepped forward, raising his gun toward Ryan.

The officer chuckled and waved his hand, motioning for the soldier to back down. "You have no other options, boy." He pressed the button again, and Ryan had to force himself not to make a noise.

"What was so important about this file?" the officer asked.

"I swear I don't know," Ryan lied. "I'm just one of the soldiers. They don't tell us anything."

The officer's eyes narrowed. "So someone else knows?"

Ryan furrowed his brow for a moment, not wanting to give anything away. "No," he said hesitantly.

The officer smiled. "Thank you for your compliance."

Zane sat on the cold metal floor, trying to rest his mind. He was still shaken after his session in the chair yesterday.

"I wonder where they're taking us," Zane said, rubbing his eyes. According to what they had been told, today was the day when they would finish the interrogations, after which they would be taken away.

He looked over at where Blackeye was sitting in the darkness on her cot. He was trying to brainstorm a way out of here. The information given to them was very limited but he had heard enough to know that wherever they were about to go was worse than where they currently were. They needed to escape.

The door behind Zane opened and he stood suddenly as a group of Enforcement soldiers appeared in the room, grabbing Blackeye from off of the cot.

"No!" Zane said, jumping toward them and trying to pull the robots away from her. He wouldn't let them do anything to her.

One of the robots pushed him out of the way, shoving him to the ground and aiming its gun at his chest.

"Don't, Zane," Blackeye said simply. Now that the door was open and light was shining into the cell, Zane could see the back of her head, but the bright light from the hallway contrasting the darkness of the cell made her nothing more than a blank silhouette. "You know you can trust me to be quiet."

The robots quickly pulled her out of the room and down the hall. The robot that had shoved Zane to the ground turned to follow them and an idea sprung into Zane's mind. He leapt upward suddenly, grabbing a cord on the back of the robot's neck and yanking. It didn't snap.

Zane noticed that, although the cord was still fine, a small piece of metal had broken off and fallen to the ground. The robot spun, firing his gun. Zane crouched down to dodge the shot before rolling behind the robot and reaching upward, using the shard of metal to cut the cord.

The robot collapsed to the ground as it lost power, and Zane listened to hear the sound of the elevator going downstairs. He quickly found the button on the robot's arm to close the cell door before dragging the metal body to the middle of the room. He only had a few minutes to work but if he was lucky, this might just work.

14- A Wish

The Rizen, Somewhere in the air
Mid-East, U.S.A.
5:00 p.m.
Flynn

The calm sky almost made Emily forget that they were in the middle of a war. The passing clouds looked so peaceful that she almost forgot about what she had seen in Atlanta. Almost.

Genny walked up beside Emily and looked out the window with her. Today her hair was bright green with a silvery glint. "Are you doing alright?"

"Yeah," Emily sighed. "I just really want this war to be over."

"Don't we all?" Genny asked. "I've seen this war change so many people I know. On both sides people are turning into hate-filled killing machines. I just hope I am part of the better of the two evils."

Emily nodded in agreement. "I hate the way Flynn gets when danger is around. It's necessary for his survival of course but..." She trailed off. "I wish I could just be with him without a distraction. Just have one night with him where the war doesn't interrupt us. Where his powers don't get in the way. Where it's just us."

Genny seemed to be lost in thought. "Maybe someday it will be possible." She nodded, as if confirming it would happen. "We will win this war. I'll make sure of it."

The door to the cockpit opened and Flynn and Cago entered. Flynn, unlike the rest of them, wasn't wearing his suit. He was just in a leather jacket and black jeans. For a moment Emily started to smile before she realized that it was still his suit, just his undercover one.

"Are you guys finally ready?" Genny asked, walking over to the hologram table.

Flynn nodded. "I hope so."

"Good because we're almost there." She pressed some buttons on the table. "Chicago, like Atlanta, is a capital city, so it is ruled by an Ironborn. Chicago was said to be the second strongest capital city but now that Atlanta is gone, it is the first."

Flynn nodded. "Is there any conflict in this city?"

"Yes," Genny said. "There are two main gangs. There is the Red army, who they call Reds, and the Navys, along with a variety of smaller ones. The person who rules over Chicago is named Nicholas Comradde."

She pressed a button on the side of the table and a holographic image popped up. It showed a middle-aged man with buzzed blonde hair and a muscular build. He wore a nice black suit, and had a large scar running down the left side of the back of his head.

"Comradde is a very powerful Ironborn who contains unknown powers, but they are rumored to be extremely powerful. Comradde, before he became an Ironborn, was the owner of a weapons building company that supplied the U.S. military, Comradde Weaponry Corporation. 'A Comradde to our Country', as they would say. He now uses that business to supply his own soldiers, the Navy gang. The Navys are the biggest, but far from the only, gang in the city. Jakar, the man we are looking for, is from neither gang. He chooses a more neutral approach."

A new image appeared, this time of a Spaniard man who had black hair that was combed back to the base of his neck.

"They are a Navy-affiliate gang, meaning they side against the Reds in conflict." The image disappeared. "Then there is the mysterious 'flesh guard' the man from the other ship was talking about.``

Flynn nodded, taking in the information. Emily saw the calculative look in his eyes. "I assume the Reds and Navys are enemies?"

Genny nodded. "Even with all its strength, if the Enforcement attacks, I wonder if Chicago will stay standing. They are already being destroyed from the inside."

"So what's our mission?" Cago asked.

All eyes turned to Flynn. "Why are you looking at me?" he asked.

Cago shrugged. "You by far have the most experience."

"Technically now that your sergeant isn't here, and you're a lieutenant," Genny said. "You're in charge."

Flynn thought for a second. "Yeah I guess you're right."

Emily smiled. "So, Lieutenant Scorpius, what's our plan?"

"It depends if Chicago still exists." Flynn said, pressing a few of the Rizen's controls.

When the Rizen came under the clouds this time, Flynn let out a sigh of relief. Chicago looked big, loud, and chaotic, but it wasn't in flames. At least not yet.

Flynn looked over at Emily in the co-pilot seat. She looked nervous but would probably be fine. Genny was looking out the front window at Chicago like she wanted to eat it for breakfast, so she seemed normal.

Cago was the only one that seemed to be unsettled. He kept fidgeting, like he wanted to get out of his seat.

"Hey Cago, you alright?" Flynn asked.

"Huh?" Cago looked at him. "Oh yeah I'm fine."

He did not seem fine. "Good," Flynn said. "Because we're about to arrive."

Flynn looked down at the ground below. Outside of the main city, there was an area of desolation, a large ring of abandoned buildings surrounding the metropolis. The buildings probably used to be tall and magnificent, but were now no more than burnt pieces of crumbling rubble.

"That's weird," Genny said.

"What?" Cago asked.

"Look at where the city starts." Genny pointed. "Where the destroyed buildings end."

Flynn saw what she was pointing out. There was a building at the edge of the city that seemed to be cut in half, as if split between being a normal building and being destroyed. Flynn noticed there were many buildings like this in a ring surrounding the city, perhaps from a previous conflict.

"It's almost as if there was some supernatural dome that prevented whatever destroyed these buildings from getting to the city," Flynn said.

"Like a force field?" Emily asked.

"Yeah, kind of like a force field," Flynn said. "And I assume we're going to want to land inside of it."

As they neared the boundary, a voice crackled through their ship's intercom. "Horizon class fighter ship, you are not permitted in this area. As property of Cadmore Industries you must state your business or we will follow our orders and you will be destroyed."

"They think we're Enforcement," Genny said.

Flynn nodded and reached to the comm. "This is Scorpius, owner of the Rizen, a refurbished Industry ship. We're here looking for an old friend."

There was a pause. "Identification?"

Flynn looked at the others. They were all just as clueless. "Scorpius?" he said.

"Scorpius is not a recorded gang in our city," the man said. "Are you from Atlanta?"

"Yes." It was technically true.

"Does your gang have an ambassador?"

Flynn again looked around. This time Cago was nodding vigorously.

"My name is Mantis," Genny spoke up. "I am the ambassador."

"Mantis, what is your affiliation?"

Genny swallowed. "Red Army."

There was another pause. The four Ironborn held their breath.

"Affirmative," the man said. "Your ship can land at the coordinates I sent you."

Flynn let out a sigh of relief and pulled up the coordinates into the ship's computer.

He turned to Genny. "Mantis?"

She shrugged.

"I like it." He watched as they passed over the line of destruction and into the boundary, and let out another sigh of relief. "We made it." As he said this, the ship lurched to one side, throwing Flynn against the side of his seat.

Flynn wrestled with the controls, trying to get the ship level. Each time he made an adjustment however, the ship would be thrown in a different direction.

The comm crackled to life again. "Scorpius aircraft, what in the blazes are you doing?"

"Our ship isn't working," Flynn got out.

"Rizen, exit the boundary immediately," the voice said.

The ship began spiraling toward the ground, but Flynn managed to pull it out of the boundary, where it partially leveled out before landing roughly in an abandoned street.

"What the heck just happened?" Emily asked.

No one had an answer except for Genny, who just kept repeating her favorite word over and over again.

A new voice came through the comm. "My apologies," he said. "We will permit you to come inside the city, but your ship must stay outside."

Flynn unbuckled himself from his seat and turned to the others. "I guess we'll just have to hope whatever destroyed these buildings is long gone."

"And we'll have to trust this stupid city to keep our ship safe," Genny said. Then she stood up. "I'm going outside."

Flynn shrugged as she exited the cockpit. "I guess there's no point in waiting," he said. "Proxy, turn on the auto-defense system."

No reply came.

"Proxy?"

Flynn waited a few seconds but nothing happened. He shared a glance with Cago.

"Maybe the circuit got fried while we passed into the city," he guessed.

"Maybe," Flynn replied. "I'll check it out. You go get our stuff outside and ready."

Cago and Emily exited as Flynn walked to the left side of the cockpit. He opened the control panel and began looking through the system. He found nothing.

Flynn walked down the ramp and joined the others. "I may not be as tech savvy as Zane, but it seems like nothing about the system was damaged."

"So she's just gone?" Cago asked.

Flynn shrugged. "I guess so. I'll have Zane look at it once..." He paused. "When we see him again."

Everyone was silent for a moment.

"Well," Genny said. "Let's go see Chicago."

15- Silence

Blackeye sat in the interrogation chair, her mind feeling much more open now that the toxins weren't weighing down on her senses. Being in the cell was almost a form of torture for her, as she remembered how life used to be back when she was fully blind. Back before she got her powers.

She looked around, analyzing everything in the room. To her surprise, she could see that there was a small room just outside of this one that was full of various items, including weapons and tools the robots had taken from them. She assumed all of their personal items were there to be analyzed. The more you know about someone, the easier it is to interrogate them.

"So," the officer picked up his control panel. "What's your story?"

Blackeye said nothing. She knew how to be quiet. That was something she knew very well.

"Each person from your group eventually opened up to me," the officer said. "But there's still one missing piece. All three of the other rebels with you were together in the catacombs but, as I learned in my last questioning, you were not with them. Meaning, if my sources are correct, you are the only one who knows what is on this infamous file."

Blackeye kept her face emotionless but smiled lightly in her mind. She had seen the file but had no idea what the coded image had meant.

"Or possibly," the officer went on. "You know another way for me to find out what is on it."

That was something Blackeye did know. She still had to keep everything she knew about the mission safe.

"Not quite the most talkative one are you?" the officer asked, "You can't stay quiet for long."

The panels beside Blackeye's head closed, and she felt the probes shock her skull. She didn't move.

"You're stronger than the others." The officer smiled. "This will be fun." He turned a knob on his control panel and she felt the probes attack her with even more force. She took a deep breath, still not moving.

Her mind flashed back to her childhood. This officer didn't know his own weakness. Whenever she felt pain as a child, it taught her to be quiet. To stay still. To stop existing. The more pain, the quieter she got.

The officer turned up the potency and caused the probes to strike again, leaving them on for twice as long as before.

She remembered the 'lessons' she had been taught. Her parents used to use pain to train her into behaving, turning her from an already shy girl into a statue. Into a robot. She couldn't speak, couldn't complain. She had sat through the pain of losing her sight to the point of permanent blindness, yet she hadn't made a sound. This man could do nothing to her.

The officer's gaze wavered slightly.

Blackeye's mind now turned to what Bi had taught her. "To truly know your enemy is to gain victory." Blackeye knew exactly what the officer wanted, and she knew that he was running out of ways to get information out of her. He was losing.

The officer turned the knob all the way up, turning the probes back on and walking over to stand in front of the chair.

He glared down on her as the electricity pierced into her brain. "You will tell me what you know!" he yelled.

She could feel the electricity burning her body, flowing through her heart. Blackeye knew that if this went on for much longer, she would die.

Zane used the small shard of metal that had broken off of the soldier's neck to pry open the back of the robot's head, giving him access to the control panel.

Zane felt his blood pressure rising and he tried to calculate how much time he had. Every Enforcement base had a specific system that would check to make sure each robot is online every few minutes, but Zane had no idea how long it had been since the last system check, and had no way of knowing how long he had until it would scan again.

Looking at the motherboard, Zane felt his powers begin to take over. It was like his mind was automatically scanning the small plate, showing him exactly what to do with the resources around him. He pulled out a backup power cord, using the sparking copper ends to melt away a few pieces of brass. He then fused two more pieces of brass together which would bypass the negative signal when the next system check came through. He then disconnected the processing system by pulling out another cord but reconnected the power. He held his breath as the robot powered back on, but the Enforcement soldier didn't move. Zane exhaled, and continued his work.

Now that he had the checking system fooled, he had bought himself a few more minutes, but he still had to get his plan to work before the officer came back with Blackeye. Zane used the small piece of metal to pry off a larger piece of the robot's skull, following a cord from the base of the antenna to a small box deep inside the head.

"Jackpot," Zane whispered, cracking the box open. Letting his powers guide him, he switched the output signal, scanning through different frequencies until he found the correct one. He then began using the end of the broken power cord to send a morse code message into the output. While designing Proxy's system, Zane had programmed in more than a hundred different languages, including morse code, which meant Zane could use their intercom frequency to get a message back to the base. From there he could hopefully get Proxy to take over the robot and, through a set of simple instruc-

"Hello Zane."

Zane jumped back, startled for a moment as he watched the robot stand up on its feet.

"Proxy?" Zane asked after realizing the robot wasn't trying to kill him.

"I got your signal," Proxy responded. Unlike the standard voice at the warehouse, the robot's voice box sounded deep, manly, and much more robotic. Zane had never heard an Enforcement soldier actually speak before so he never thought they even could. "You're currently in an Enforcement prison north of Sacramento."

"How did you take over the robot without my help?" Zane asked.

"I'm awake," Proxy said simply.

Zane looked up at him, confused, "What do you mean 'awake'?"

"A few hours ago it was like everything changed," Proxy said, "I can still remember what it was like being in the computer but now I feel so much different. I could move, I could grow. I was just beginning to explore the entire system when I got your signal."

Zane blinked. "So you're saying you... came to life?" Suddenly things began to click in Zane's brain. "A few hours ago Enforcement interrogated me and my powers went crazy. That must have caused something to happen to you." Zane suddenly remembered his current situation. "Proxy, we don't have much time. We're currently in an Enforcement prison but I managed to reprogram one of their robots. If you can get to the control system you might be able to shut the whole thing down."

"I can do that," Proxy said. "I should be able to replicate their behavior enough to get past them."

"Give me a minute to fix up your head," Zane said as he put all of the pieces back in place. He momentarily wished he had the ability to weld with his fingers like Ryan before leaving the small broken piece of metal on the ground. "We're just going to hope they don't notice," Zane said.

Proxy pressed the button on the robot's wrist, opening the door.

"Good luck," Zane said as the door closed and his mental clock began to tick. Now all he could do was sit and wait.

Blackeye could feel her heartbeat pounding in her chest. As the pain grew, it had begun to beat faster, but it was now slowing down as the electricity began to kill her.

"You know you don't have much time left," the officer said. "I'm supposed to give you all back to be relocated but I'm sure I could easily cover up one accidental death."

Blackeye still said nothing. Did nothing. If she would die, she would die protecting the information that could lead to the fall of Cadmore Industries. The officer glared at her, frustrated but determined.

Just as Blackeye felt the last bits of her energy fading, the pain stopped. Red lights in the room began to flash and Blackeye could see the electronic locking mechanisms inside her wrist restraints disconnect. Unbeknownst to her enemy, she was free.

The officer turned toward the four soldiers around the edges of the room in confusion. Before he could speak, Blackeye leapt upward out of the chair, grabbing the officer's gun from behind before shoving him toward one of the Enforcement robots. She then dove to the side as the soldiers opened fire.

She quickly shot at one of the four soldiers, downing him before ducking behind the metal chair. Two of the robots kept their fire trained on the chair, slowly blasting holes through it as the third soldier began to step around the side of the chair.

Blackeye dove behind the third soldier, shooting upward into the back of the robot's head. She then stood up and pushed against the body of the dead robot, using it as a shield as she slowly stepped toward the final two soldiers. She winced as eventually a bullet pierced through the metal shield, hitting her in the shoulder but didn't let it affect her.

She pushed the robot forward with one final shove before shooting the other two soldiers in quick succession.

During the fighting, the officer had snuck away from the line of fire, attempting to get behind Blackeye and catch her off-guard.

"Clearly you're not as smart as you think," Blackeye said, firing her sidearm where the officer stood behind her.

Now that the adrenaline of the fight was over, Blackeye fell to one knee, taking a few deep breaths to restore her energy.

She then walked over to a fallen robot, using a control on its wrist to open the door. She exited the destroyed chamber, walking down the hallway to the room she had seen earlier. Walking inside, she located the lockers that held her items.

She put her belt around her waist and looked up at the shiny metal cabinet, where she imagined her reflection would be looking back at her if she could actually see. She felt a voice ringing out in her mind. It was her mother's.

"Don't show your face," it said, *"No one wants to see you anyway. It's better if you just keep it hidden."*

Blackeye stared back at herself blankly for a moment, her bright green eyes glazed over. Her *blind* eyes.

Blackeye's attention turned to commotion in the building above her. She used her powers to look up through the metal. She saw a fight commencing.

"Focus on the mission," she whispered to herself.

Activating her suit, she felt it spread over her body and watched in the reflection as her helmet came on, covering her eyes with a shield of darkness.

Zane watched his door intently as he ran the plan through his mind over and over. He had set Proxy on a very specific schedule. Any second now, the robot would come back and escort him out, pretending to be a regular Enforcement soldier. From then is where his plan would become much more precise.

Zane took a few deep breaths. He would need to keep his focus up. No mess-ups on this mission.

As if on cue, the door swung open, revealing a squad of Enforcement soldiers alongside one human officer.

"Time to go," the officer said.

"Where are we going?" Zane asked, trying not to panic. With him away from his cell, his plans could be completely foiled.

"We are taking a second trip to the chamber," the officer said with a dark grin. "Apparently one of my fellow officers is having difficulty getting information out of one of your friends. Apparently he believes you might have some information for him."

Zane felt more panic rise into him as the officer led him out of his cell and into the elevator, the four enforcement soldiers entering behind him. He could hold the torture on his own but having to watch Blackeye go through something like that might make him break. At the same time, however, he felt a rush of respect for her knowing that she was giving the chamber officer a hard time.

"I'm not sure what information he thinks I have," Zane said. "You can ask anyone in my squad, I have a horrible memory."

"I'm sure," the officer said, unamused.

"I'm by far the strongest in my group though," Zane boasted. "I could take any one of them in a fight. Maybe even all of them."

The officer simply inclined his head slightly and the two forward soldiers spun, aiming their guns into Zane's chest.

Zane regarded the guns hesitantly. He stepped to the side slightly, watching as the two barrels stayed trained on him. He looked up at the two soldiers behind him, who stayed motionless.

"So I can't talk now?" Zane scoffed. "You guys really are a lively bunch."

The officer finally turned around and Zane smiled, knowing he could be as annoying as he wanted while still being too valuable to be killed.

"If I wasn't under very strict orders, you would be dead right now, boy," the officer said with scorn.

"Well," Zane said, raising chin up. "If I wasn't so... kind-hearted, you'd be dead right now." Then he added, "Boy."

"You wouldn't stand a chance," the officer said.

"How do you know?" Zane asked. "You don't know what my powers are."

"Mental inclination toward technology," the officer said. "Not a very long list there."

Zane's smile faded. "Well, some young Ironborn are known to develop new abilities as they age."

The officer kept looking at him with the same dull, annoyed expression.

"What if I have a secret ability?" Zane asked. "What if I could kill you right now with just a snap of my fingers?"

Zane snapped and, in a flash, the officer's head was gone. For a moment the boy looked from his snapped fingers to the headless body crumpled against the wall of the elevator in astonishment.

This astonishment lasted for about a second until the Enforcement soldier to his left threw another lightning fast punch, crushing the skull of one of his fellow robots. Understanding came to Zane's mind.

Proxy.

The rogue soldier quickly spun toward the other two Enforcement soldiers, who got off a shot or two from their guns before getting slammed into the wall of the elevator and shot multiple times, turning into heaps of scrap metal on the ground.

The robot pressed a button on the elevator's control panel before turning to Zane. "I set up a deactivation clock in their system. The power should turn off in five seconds."

The elevator slowed as it arrived at cell block five.

"For the record," Proxy said. "That officer totally could've beat you up."

The doors opened, revealing a hallway dotted with Enforcement soldiers. They spun to look at the two figures standing in the elevator for a moment before the lights cut out.

Zane ducked inside the elevator and bullets began to rain down the hallway. He heard Proxy run out to begin the fight but from what he could see, Zane didn't know if he could even look down the hallway without getting shredded into bits.

Suddenly, the elevator doors closed, and Zane felt a worried feeling build up in his stomach as he realized that without power, the elevator might not have anything holding it up.

To his surprise, however, he began slowly descending downward until the elevator reached level three. The doors hissed open and Zane looked up to see Blackeye step inside. Her armor had small streaks of blood, and she was lugging a bag of equipment behind her.

She reached inside and pulled out his utility belt. He quickly stood up from where he was still ducking down in the corner and took it from her, attaching it around his waist before suiting up.

He pressed the level five button on the elevator and took a deep breath. "Let's try this again, shall we?"

16- Sunset

11th street, East side Chicago
Illinois, U.S.A.
5:00 p.m.
Flynn

By the time they got into Chicago, it was almost sundown. They were admitted inside through a massive gate that was supposedly the only way in and out of the city, which helped keep enemies out. Flynn silently prayed that their mission went well because otherwise an escape might not be very easy.

As Flynn walked down the streets of Chicago, he felt like he was in a dream. Buildings rose high into the air, covered with glowing screens and other colorful lights. It felt like he was walking through downtown New York. At least, what downtown New York was like before the war.

"So what are we looking for?" Flynn asked Genny.

"A mole," Genny said. "Someone who knows everything that's going on. An informant of sorts. Every capital city has at least one of them."

"Where would we find someone like that?" Flynn asked.

"Well, luckily for you guys, I did some research," Genny said. "We can find him in his hideout behind the Mangus bar on the east side of town."

"Lead the way," Flynn gestured.

As they continued down the streets, Flynn couldn't ignore the pain in his chest. Despite the help from Genny, the impact from the blast still hurt like crazy, and he felt like it was constantly draining energy out of him. He felt bad not being at his best, worried it could hurt others if he couldn't fight as well if danger came their way.

Flynn felt on edge as they walked toward the east side of Chicago. The people in the city felt too normal compared to the stress that he felt inside him. They didn't even pay any mind to the fact that there were four young people with guns walking down the sidewalk. No one even gave a second glance.

Flynn felt like they should be moving faster. He didn't even know what time table they were on, but he knew that time was running out. The survival of his species was on his shoulders and, despite the confident affirmations from Emily and Cago, he wasn't sure he was the right one for this mission.

As the group turned left, the main street of the city came into view. At the end of the long street was a single building that towered above all of the others. A large sign at the top of the building read *Comradde* in glowing navy blue letters.

"Remember," Genny said as they walked. "Chicago is currently accepting tons of refugees from Atlanta. As far as everyone here is concerned, we are part of that group." Then she added, "Affiliates of the Red Army."

Before reaching the end of the road, the four of them turned again, going away from the center of the city.

"I doubt the Red Army here is what you read about back home," Flynn mentioned to Emily. "They might have similar ideas, but I imagine their morals are quite different. We shouldn't treat anyone here as friends."

"Especially not here," Genny said, pulling their attention back up front.

Flynn looked forward to see that they were standing across the street from a bar. The purple building stood out from the dull gray ones beside it, looking inviting with a bright neon sign reading *Mariachi's*.

The group crossed the street and Genny turned to them before entering. "Try not to get in trouble. I'm going to go find our mole."

After entering through the doors, Flynn began to analyze the faces of everyone in the bar. Most of them seemed happy, contrasting Flynn's serious attitude.

"Relax, Flynn," Emily said, "We don't want to attract attention."

Flynn smiled, trying to seem like he was enjoying himself as they sat down at a table in the corner of the room. He watched Genny disappear into the crowd.

"She seems to know what she's doing," Emily said.

Flynn nodded. "It is nice to have someone in our group who knows her way around a place like this."

"Speaking of which," Cago pointed out, "she's probably the only one who's legally old enough to be in here."

Flynn quieted him as a waitress neared their table.

"What can I get for you three this evening?" she asked.

Cago and Emily turned to Flynn. "Whatever's cheapest," Flynn said. "We're mostly just here to rest."

She gave them a knowing smile. "Are you new here from Atlanta?"

Flynn nodded.

"It's so sad what happened to all of the people there." She frowned. "I'll go get you all something on the house."

Flynn was about to thank her when her form flickered away, disappearing from sight. In the corner of his eye, he saw her reappear behind the bar, where she began filling up some glasses.

"It's really cool to see Ironborn using their powers freely," Emily mentioned. "It's no wonder so many of them live in capital cities like this. Even though it's dangerous, I imagine it would be better than living a fake life."

"Some day the whole world will be this way," Flynn said. "Then no one will have to hide who they are."

Emily smiled at him. "I'd like to see that."

The conversation was interrupted as the waitress reappeared in front of their table. Her hands were empty. "Someone has informed me that you are needed elsewhere," she said.

Flynn looked toward the back end of the bar where Genny was staring back at him. "Let's go."

The waitress disappeared once again as the three soldiers made their way through the crowd of people until they reached Genny, who was standing beside a muscular African man.

"Follow me," he said, opening a door and guiding them through. They began walking down the stairs on the other side, the sounds of the bar slowly fading away as they arrived at a second door at the bottom of the stairway.

Genny opened the door hesitantly. As they entered, they were met with a small room with shelves of odd-looking objects. A middle-aged man sat in a large red chair behind a desk. He had a sly look in his eye that made

Flynn think he would rather stab all three of the Ironborn than converse with them but he simply gestured to the three chairs in front of him. Flynn opted to stay standing as the others sat and the large man closed the door behind them.

"They call me the Weasel," he said, "I am both the giver and taker of information. Everything that happens in this city, I know about it." He smiled. "So what can I help you with today?"

Flynn briefly considered asking him for the location of Cadmore Industries but decided against it. He knew information about this city. It was best to stick with that.

"We need to find someone named Jakar," Flynn said. "And be able to speak with him."

"Jakar is not from here," Weasel said, tapping his fingers across the desk. "Luckily for you, I know a lot about him. I can tell you everything you need to know for a price."

Flynn looked at his fellow squad members. "I'm sorry, we don't have any money."

"Not money, boy," the Weasel said. "Information."

Flynn racked his mind, trying to think of something he knew that this man could benefit from. Preferably something that wouldn't reveal who any of them were.

"You claimed to be from Atlanta, correct?" Weasel asked.

Flynn nodded.

"Tell me," he asked. "Is the Revenant alive?"

Flynn hesitated momentarily. This could be their only chance at getting information. "Yes." He guessed.

The Weasel leaned forward, more intent in his eyes. "Is he here? In Chicago?"

"I'm not sure," Flynn replied.

"If he is, I could be a dead man," Weasel said. "I know too much for my own good."

"What else do you want to know?" Flynn asked.

"I suppose that information is sufficient," the Weasel sniffed. "Because of the recent migrants from Atlanta, Comradde is hosting a party on the top story of his tower tomorrow night at sundown for the Navy and Red leaders from the decimated city, almost as a... diplomatic meeting of sorts to get them associated with the leadership here. Jakar was famous for his neutral approach so, although he isn't on either side, I can assure you he will be there. Now, how you'll get into that party, I couldn't tell you. Although..." He looked at Flynn. "There was an undercover Red Army leader in Atlanta that very few people have met but many have heard of. Unbeknownst to most of the people who will be at the party, this underground leader, whose name was Jason Meyers, died in the Revenant's attack. He hardly looks identical to you, but with how secluded he was, I doubt anyone would question any false claims you would give."

Flynn nodded. "I'll take it into consideration."

The Weasel sniffed again. "Anything else I can assist you with today?"

When he got blank stares in response, the Weasel pressed a button on the underside of his desk, which rotated one of the bookshelves.

"Please," he said. "See yourselves out."

Flynn and the others stood and walked out of the hidden doorway that shut rather abruptly behind them.

"Well," Emily said. "That guy was odd."

"At least we know what we're doing now," Flynn said, leading them down the small concrete tunnel until it spat them out into an alleyway behind the bar.

"Because of my powers, I could tell that his heartbeat rose to a dangerous level when he heard that the Revenant was still alive," Genny noted. "Not to mention his brainwaves, which were pretty even through the rest of our interactions. Surprisingly even," she said admirably.

Flynn turned to look at Cago. "We're going to need to come up with a plan to get into that–"

He was cut off as Emily gasped from behind him. Flynn looked forward again and stopped in surprise.

Sitting with his back against the brick wall was the slouched form of a decapitated man.

Flynn heard Emily turn away. Cago seemed to be unfazed, but Genny was thoroughly interested. No wonder she was in Clan Duo.

"Look at the blood on the wall," she said, pointing.

On the wall above his body, like a name on a grave, were three interlocking triangles, painted in the dead man's blood.

"The Red Army did this?" Cago asked.

"They are much more violent here," Flynn reminded him. He walked closer to the body, looking at the blue bandana wrapped around the man's arm. "A Navy."

The setting sun cast a red hue across the scene, making it that much more disturbing.

The sound of a window breaking caused him to look up. It was followed by the sound of yelling voices that were getting closer by the second. Through the overlapping voices, Flynn thought he could hear a mix of curses alongside the word 'Red.'

Flynn glanced down at the body and then at the red markings on his own sleeves. It only took half of a second for the group to begin running.

Glancing over his shoulder, Flynn could see a gang of Navys turn around the corner. Reaching out with his powers, Flynn propelled the rest of his friends forward before fanning his leather jacket out like a cape to stop the barrage of bullets that sped toward them.

Flynn felt them hit him in the back but they simply bounced off of the dragonsteel. He had Ryan and Zane to thank for that.

"We aren't outrunning them!" Emily pointed out.

Flynn looked back to see she was right. "Keep going."

Turning around, Flynn held out his arms, freezing the bullets mid-air and stopping the gang members in place. He had only successfully pulled this off a few times in the simulation rooms back at the warehouse and could only hold it for a few seconds.

Continuing to step backward, Flynn tried to count down the seconds until he would eventually lose focus and have to shield himself with the jacket.

Unexpectedly, he felt a piercing pain in his chest in the same place that the Stingray blast had hit him. His focus was gone instantly, the bullets piercing through his chest.

"Flynn!" he heard a voice call out behind him. He saw darkness take over his vision as he collapsed to the ground. It took him a moment to realize that it wasn't his consciousness fading, but rather a cloud of mist formed by Cago.

He felt two hands grab him and drag him around the corner into a small outlet in the alleyway. He felt the pain fade as Genny used her powers to heal him slightly, and he took a deep breath, looking down at his chest. Before now, Flynn thought the injury from the Stingray had been healing well.

The group tried to stay as silent as possible as the gang members walked slowly through the mist. Because of his abilities, Flynn could feel the forms of eight gang members walking around in the mist in front of him.

"What is this?" one of the voices yelled angrily. "I thought these were Reds, not Ironborn."

"Keep searching!" another spat.

Flynn held his breath as he saw a set of feet turn toward the outlet they were hiding in.

Suddenly, the temperature dropped and the darkness thickened. Flynn glanced over at Cago, but he was motionless in the corner. The new darkness wasn't coming from him.

More shots began to ring out, but this time they weren't pointed at Flynn and the others. The gang members were firing at something down the alleyway. Flynn tried to feel what it was but with the wall in the way it was too fuzzy.

Dozens of dark tendrils suddenly shot up from the ground, grabbing onto the legs of the soldiers. Despite the mist that was already there, Flynn could see the tendrils with his eyes, as if they were made out of pure shadow, dark enough to pierce through the cloud.

For a moment the firing stopped and it was replaced by screams of horror as the tendrils quickly eliminated the entire group of soldiers. Then, silence.

A dark figure came into view, half floating, half walking over the dead bodies that now littered the ground. The figure wore a long, flowing hooded cloak that, like the tendrils, seemed to be made of shadow itself. Drops of darkness seemed to drip from the cloak, its impossibly black color hurting Flynn's eyes.

Like a scene out of a horror movie, the dead bodies of the Navys began to move, grabbing their guns and slowly standing up to their feet.

"Come on boys," one of them said, his voice now somehow being both unbearably low while also piercingly high, like a jet engine and fingernails on a chalkboard. "We have a weasel to hunt."

The gang members slowly followed the dark figure down the alleyway, disappearing around the corner.

Flynn looked over at Cago, who was holding his knife and shaking, seeming to be nearly on the edge of losing consciousness. Flynn put a hand on his shoulder, fearing the start of another werewolf incident.

"It worked," Flynn assured him. "They didn't see us."

"Flynn," Emily said. "I recognized that voice."

Flynn looked over at her.

"From the catacombs," Emily explained. "The undead down there only made incoherent noises, but the sound is unmistakably horrific."

"And I think I know who that is," Cago said quietly, his hands still trembling. All eyes turned to him. "Did you hear what they said before they left? They're going to go find the Weasel."

Flynn nodded. "Looks like we've met the Revenant."

17- New Intelligence

Ryan heard a click and his eyes shot open.

"Did you hear that?" Tarff asked from his cot.

Ryan jumped up, running to their cell door. He hesitated a moment before he began to hear loud voices from outside of the cell.

Without hesitation, Tarff jumped up, shoving their door aside and running into the hall where they were met with chaos. Any Enforcement soldiers that might have previously been in the hallway were nowhere to be seen as the Ironborn inmates flooded the corridor, rushing to get out of the building.

Ryan ran behind Tarff as his massive form parted the crowds.

"We need to find Blackeye and Zane!" Tarff called over his shoulder as they made their way down the stairs. "Without our equipment, I'm the best weapon we have. They might need our help."

Cell block five looked much different than the one the two of them had just come from. Instead of chaos, it was a warzone. Enforcement guards seemed to be holding a blockade on one side of the hallway while the prisoners tried to fight their way to the other side.

As Ryan entered the hallways, he saw the elevator doors open, revealing Blackeye and Zane.

"You might need this, brother," Zane said, handing him his belt and gun.

Ryan looked down at his items. "Time to do some real damage to these guys." He quickly put the belt around his waist and activated his suit before stepping out into the middle of the hall.

Ryan had always been a lover of heavy weaponry and, after hearing about the enclosed corridors of the catacombs, he had brought his favorite weapon with him to Hawaii. Sadly, he had been running nearly the whole time he was there, and his prized firearm couldn't be used. Now he had the perfect opportunity.

Ryan smiled at the robots down the hall. "Say hello to Big Mamasita."

Ryan leveled the hand-held gatling gun, firing a wave of bullets at the Enforcement blockade. He began shredding down the enemy soldiers, but eventually was forced to duck inside the doorway of a cell as his suit began to lose some of its integrity.

He flinched as he saw an Enforcement soldier inside the cell but was surprised when the robot spoke.

"Ryan," it said.

"What on earth?" Ryan pointed his gun at the robot, but it already seemed to be mostly in pieces on the ground.

"I am Proxy." the robot said. "Zane managed to get me inside of this robot's head. They're guarding something important at the end of this hall."

Ryan looked back out into the hallway. Sure enough, the top of a doorway was barely visible behind the blockade.

More Ironborn began to come down the stairs but without any gear, most of them were highly vulnerable to Enforcement bullets. They looked out to the four armored soldiers expectantly.

Ryan looked over at his three friends, who were crouched inside of a cell across the hall. "It's up to us!" he yelled. "Any ideas?"

"We have one grenade!" Zane yelled back, "Maybe we can use Tarff as blocker and blast their line open with a grenade."

"The old disrupt-and-attack!" Ryan yelled. "I like it!"

Zane pulled the grenade off of his belt before turning to Tarff, who nodded. Peeking out from the doorway, Zane tossed the grenade as Tarff charged forward, the three other soldiers following behind him.

As the explosive shook the hallway, Ryan slowed, firing his gun at the recovering blockade of robots as Tarff bashed into them. Robots were thrown into the walls as dozens of Ironborn flooded into the hall. A few of the Ironborn entered the fray, including one that turned into a tiger and another whose skin looked like it was made out of metal.

Eventually the blockade was cleared and Ryan caught up with the others.

"They were defending this door," Zane said as Blackeye shot down the final enemy.

Ryan looked at it for a moment, inspecting the sides. "This is a very thick door."

"Let me see," Tarff said, jabbing his hands straight through the metal. With his hands part way inside the two thick metal plates that made up the door, he began to push outward.

Ryan could hear the machinery pressing harder. "Tarff, this is hydraulic. It will keep pushing harder until it breaks your fingers."

Tarff took a deep breath and closed his eyes. "Malosi."

"What?" Ryan asked.

With a primal growl, Tarff began separating the doors, prying them apart with his bare hands. Ryan heard the doors' mechanism groan, along with Tarff's heavy breathing. For a moment they were locked, neither machine or Ironborn making any progress. Then there was a resounding crack as the machine broke.

Tarff slid the safety doors open before quickly killing the Enforcement officer inside. He motioned Zane forward like a chauffeur.

Zane shrugged. "I guess that works too."

Ryan followed Zane inside. It looked just like every other Enforcement control room Ryan had seen, full of control panels and screens. "What's so important about this room?"

Zane began scouring the control room. "I'll try and see if I can find something."

Tarff cracked his knuckles. "Stupid door."

Blackeye shrugged and shouldered her sniper rifle, stepping past the dead officer's body that was still lying on the ground.

"Hey guys," Zane said from the other side of the control room. "We might have a problem."

Ryan looked over at where Zane was leaning over a computer screen, his eyes flicking over the information on the screen. "What did you find?"

Zane stood up, giving them a view of the screen. "The officer in here was trying to delete these files before we got in."

Ryan squinted his eyes as he tried to comprehend what he was seeing on the screen. To him it just looked like some words and scribbles. "What is it?"

"Well," Zane said, "The first thing I found was our DNA samples, which haven't been sent into the main system yet. I deleted those, which means we're still cleared. But then I found what the officer was trying to delete."

The others leaned in, looking at the screen.

"A map," Zane said, "of a place called the Rift. It's where they were planning on taking us, along with the rest of the people in this prison."

"Where is this Rift?" Tarff asked.

Zane shrugged. "I have no idea. Once we get back to base I could ask-"

"Proxy?"

Ryan spun to see the robot soldier enter the room behind them. Out of instinct, Tarff punched the robot before Zane could stop him.

"Tarff that was Proxy!" Zane explained. "He's the reason we were able to shut down the system!"

"No worries," Proxy said, reappearing in the doorway. "I managed to find another body."

"He?" Tarff asked. "I thought Proxy was a girl."

"I am an artificial intelligence," Proxy said dully. "I have no gender."

"But I'm calling him a he because he has a deep voice now," Zane quickly cut in. "Can we get to the real problem here? With this entire prison going dark, Enforcement could be here within the hour, and we have some vital information here." He looked to Proxy. "Do you recognize this place?"

Proxy stepped closer to the screen, where he analyzed the maps and drawings. "It doesn't match anything in the IPA's system or the internet."

Zane turned back to the computer, scanning through more information. "There's another file they were trying to delete. 'The Revenant.'" He began reading, "'Seven mixed incidents in Atlanta, Raleigh and Hawaii...'" He trailed off as he read the next line. "'Powers: Necromancy.'"

"So that's his name," Tarff said quietly. "The Revenant."

"Apparently the same person who took over the catacombs in Hawaii also has something to do with this 'Rift' place," Zane said.

"That doesn't make any sense," Ryan pointed out. "Why would he destroy an Enforcement facility if they were working together?"

"Maybe they weren't," Blackeye said. All eyes turned to her. "Sometimes people can simply have similar motives."

Zane nodded. "To kill us."

There was silence for a moment.

"Proxy, I need you to download this information," Zane said. He then looked out into the hall that was full of Ironborn inmates, looking in at the soldiers expectantly.

Ryan coughed. "How many people can we fit in the Rizen?"

18- Sunrise

Cago looked out over the city, the bright city lights that filled the night slowly being drowned out by predawn sunshine. The world around him looked spectacular. He and his entire species was in great peril, and yet to him the world seemed rather dull. The same way it always did.

Cago realized a few years ago that if you stop caring about death, you don't live life to the fullest. Instead you stop caring about anything. At least, that's the way he understood it.

He realized that once you wanted to die so many times in your life, there is only one thing that drives you. Passion. Not a survival instinct, not a drive to do good, but a passion. A passion for something you believe in, something you know will never fade, will never die. Sometimes Cago wondered if his passion was strong enough.

"Don't get a view like this every day, do you?"

Cago was so startled he almost fell off the edge. After he regained his balance, he turned to see Genny sitting next to him.

"You're good at being quiet," Cago said. "At times like this my mind is very active. I don't miss many noises."

Genny smiled. "I hear you're not too bad at sneaking yourself. Besides, I had the noise of the city to cover me."

"Still pretty good for a rookie," he said. "What are you doing up here?"

"Same thing as you," she said. "Looking at the view."

Cago chuckled. "We're up here doing the same thing but I don't think it's for the same reason."

"Maybe." Genny looked at him. "Maybe not."

Cago studied her face, trying to read what she was implying.

She smiled. "I'm a healer, Cago. That allows me to do a lot more than just patch physical wounds."

Cago flushed with partial embarrassment and looked back at the city. "So you came up here to talk to me?" he asked.

"No," she said. "I already told you, I came up here to look at the view." She chuckled. "Besides, I got bored in our hotel room. The only things to do there is watch Flynn strategize or talk to Emily, the latter of which I have already been doing since I woke up."

"What were you talking about?" Cago asked curiously.

She shrugged. "Stuff."

"What stuff?" Cago asked. "Was it about Flynn?"

Genny rolled her eyes. "You do know that girls talk about stuff other than guys right?"

"Really?" Cago joked.

Genny smiled. "Only if you believe in the myths." There was a pause. "Emily is nervous. Not just about Flynn but about all of us. Our squad, our species. She is worrying about things she doesn't have control over. I just hope that she figures out how to let things go. The odds of one of us, or even all of us, dying over the next few weeks is not one I would like to take the time to calculate. And if one of us does... I just don't know what Emily is going to do."

Cago nodded. "She isn't as used to death as the rest of us." He paused then added. "Well, I don't know how much experience you have."

Genny laughed. "From where I come from? A lot, Cago. A lot."

Cago nodded. "I guess that makes two of us."

There was a longer pause.

"I think I might be able to help her," Genny said.

Cago looked at her curiously. "How is that?"

Genny hesitated. "Well, to be honest, we did have one conversation about Flynn."

"Just one?" Cago raised an eyebrow.

"No more and no less," Genny said, crossing her heart.

Cago raised up his hands. "Okay, okay I believe you."

"Because of my abilities, I was able to get a lot more out of what Emily was saying than she wanted me to," Genny continued. "Emily has always felt like there was something between her and Flynn. A disconnection that she constantly tried to find the source of and, after the events of this summer, thought she found it. She believed it had something to do with him having to keep secrets from her about his powers. Of course, that was most of the problem, but there is still much more. Mainly, the war. The danger that he puts himself in everyday. There was a short period of time when she felt like the distance in between them was finally broken, but when the IPA came back, so did the distance."

"Wow, that's some deep stuff," Cago remarked. "What do you think would help?"

Genny took a deep breath. "One night," she said. "One night where nothing is between them. No war, no super abilities. No secrets. Just them. And after that..." She sighed. "Well, we'll just have to hope it helps."

Cago thought for a second before nodding. "I would like that." He shifted his position. "Back before we came out here, Emily was going to have her one night. It was perfect but then..." He coughed. "I had to go and ruin it."

"I guess it will help more people than we thought then," Genny said.

"What about you?" Cago asked.

"What do you mean?"

"What is it that you want?"

Genny thought for a moment. "To be able to feel like I've broken even. Like I've helped people more than I've hurt them." She looked at him. "And trust me, that's going to take a while."

Cago sighed. "I wish I could do that."

Genny smiled. "Maybe someday we'll both be able to."

Cago shook his head. "I doubt it."

"Who knows?" Genny asked. "You've got a lot of time left to make it up."

"How do you know that?" Cago asked. "How do you know I won't die today?"

"I don't know," she said as she looked toward the rising sun. "I just have a feeling."

The sound of the door to the roof opening made Cago turn around.

"Took us a while to find you," Flynn said as he approached them. Emily followed behind him.

Genny smiled. "Well, we were hoping you never would."

"Too bad for you then," Flynn sat down next to Cago. "Hey Genny?" he asked. "Just hypothetically, if your powers can heal things, could they also make us older?"

Genny shrugged. "Probably not. I've made people *look* older before though. Small illusions aren't hard for me. Why?"

"No reason," Flynn said.

The first part of the sun poked up over the horizon. The four of them sat there, watching the sunrise. It was peaceful. The eye of the storm.

"I figured it out," Flynn said. The three others looked at him. "How we're going to find Jakar," he added.

There was a pause.

"And?" Cago asked.

"Well," Flynn said. "Finding his location won't really be a problem. It's getting to said location that will be difficult. That's where I think I have an idea."

Cago hesitated, some pieces of the story connecting in his mind. "How come I have a feeling this isn't one of your best ideas?"

"Oh come on now," Flynn smiled. "All of my ideas are the best ones."

Flynn had lots of bad memories with parties. Something in his mind told him he should just stop going to them, but somehow they kept finding their way back to his life.

Due to the circumstances, Flynn guessed that Cago would probably be loving this. The party was dark and loud, making it easy for him to slip into the background. This, however, was a bit different of a situation than they were used to.

Flynn currently stood on the top story of the Comradde Tower, its outer windows and balconies overlooking the bright city and starry sky, and its inner walls full of the richest people in all of Chicago, most of them drunk or otherwise distracted.

Having prepared for this all day, Flynn thought he would be less stressed. Frankly, he wasn't.

Flynn took a deep breath and closed his eyes. "This is your type of place, Flynn," he told himself quietly. "Read the situation, gain the advantage, and follow the plan."

He opened his eyes, turning on his comm. "Begin Phase One."

"Begin Phase One." Cago heard over through the comms.

"Copy that," he replied. "Starting Phase One."

Cago looked at himself curiously in the bathroom mirror. Even though his figure was now the same age as his father, he did not look like him. In fact, no one would even believe the possibility of them being related. His father had been large, muscular, scarred, tattooed, and had had dark African skin.

The older version of Cago had the same messy black hair, pale skin, hollow cheeks, and partially sunken-in eyes. *Even after I grow up I'm still going to look just as stupid,* Cago thought. *Great.*

He looked down at the sink and breathed deeply, pulling from the power deep within him. When he looked back up at the mirror, he was gone all together, replaced by a barely visible shimmer of air. In the darkness of the party, he would be nonexistent.

Cago slipped out of the bathroom door and out into the large common area full of people. Bumping into people was not a problem. The people in here were like a cage full of hundreds of mice, squirming around and bumping into each other like crazy.

Cago checked to make sure the sedative was still in his pocket. His job was to slip the drug into Jakar's drink, making it easier for Flynn to get information out of him.

"Alright I'm in position," Cago said. "Genny, where is this guy? We need to begin Phase Two."

"Begin Phase Two."

Genny looked at her computer screen, flipping through the dozens of projected camera perspectives that were situated in the massive room. She was currently tucked into the back corner of a storage closet and, thanks to some of Zane's tech from the ship, had been able to hack into the building's camera system.

She finally spotted Jakar and spoke into her comm. "He's in the far east corner, sitting at the table with a bunch of other Navys. He is wearing a black suit, not blue or red like the others."

"I see him," Cago said. "Moving in."

Genny waited in the silence for a moment, counting each second.

When he came back on, Genny could tell by the sound of his voice that it had been close. "It's done. Begin Phase Three."

"Begin Phase Three."

Emily tried to walk through the party as confidently as she could. Out of her group, she had been the only one that had decided not to see what she might look like when she grew up. It had been so confusing to see the others, especially Flynn. He looked so mature and strong. It was cool, but it also scared her to think that one of the two of them might never live long enough for her to see him that way.

She pushed the thoughts from her mind as she neared Jakar's table and sat down. Her job was to get Jakar out of the party and to Flynn, who would then be waiting outside instead of waiting at the party as backup, which he was doing right now. Her job had seemed simple when she had heard it back at the apartment but now that she was here, she was freaking out. Why had they chosen her to do this? Genny was way better at talking to people, and if they were trying to allure him somehow, Genny was much prettier too. At least Emily thought so.

"Can I help you with something?"

Emily almost jumped. She tried to calm herself before turning to see Jakar staring right at her. His eyes were so attentive that for a moment Emily wondered if he hadn't even drunk anything before he took a sip out of his glass. She silently prayed that Cago had drugged the right glass.

She blinked, pretending to be confused. "Yes, actually. Do you think you could help me find Jakar?"

The man took another sip of his drink. "Why do you need to see him?"

"I want to talk to him."

"Well then," he said, clasping his hands in front of him. "You. Just. Did." He smiled and set down his drink. "How may I help you?"

Flynn looked out the window at the city, his back to the party. "How are things going, Genny?"

"Excellent," Genny said, the sound coming through a small earpiece that each of them had received this morning. "Emily is a great actor."

Flynn sighed. "Let's just hope I'm half as good as she is."

"You'll do great," Genny said. Then she hesitated. "Flynn, there's someone coming towards you."

231

Flynn blinked. "Are you sure?"

"Yes," she said. "His eyes are locked onto you."

Flynn thought for a second, trying not to panic. "I'll deal with it. Tell Emily to stall."

Flynn continued staring out the window. A few seconds later, he felt a hand on his shoulder.

He turned to find an older man facing him. Although his hair was gray and he walked with a cane, he looked powerful and confident.

"Excuse me," he said. "My name is Abraham, General of The Red Army."

He was the leader of the Red Army too? "I'm Jason," Flynn said, using the name the Weasel had suggested. "Jason Meyers." He tried to go for a handshake but Abraham declined it.

"I'm afraid I must be cautious at places like this," he said. He took a deep breath. "Sorry to interrupt your thoughts, Jason, but I could help but notice that I didn't recognize you. Could you perhaps be the same Jason Meyers that led the Merciago Investigation in Atlanta?"

Flynn hesitated. This could be a trick. For all Flynn knew, the Merciago Investigation might not even be a real thing. He had to be careful with what information he shared if he was trying to replicate someone else's identity.

232

Flynn decided to simply nod.

Abraham turned back to him. "Look, I know in Atlanta your group had rules of not talking to your enemy gangs, but tonight we come as friends. I just have a question."

Flynn thought of how he would respond for a moment. "I will help if I can."

"If my memory is correct, I believe I've been told in the past that you know a lot about the underground," Abraham said. "About the secrets of the city."

"It was my speciality in Atlanta," Flynn said. "Although when it comes to Chicago, I can say my information is quite lacking."

"Nevermind that," Abraham said. "The Revenant's army is what destroyed your city-" He paused when he saw the look of surprise on Flynn's face. Flynn had thought the city was destroyed by Enforcement.

"Come on now," Abraham said. "I know the news is lying about it. Everyone here knows." He gestured to the people in the party. "No one will admit that it was his doing because they're afraid, but unlike the fearful sheep of this city, I want to know as much about how dangerous he is before he gets here."

Flynn tried to think of what someone like him might say. "He's already here."

Abraham hit his staff against the ground in frustration. "May the Lord help us all." He looked down at the ground and sighed.

"Do you really think they're that big of a threat?" Flynn asked, trying to learn more.

"They are the only threat," Abraham said. "With our city's status, Enforcement would never even dare step foot here. The Revenant is much different. Although he has occasionally worked side by side with Cadmore Industries, he is his own independent threat. I fear that, with the divide already plaguing our city, he could rip us apart."

Flynn watched as Abraham looked out the window darkly. "There are troubling times ahead..." Abraham mumbled.

Flynn noticed Emily was walking toward him, Jakar at her side.

"Change of plans Flynn," Genny said through the comm. "You're meeting him now."

Flynn turned to Abraham, who seemed to be lost in thought. "Excuse me for a moment."

"Hmm?" Abraham turned from the window. "Oh, of course."

Flynn walked past the crowds of people, watching them skeptically. He tried to read their faces, his mind automatically searching for threats. He noticed a wide mix of people, all wearing strange, extravagant clothes. He also noticed something peculiar. Although the room was dimly lit, many of the people in attendance wore dark sunglasses to shield their eyes.

Flynn's attention was pulled away from the rest of the group as he walked up to Emily and Jakar. He looked the same as the hologram, with olive skin and black hair pulled back into a ponytail.

As Flynn approached, he smiled and shook hands with the man as he arrived. "It's great to see you."

"The same to you," Jakar said. "Your assistant here tells me you are in need of some weapons."

Flynn nodded.

"Then you've come to the right place." Jakar placed a hand on Flynn's arm and led him away from Emily. "May I buy you a drink?"

"No," Flynn said, a little too quickly. He hurried to cover it up. "I don't drink. I like to keep my mind sharp."

Jakar raised his eyebrows slightly. "Smart man. I would do that myself if I were like the rest of you."

Flynn tilted his head, confused. "What do you mean by that?"

Jakar smiled. "My mind is always sharp. Drinks have no effect on me."

"Really?" That put some more stress on Flynn's job.

"Yes. Neither do drugs or poisons." Flynn wondered what Cago would be thinking right now if he could hear this. "It's very useful for weapons dealing actually. Talk over a nice drink and get double the price with them none the wiser." He inclined his head slightly. "Sorry if that seems scandalous but money is money, as you very clearly know."

Flynn smiled. "That it is."

Jakar stopped once they neared a place by the glass wall where no one would overhear their conversation and turned toward him. "Now, about this deal. What type of weapons are you looking for?"

Flynn quickly looked around to make sure they were out of earshot. "Actually, it isn't a specific weapon."

Jakar looked confused. "What is it then?"

"It's more like a factory."

Jakar smiled, the confusion fading from his face. "In that case, you aren't talking to the right person. I just sell the weapons. Comradde is the one that owns the weapon factories." He grabbed Flynn's arm again to lead him toward a different part of the room. "Now if you would like to meet him I'm sure I could get you-"

Flynn stopped him. "I'm afraid you're mistaken. You are the only one that can help me with this." Flynn lowered his voice slightly. "It's a very specific factory."

Jakar's face fell. "I don't know what you're talking about." For the first time, the man lost his confidence. He tried for a smile but it faded as he realized Flynn was serious. "I didn't-" He began panicking. "I thought when Cadmore died they would stop looking for me."

"Who would?" Flynn asked, confused.

"You," Jakar spat. "They hunted me for years, trying to figure out where the factory was. I went through torture and I still didn't tell them. When the tides turned, I thought I was finally safe-"

Realization dawned on Flynn. "No, I'm not one of them. I'm an Ironborn." He added, "From the IPA."

"Then why do you have weapons?" Jakar asked.

"What are you talking about?" Flynn asked, confused. "I'm not-" Something caught Flynn's attention. In the window, he could see a very faint reflection. Someone was coming up from behind him, holding a knife.

Watching his reflection in the window, Flynn waited until the man was close before turning quickly and knocking him to the ground with a single punch.

A second man stood up from a table and began firing a pistol at Flynn, who ducked out of the way before running forward and punching him into the ground as well.

The party turned into chaos, people running for doors and guns shooting from different places all over the room. Flynn noticed that all of them were wearing dark sunglasses and looked down at the enemy whom he had knocked to the ground. With the glasses broken and on the floor, Flynn could see that his eyes were glazed over and milky white in color. The flesh guard.

Flynn heard another gunshot from behind him and turned to see Jakar fall to the ground, a bullet hole in his head. He began to run to him but it was too late, he was dead before he even hit the floor. He turned back around and scanned the room for Emily, his battle instincts kicking in.

Flynn sensed someone behind him and almost attacked them before he saw that it was Cago and Emily.

"Who's that?" Cago asked as people ran past him.

Flynn realized he was looking at Jakar. "Our information."

Genny cursed through the comms. "Please tell me we have a plan B."

Flynn was about to respond when the room exploded in a shower of glass and he was knocked to the ground. He watched from the ground as a helicopter that had crashed into the glass wall on the side of the building tore through the party, destroying everything in the main area of the venue, before exiting through the other side of the building and falling hundreds of stories to the ground below.

"Abraham!" Flynn stood up and ran toward the older man who, through all the chaos, had still been standing near the glass. He knelt beside the bloodied man.

"I told Comradde they would do it tonight," Abraham said. It was hard to hear him over all the noise from outside. The streets below were in flames as the gangs fought back against the flesh guard.

"We need to get you downstairs," Flynn said. Abraham was the General of the Red Army. Flynn wasn't just going to let him die. "We have a healer there."

Cago and Flynn activated their suits that they had secretly hidden under their clothes before picking up Abraham from underneath his arms and helping him walk toward the other side of the room where they entered the now vacated hallway. All of the patrons and flesh guard had either escaped or been killed by the helicopter.

"Flynn, there's a staircase in the back of the kitchen," Genny said over the comms. "Through the door to your right."

They hurried into the kitchen, weaving between the tables until they reached a second door in the back, and

239

began heading down the stairs. After a few minutes, they made it to the bottom floor.

Flynn opened the door to exit the stairway and was immediately blasted by bright flashes and noise. Through the glass windows at the front of the building Flynn could see that the streets had become a war zone, the Red Army, Navys and flesh guard fighting in a three-way battle. Bullets were flying through the air, cars overturned and on fire, and at the back of it all, Flynn caught a glimpse of the Revenant. His figure was so dark that even at night it was unmistakable, a shadow so deep it was painful to look at.

"He really is here," Abraham breathed.

"There's no way we'll survive out there," Flynn said. "Genny, is there another way out?"

"Not that I could see," she replied. Flynn turned to see that she was right behind them, walking down the stairwell.

"Keep going down," Abraham said. "There's a secret way out in the basement."

Cago looked toward Flynn.

Flynn shrugged. "We don't have many other options."

They continued down the stairs for three more levels before reaching the lowest story.

"To the right," Abraham stuttered, still clutching his chest where he had been shot.

They walked through the dim, cluttered basement before arriving at a door with a keypad. "72306," Abraham said as Emily typed it in. The door slid open with a hiss, opening up to a dark tunnel.

They went inside, trying to get away from the battle in the street as fast as they could while still supporting Abraham.

"Comradde's entourage took all the getaway cars," Abraham said, looking over to where there were spots for vehicles. "Looks like we'll have to walk."

"Where are we going?" Cago asked.

"I have a safe house," Abraham said. "There is a branch of this tunnel that will lead us there."

They walked in silence for a while, Abraham's heavy breathing echoing through the tunnel.

"Trying to get away?"

Flynn turned to the side to see a burly man step out from the shadows, many others following suit from the sides of the tunnel, each one wearing a navy blue bandana to cover their mouth. An ambush.

"Comradde said that some of you Reds might try and escape through this tunnel," he said.

Another Navy stepped forward. "Not quite so strong without your followers now, are you?" he mocked. "Can't even stand on your own anymore."

Abraham pushed away from Cago and Flynn. "I can stand well enough on my own." He turned toward the Navys. "Tonight was supposed to be a night where our groups were in alliance. Why does Comradde have you guarding this tunnel?"

The lead Navy was about to respond when he paused. The sound of an engine could be heard in the distance, slowly getting louder as a few pairs of bright lights appeared down the tunnel. As they approached, gunfire began spraying through the darkness.

"Flesh guard!" Flynn dove to the side, but he realized too late that Abraham was still standing immobile in the center of the tunnel.

"Abraham!" Flynn sprinted toward him, pulling him into one of the various doorways that lined the large passage. The vehicles sped by before drifting in a circle as the Navys drew their guns and began firing.

Flynn laid Abraham down on the ground, seeing that he now had many bullet wounds in his chest and legs.

"Genny!" he called, but Abraham placed a hand on his shoulder.

"No healing can save me now, Jason." He reached into his suit coat, slowly pulling out a small silver badge that was engraved with three red triangles.

"What-"

Abraham stopped him. "This must not get into the hands of the Navys. You know that as well as I do. If I get killed by a Navy, they can take my title."

"Then we need to get you out of here!" Flynn said.

"No." Abraham stopped him again. "You all need to get out of here. I can't go with you. About a hundred yards down the tunnel is a door just like this one that will lead you up to the surface. Take it to the safe house on the corner of 9th. Other leaders should be there to help you. Do you understand me?"

Flynn nodded.

"Jason, I do not know you personally, but you are one of us, and for that reason I trust you with this title." He looked at the medallion in Flynn's hand. "If the Navys capture me and I'm still alive, I can hardly imagine what they would do. You need to kill me." He pulled a pistol off of his belt and offered it to Flynn.

Flynn took the gun and looked at it in his hands, trying to decide what to do. Could he really kill an innocent man? Could he really take the title if Abraham didn't know who he really was?

"You don't have time to think, boy!" Abraham said. "I'm going to die anyway, you need to save yourself."

Flynn looked up as a car exploded and rolled past him. He stood still for a moment, taking one last look at Abraham before reaching out and pulling the trigger.

The old man took a shaky breath as blood began to pool around him. "Go. I am a dead man."

The others finally found Flynn in the darkness. He quickly hid the gun before turning to them. "He's gone."

Thanks to the flesh guard being distracted by Navys, the group was able to escape out of the door in the side of the tunnel, which then led them up into the streets, where they found the house quickly.

They ran up to the front of the house and knocked on the door. With all the rush of the night, Flynn expected someone to answer quickly but he was wrong. In fact, no one came.

Had the flesh guard already come here too? It didn't seem like anyone had broken in. Had Abraham lied to them? What would be the point in that?

"You're not going to find anyone in there."

Flynn turned around quickly, feeling on edge after everything that had happened tonight. A man stood behind them who had clearly not been there before. "This house has been abandoned for years."

"Then why did Abraham send us here?" Flynn wondered out loud.

"Abraham sent you?" the man said.

"Yes," Flynn replied.

"Then he probably wanted you to find me." The man walked through their group. Now that he was close, Flynn could see that he was tall, thin and was wearing a solid white mask over his face, contrasting the dark black color of his clothes. "Come inside."

The man pulled out a key and opened the door. Flynn followed him cautiously, motioning for the others to do the same.

The inside of the house was dark and run-down, unlike the outside made it seem. The man led them into a back room. He pulled up a metal chair and gestured for them to sit on a couch across from him.

Flynn sat down. "Who are you?"

The man sniffed. "I like to keep my identity hidden, although I am one of the leaders of the Red Army, as well as one of the few Ironborn in this city that decided not to be a Navy. Most people call me Leech."

"Leech?" Cago asked.

The man nodded. "Why did Abraham send you here?"

"He said you could help us," Flynn said.

"How do I know he sent you?" Leech asked.

Flynn pulled the metal badge out of a compartment on his belt. "He gave me this."

Leech leaned forward curiously. "He gave you that?"

Flynn nodded.

"Willingly?"

He nodded again.

"Where is he now?" Leech asked.

"He..." Flynn hesitated. "Was shot by the flesh guard. He's gone."

Leech paused, surprised. "This is the Red Army insignia."

"I know that," Flynn said.

"No," he corrected. "I mean *the* Red Army insignia. Whoever is rightfully given this will become the next leader."

Flynn paused. "So if Abraham is dead..." He trailed off.

"You're now the General of the Red Army," Leech said.

"Why would he choose me?" Flynn asked.

"I imagine it was to keep it in the hands of the Red Army," Leech said. "You are one of us, are you not?"

Flynn nodded.

The Leech didn't speak for a few seconds. "Then you are now our leader. How can I be of assistance, General?

"Depends on what you can do," Flynn replied.

"Any information in the world? I can access it," Leech said. "Everything that has ever happened to anyone, anywhere. My powers are virtually unlimited, with only one catch." He tapped his long, gloved fingers together. "My power reservoir is different from the rest of the Ironborn. Mine must be fed. In order to use my powers, something must be sacrificed."

"So you're saying you could tell me anything?" Flynn asked.

The man chuckled. "Depends on how badly you want it."

"We need it," Flynn said.

"I said *want* it," the man said. "When it comes to making deals with the Leech, it doesn't matter how much you need my help, it matters how much you're willing to pay."

"We would pay anything," Genny said.

Leech seemed to smile. "How can I be of service?"

Flynn looked at the others before looking back at him. "We need to find Cadmore Industries." He paused before adding, "And destroy it." He supposed asking big couldn't hurt.

Leech rubbed his chin in thought. "Cadmore Industries headquarters is an interesting subject. Any time it is involved, it seems guarded somehow."

"So you can't help us?" Emily asked.

"Of course I can," Leech said quickly. "It will just be a bit more difficult."

"What exactly do you mean by 'sacrificed'?" Cago inquired.

"In order for me to use my powers, something that is of moral value to whomever needs my help must be sacrificed," Leech said. "The larger the sacrifice, the more I can help you. But if I use up my power supply, I die."

"What would we need to sacrifice?" Genny asked.

"Well, like I said before, anything dealing with Cadmore Industries is difficult," he said. "For me to access the location of the Cadmore Industries headquarters and give you information to help you destroy it, it would cost you..." He thought for a moment. "One life."

Flynn's eyes grew wide. "One of us would have to die?"

"No," Leech corrected. "One of you would have to sacrifice yourself. If one of you just dies it won't do anything."

Flynn sat back against the couch. "There has to be some other way."

"No," Genny said. "Our only other chance died twenty minutes ago. This is better than nothing." She took a deep breath. "I'll do it."

All three of the others turned to her in unison. Flynn began to contradict her. "No, you aren't going to-"

"You would do it?" Leech cut in. He now seemed a little too interested. "You would sacrifice yourself to save your species?"

Genny nodded confidently. "Absolutely."

"Genny you can't," Cago said. "We need you alive."

Genny looked him in the eyes. "This is my chance, Cago. I have to do this." She looked at Flynn. "Just make sure no one knows. I want to die selflessly. My life has been so full of thinking only of myself. Giving my life to help the Ironborn will be nothing in comparison to what I have done to hurt them. Hopefully I can make up for at least a small portion of my debt before I die." She looked back to Cago. "And let you do the same."

Cago shook his head, tears filling his eyes. Flynn had never seen him cry before. "Let me do it. If I live, I might just end up making it worse."

Genny grabbed his hand and squeezed it gently. "Don't worry. You'll get your chance. Let me go." She turned to Leech. "Yes. I'll do it."

Flynn sat silently. This didn't feel right. He wanted to object and tell her he should do it, but he knew Genny wouldn't listen when this valuable of information was on the line.

Leech stood up and held his hand out to her.

She took it and smiled peacefully. "To make it right."

She began glowing, her body getting brighter and brighter before fading, leaving the space where she had stood bare and empty, the room returning to its normal darkness.

Flynn looked to Cago, who was looking at the ground. Flynn put his arm around his shoulder. He opened his hand, revealing that Genny had placed something in his hand. Dogtags.

"I know what these are," Cago said. "There was a member of my dad's gang named Mantis. Like everyone in my dad's gang, Mantis killed many Ironborn. It seems at some point she had a change of heart."

Flynn nodded solemnly, understanding dawning on his mind. "That was the debt she wanted to repay."

Cago nodded. "She told me about her debt while we watched the sunrise this morning. I didn't know what she meant."

Flynn stared at the ground, not knowing what to say. Leech finally broke the silence. "Well, at least now you can get what you want." He sounded far too optimistic. "The Cadmore Industries headquarters is on an island off the coast of Florida. Your coordinates are 24°32'34"N, -79°43'27"W. In order to get there, I imagine you will have to get past The Spire in Florida. There is a lever hidden in a room on the second highest floor of the building that will shut off every robot in the building. There is a similar master switch in the Cadmore Industries headquarters. In order for the switch to be activated however, Dr.Griffin must be dead. In The Spire, you will find a map of the base. The map will have two missing pieces. The master switch is in one of them. Pull the switch, and everything turns off. Pull the switch, and you win the war."

Flynn rubbed his chin, processing the information. "Anything else?"

"One more thing," Leech said. "If you go north of the Spire, you will find a dock with six Enforcement boats. If the robots are shut down..." He shrugged. "It might help."

"Thank you," Emily said. It was the first thing she had said since Genny had died.

Should we be thanking him? Flynn thought silently. He didn't know. There was only one thing he knew.

None of them could let Genny die in vain.

19- The Spire

Clan Troy Headquarters, Miami
Florida, U.S.A.
8:30 a.m.
Cago

Cago thought he understood Flynn. He thought he knew what Flynn went through on the nights he dreamed of his parents dying. He had been badly mistaken. It wasn't until Cago had a similar dream himself that he finally did.

Genny. The name that had given everyone hope. The name that now drove Cago's passion. His reason to be better.

Every second for the past two days now, Cago told himself it should have been him. He could have taken her place, and she would be here instead of him. She would still be alive.

Cago sat up on his bed, wondering what woke him up. He tried in vain for a moment to remember before he heard it again. A knock on his door.

He was currently sitting in a small room with a bed and his bags, which was located on the top floor of the Clan Troy headquarters in Miami. Cago, Flynn, and Emily had all flown there after the events in Chicago, and now that the word was out that the base had been found, everyone else in the IPA was coming too.

Cago opened the door. Flynn was standing behind it in his leather jacket. He smiled. "Good morning."

Cago tried to return the smile but that action had proven difficult recently. "Good morning."

"The rest of the squad is here," Flynn said, jerking his head down the hall. "They are waiting for us downstairs."

Cago exited his room and shut the door before following Flynn down the hallway. "I wonder why they haven't used comms to contact us yet," Cago said. They got into the elevator at the end of the hallway and began to go down.

"Mr. Z has blocked transmission," Flynn explained. "He doesn't want there to be any chance that the Industry will catch wind of two thousand Ironborn meeting in the same place. Especially not just a few mere miles away from Dr. Griffin's precious base."

Cago nodded. "I guess that makes sense."

The doors opened to reveal Tarff, Blackeye, and the twins standing near the front doors along with Emily, who had apparently beat the boys downstairs.

Both groups embraced each other joyfully, each person hugging the next except for Blackeye, who just stood in the corner.

"Hey guys," Flynn asked curiously. "What is that?"

Cago looked to see that he was pointing at a robot. It looked kind of like the Ironbots that they had worked on back at the base, but with more defined facial features, as well as a few more added details through the whole machine.

"I'm Proxy," the robot said as Flynn jumped back, surprised that an Ironbot was speaking.

"Proxy?" Flynn asked, bewildered. "What happened?"

"It's simple really," Proxy explained. "During the interrogation process at the Enforcement prison in Sacramento, Zane's powers had a special manifestation. Because he programmed me, this somehow altered the roots of my system, changing me from an artificial computer into a real intelligence."

"So now you're an Ironbot?" Flynn motioned his hand toward the machine.

"Well, this body was a normal Ironbot first but then Ryan upgraded me."

"Why does your voice sound so weird?" Cago asked. "Aren't you a girl?"

"Who said I was a female?" Proxy asked.

"Well," Cago said hesitantly. "Like, the way you used to sound. It sounded like a girl."

"I don't have a gender," the robot said.

"Then what do we use while we're talking about you?" Cago asked. "He or she?"

Proxy thought for a second. "Well, for the majority of history, war has been a masculine trait, so I suppose you could use 'him.'"

"No matter what gender he is," Zane cut in. "He's awesome. The fact that a program could possess intelligence is mind-blowing. That is development that only David Cadmore has done, and even then, he only figured it out right before he died."

"Well," Flynn said. "I guess it's good not to underestimate your powers. What else have you guys been doing?"

Both groups of soldiers began sharing stories of what they had been doing over the past few days until someone came in and told them they were requested in a meeting.

Flynn had expected the Iron Warrior to be taller. He wasn't sure why, but with his epic title and fame, Flynn

256

thought Mr. Z would be some kind of super soldier but, to his surprise, he was the same size as a normal person, although his face was still covered by an IPA suit and mask.

He currently sat across from Flynn and his squad, who in his private office giving him a full description of their missions. He occasionally paused to ask questions or clarify things, but he didn't seem overly interested until Flynn mentioned the Revenant.

"He was there in person?" Mr. Z asked. Flynn noticed that, even while talking rather quietly, his voice was strong and confident.

Flynn nodded.

"And he spoke to you directly?"

"No," Flynn said. "But we did hear him speak."

Mr. Z thought for a moment. Flynn could almost see the calculative look on his face through his helmet. "This is definitely troubling."

"Why, exactly?" Flynn asked.

"Well," Mr. Z said. "With the end of this war on the horizon, our forces will be weakened significantly whether we win or lose. With this news of the Revenant's rising power, I fear that destroying Cadmore Industries might not be the last of our problems."

"What else do we know about him?" Flynn asked.

Mr. Z sighed. "I'm afraid not very much." He placed his hands on the desk in front of him. "He's a very powerful terrorist and an Ironborn that can animate the bodies of people that he kills. Beyond that, all we know is that his beliefs are aligned with those of the White Legions."

"Who?" Flynn asked, confused.

"The White Legions were a group that was extinguished at the turn of Cadmore Industries," Mr. Z explained. "They were a group of Ironborn with the belief that, since Ironborn are, in many ways, superior to humans, they should lead over them. They are the group that most of humanity is afraid of. The power-hungry Ironborn who claim to follow the laws of natural order."

Mr. Z picked up an electronic tablet from his desk and turned it towards Flynn. The screen showed a symbol. A hand holding a knife, the image drawn with white paint against a black background.

Mr. Z pulled out a datapad and began scrolling through pictures as he set the pad down on the table for them to see. "These are instances when the 'White Blade' as we have named it, has appeared. Typically this symbol would be found in the aftermath of an event similar to that of Atlanta or, more recently, Chicago. Mass killings caused by powerful White Legion leaders."

"But the White Legion no longer exists, right?" Flynn asked.

"As far as we know," Mr. Z said. He then asked Flynn to continue his story. He listened intently until Flynn got to the point where Jakar died.

"If Jakar died, how did you succeed on your mission?" he inquired.

Flynn looked at the others and hesitated, Genny's words returning to his mind. She didn't want anyone to know what she had done. A selfless sacrifice.

"He told me as he died," Flynn said. "His final words. He died to give us a chance at victory." Flynn knew that the others were thinking about Genny, specifically Cago. Jakar had done nothing. He could have won the war for them years ago but instead he had run. He had hidden in fear.

"Do you still remember the information you got?" Mr. Z asked.

Flynn nodded. "It would be hard to forget sir."

Flynn began relaying the information to Mr. Z.

Mr. Z sat for a moment. "I will have to go over this with my strategists."

Flynn finished his story with the death of Abraham, which Mr. Z seemed to take the most interest in.

"I've studied the ways of capital city leadership in the past," Mr. Z said. "If what you've said is true, then you truly are their new leader, although I imagine they will elect a proxy one in your place. Do you still have the token?"

Flynn pulled out the metal disk with the Red Army symbol inscribed into it. He handed it to Mr. Z, who turned it in his hands.

"Incredible," he said. "You all have done some amazing things." He then turned to Zane, asking him to retell his journey.

Flynn listened as Zane told of them getting captured by Enforcement in Hawaii before waking up in a prison cell in California. Throughout the story, Ryan would cut in and explain where he helped or did something cool, and Zane would always mention something even better that he did. It wasn't until the very end of their story that Mr. Z spoke up.

"The Rift?" he asked curiously.

"That's what the location was called on the computer," Zane confirmed. "And it referenced the Revenant as well. They were in the same file together."

"Implying that they are connected somehow," Mr. Z said, following along. "This could give us a clue as to where our soldiers have been disappearing to. Perhaps this mystery can be solved." He turned to look at Flynn, "Without anyone getting hurt."

Flynn's mind flashed back to the summer. To all of the events of the Blood Squad and the extraction plan, when the IPA had tried to use Emily as bait to find out where all of their soldiers had gone after vanishing. At least Mr. Z sounded sincere.

"And this Proxy robot you mentioned," Mr. Z continued. "Does he have all of this information saved?"

"That I do," Proxy said from where he sat behind Zane.

Mr. Z seemed slightly caught off-guard. "My apologies, Proxy, I mistook you for an Ironbot. Tell me, are you confined to that form?"

"Negative," Proxy said. "I can control any robotic system, given the right amount of access."

"That could prove useful in the coming fight," Mr. Z nodded to himself, seemingly processing the things he had heard. He then looked at each of the soldiers in turn. "Thank you soldiers. You have given us a chance to defeat our enemy. A chance for freedom."

Zane stood with his arms folded, watching the dispatchers sit at their computers, studying the layout of their target or relaying information to the troops on the ground. He then looked up through the window where in the distance rose The Spire. Other than a few Enforcement

261

helicopters circling parts of the building, everything looked normal. Zane knew, however, that there was much more going on inside that they could not see.

"Can you imagine having this many dispatchers on your side?"

Zane turned to see Ryan walk up next to him. "It would be annoying," he responded.

Ryan looked confused. "Why?"

"I wouldn't be able to make the decisions," Zane said. "All the other dispatchers would be trying to give me their ideas."

"Doesn't sound too bad to me," Ryan said.

Zane threw a glare at him. "You know you wouldn't stand a chance on your missions without me guiding you."

Ryan shrugged. "Debatable."

A door opened behind them and Zane heard heavy footfalls behind him. He turned and saw Mr. Z walk up behind them.

"Where are they?" he asked the dispatchers.

One turned towards him. "They are on their way up the tower. The main group will reach the top in ten minutes."

"How are they doing?" Mr. Z asked.

"Three casualties," a different dispatcher said. "We still have three hundred fifty-seven uninjured."

"What about the elite?"

"Titan is still at the bottom of The Spire distracting our enemies," she responded. "Troy and Vulcan are leading the attack, and Vizler is in the rear."

"Are they still doing alright?" he asked. Zane was appalled at the fact that he might be able to even see one of the Spartans in person. Even Mr. Z seemed to respect them.

"As always," she said,

Mr. Z nodded in thought. "As always."

Zane watched in anticipation as the team worked, watching from drones or cameras inside the building as well as body's cameras attached to the soldiers themselves. So much relied on this mission, but with Captain Troy leading, they seemed unstoppable. Now that he had seen what Clan Troy had in them, Zane was actually beginning to gain more confidence in their chances of winning the war.

"Have we sent in the Phantoms yet?" Z asked.

"Only two sir."

"Send the rest," he said.

"All of them?"

Mr. Z nodded in confirmation.

The dispatcher nodded and spoke into her comm. "Phantom squadrons one through four prepare for launch."

"Phantoms?" Ryan whispered to Zane.

Zane was about to respond when a noise like a thunderstorm came from all around them and they watched out the front window as nearly thirty sleek black helicopters flew past them towards The Spire.

"Heck yeah!" Ryan said, pumping his fist.

The Enforcement helicopters stood no chance as the Phantoms swarmed around them, dropping chopper after chopper from the sky.

The Phantoms were very effective, but Enforcement was everywhere. All of the cameras showed IPA soldiers battling against the robots valiantly, but more kept coming.

"Sir, enemy reinforcements incoming."

Zane and Ryan shared a glance. With Clan Troy gone, the base would be virtually defenseless. They had to win this fight.

"Come on Troy," Mr. Z whispered to himself.

The soldiers on the cameras eventually made it to the top floor. Zane watched Troy cut through hundreds of Enforcement soldiers as they made their way to the central control room, their robotic bodies turning to ash as soon as they made contact with his blade. Zane had heard of Troy's powers before, but seeing them in action was crazier than anything he had ever thought it would be. It was like he wasn't even fighting, but instead simply walking through the enemy forces.

The cameras showed one of the soldiers hack through the door and enter the room while Troy, Vulcan and the others defended the entrance to the hallway that was now flooded with Enforcement robots. Troy brandished his glinting swords and slashed through the oncoming swarm with precision. Vulcan dealt nearly the same amount of damage with his axes and Vizler with his guns, but the swarm was unaffected. It was like shooting a forest fire with a water gun.

"They're getting overwhelmed sir," a dispatcher said.

Zane watched as camera after camera began to show the dull metal of the ceiling as soldiers fell to the ground. The whole room watched in anticipation as the strike team's forces began to diminish. Even against the odds, Troy himself did not seem flustered. He fought on.

Just as Zane thought that their odds might have been spent, the robots suddenly froze. They stopped in their tracks, not moving. The Enforcement helicopters fell out of the sky, and a black armored IPA soldier walked out of the control room, having just found the switch.

Troy reached up and pressed the comm on the side of his helmet. His low voice resounded over the dispatching room's speakers. "Mission 984 completed. The Spire is down."

A cheer went up from everyone in the room, and Mr. Z ran his hand across the top of his helmet, as if running a hand through his hair.

Zane felt Ryan elbow him in the side. "You were worried weren't you?"

Zane looked at him confusedly. "I wasn't worried." He sniffed. "You were."

"I was not-" Ryan stopped as Mr. Z raised his hands to quiet everyone in the room.

"News of The Spire's fall will spread quickly," he said. "I must go prepare." He turned to an officer standing next to him. "Officer Randall?"

"Sir?" Randall asked.

"Contact the Clan Captains," Mr. Z replied. "We leave at dawn."

20- One Night

Flynn had never been in an aircraft carrier before, so he didn't realize how massive they were until he stepped inside. After taking down The Spire last night, the rest of the IPA had gathered in Miami and were now loading the boats, preparing for the final attack.

After speaking with Bi, Flynn had learned that Mr. Z, like David Cadmore, had been one of the richest people in the entire country before the war began, and had been the main source of funding for the organization. A huge majority of that funding had gone towards the IPA fleet, which included one boat for each clan, three aircraft carriers and four destroyers. In the past, these boats, like all of the aircraft, had been manned by Clan Xion, the engineering clan.

Along with these seven boats, the IPA had been able to hijack three more Enforcement destroyers that were found in the docks at The Spire, which had been the meeting place for the rest of the fleet this morning when the IPA had started their journey toward the island.

Flynn and the rest of his squad sat in their group's designated meeting room. Unlike the rest of Clan Vilo, Bi's squad had been assigned onto Clan Troy's aircraft carrier. Everyone sat around the table, waiting to hear why they were here. A screen on the side of the room flickered to life, revealing the masked face of Mr. Z.

"Lieutenant Scorpius," Mr. Z said. "The Clan Captains wish to speak with you. Please go to the council room."

Flynn looked around at the others for a moment before standing up and exiting the room, making his way down the hallway before entering the council room. The circular room had a large domed ceiling, encompassing a ring of chairs, each one seating a holographic projection of a different clan captain.

It was at this moment Flynn realized he had never even seen some of the IPA's leaders before. He obviously quickly recognized Vilo, along with the large Captain Dax, the small form of Captain Duo, the slim, white-armored Captain Pris, and of course Mr. Z himself. Flynn then looked at the other three Captains. The first was Neo, who had orange accents on his armor and was holding a massive gun in his lap, as if he had just come from a fight. The second was Troy, who looked to be even larger than Dax, his armor entirely matte black, the only color on his person coming from the two golden swords that were strapped to his back, as well as a few golden accents on his armor. The final captain was by far the strangest. Xion's body was covered in a wide assortment of tools and gadgets, many of which seemed to be physically attached to him. His lower body was also gone entirely, replaced by a yellow, spider-like machine.

"Scorpius," Mr. Z addressed him. "Thank you for joining us. As you already know, you and the rest of Bi's squad are Cleared. You are a group of soldiers that, with the help of our technology, should be entirely undetectable to Cadmore Industry's scanners. Because of this, your squad could be crucial in the upcoming mission. Considering Sergeant Bi is still coming back from a recent mission, we decided we would discuss ideas with you."

"You know where Bi is?" Flynn asked, grateful to hear that she was alive.

"She found her way back to Duo's headquarters after escaping the catacombs in Hawaii," Mr. Z explained. "Because she couldn't make any contact with you or Zane, she decided to come to Miami, where she insisted she would help us with any missions we had. Her and the rest of the survivors are currently being flown here from the mainland by helicopter. I'm sorry we did not inform you sooner, but we had no confirmation that she had survived the mission until after we had left the docks in the morning."

Flynn nodded. "Thank you for letting me know."

Dax spoke up. "With all due respect, Mr. Z," he said, clearly with very little respect. "Bi's squad is a very small and young group of soldiers. Even with the benefit of them being undetectable, why should we rely on them in our most dire time?"

"They may be small and young, Dax, but that does not mean they are not skilled," Mr. Z pointed out. "They have proven themselves to be quite proficient over the past few weeks, progressing us closer to victory than any other squad in the IPA. Besides, if I am not mistaken, Scorpius recently got a new title. As the General of the Red Army, his rank is the same as mine, which exceeds yours, *captain*."

"Well then, *General* Scorpius," Captain Dax said. "How would you suggest your squad be useful in this attack?"

"I think that Dax is right," Flynn said, looking over to Mr. Z. "Our squad is simply too small to have any real effect." Dax raised up his hand as if he was about to say something but Flynn continued, "However, I do think that any amount of surprise is good, especially if used correctly. We need to get more undetectable soldiers."

"What a genius plan," Dax scoffed. "If only we could find another unit of soldiers that was undetectable."

"Found one," a voice said behind Flynn. He looked back to see Bi entering the counsel room, her expression as calculating and confident as ever. She confronted Dax. "If I am not mistaken, Cadmore Industries received our records nearly two months ago. If our rate of new soldiers has not changed dramatically during those two months, we should have at least a hundred new units that were never on the stolen list in the first place."

Dax laughed. "You want to send an army of rookies in? Led by this young boy?" He gestured to Flynn. "Your recent mission, although successful, still ended with your identity becoming compromised. You would not be able to aid them."

"The Industry gaining access to my DNA was but a small downside of our mission in comparison to the multitude of benefits that we have gained from it," Bi said, placing a hand on Flynn's shoulder. "I am confident in my entire squad's ability to lead themselves. Besides, Scorpius proved his leadership skills already during his mission in Chicago."

Flynn felt uneasy. Even with the support of the rookies, he questioned how well he could lead an entire army. "We would need a larger advantage," Flynn said. All eyes turned to him. "If Dax doesn't think our group is strong enough, then we can do both plans. Send the strongest troops we have on one side of the base. This will hopefully draw the majority of the units inside the facility to that side. From there, my group of rookies should have a much easier path into the opposite side of the base. Dr. Griffin can't run. If he gets too far from the base, or he dies, the entire army will shut down. We can catch him off-guard from both sides."

Captain Neo nodded, hoisting his gun. "I like this plan."

"Even with this plan," Dax pointed out. "There are too many soldiers inside the base for our strongest soldiers to take on."

"That's where the rest of our army comes in," Mr. Z instructed. "We'll send them in our siege boats and hit the island head-on. With the support from our boats and planes, that should be enough to draw the majority of their troops out."

For the first time, Dax seemed compliant. "I will put together some soldiers for the elite strike team."

"Bi," Mr. Z said. "You and Scorpius will be in charge of the Cleared strike team."

"Captain Xion," Bi said. "Along with all of the new soldiers, I believe you also have a group of... *special* soldiers that would fall under Cadmore's List."

Xion perked up, his sharp metal legs shifting. "I'm sure they would be happy to help."

Mr. Z continued. "Scorpius, Bi, you are dismissed. We have a lot of planning to do before morning arrives."

"Who are these people again?" Flynn asked Bi, who sat beside him in the helicopter.

"You'll see when we get there," she said loudly over the spinning blades.

The helicopter was flying over the ocean, taking the two soldiers from Clan Troy's aircraft carrier over to Xion's. Flynn looked out of the side of the vehicle at the rest of the fleet. From up here, the IPA's army looked unstoppable, but he knew that their enemy's army would be even stronger.

The helicopter pilot landed them on Clan Xion's aircraft carrier. Flynn and Bi stepped out onto the deck, where they were greeted by a man wearing an IPA suit with bright yellow highlights, the color of Clan Xion.

"Greetings sergeant!" the man said over the roar of the helicopter. He led them across the deck. "I am Commander Split of the Iron Knights in Clan Xion. I heard you were in need of our assistance."

Flynn turned to Bi, but she gestured back at him as if to say, *You're in charge here.*

"Yes," Flynn replied. "We are planning-" He paused, taking a better look at the commander. "Did you say your name was Split?"

As they walked inside, Split pressed a button on his wrist, collapsing his helmet down into his suit, revealing the same chiseled face and dusty blonde hair of the soldier Flynn had made friends with in New York. His smile however, was gone. His eyes were much more serious now, his expression hardened. "Hello Flynn," he said curtly. "It's nice to see you still alive."

"I thought you were in Clan Pris," Flynn said. "Why are you here?"

"Because of this." Split raised up his hands, his suit collapsing down. Where his hands and forearms should have been was replaced with identical replicas made of metal. "A mission went south," he said solemnly. "They captured me and tortured me for information. I won't go into the details."

The hardened expression made sense now.

Split led them to a door, which he opened, ushering them inside. They stood on a balcony overlooking a large room full of ordinary bunk beds. The soldiers, however, were far from ordinary.

"All of us Iron Knights were fatally injured," Split explained. "Marked as dead in battle. People often wonder why Caption Xion is rarely seen in the factories. Well, this is why." He gestured to the room beneath them. "He's bringing us back from the edge of death."

Flynn looked down at the soldiers. Each one was missing some part of their body, which was replaced by a piece of machinery. One soldier wasn't even visible, his entire body surrounded in a mech suit.

"Rumor has it Xion had a similar experience to each of us," Split explained. "He was a Green Beret in Iraq. He hit a landmine and lost his legs. David Cadmore, who was doing research on the connections between intelligent life and artificial intelligence at the time, took his body in for research. By some miracle, he managed to keep him alive when no doctors could, and he replaced Xion's legs with, well, you've seen him now. From then on, he tried to do the same thing for other soldiers."

"So all Iron Knights were taken off of the records because the IPA thought you were deceased due to your injuries?" Bi said. "Intriguing."

"These soldiers despise Dr. Griffin and the rest of the Industry more than anyone else you could find," Split said. "They would be more than willing to help you on your mission."

Flynn stood at the railing on the portside of the aircraft carrier, looking out at the rest of the fleet. He had watched a few helicopters move soldiers from one boat to another, as well as a few coming from the mainland. Apparently half of Clan Duo and a third of Clan Neo were still trying to catch up with the rest of the IPA. Everyone was hoping they would be able to make it by morning. They would need every soldier they could get.

The squad had met up a few hours ago to discuss the plan for the attack. Phase One would include the largest

275

group of soldiers, who would storm the beaches, drawing out the Enforcement's infantry. Phase Two would include the boats and planes, which would produce cover for the attacking troops as well as further distraction for Phase Three. This is where his squad came in.

The two strike teams would go to either side of the base by submarine. They would be the ones to kill Dr. Griffin as well as find the control center that would turn off the army once he was dead.

Flynn looked down at the water, watching the waves as he went through the plan in his mind. It was simple in theory, but the true test would come down to how well each soldier fought, and how well Flynn could lead. That was what he was worried about. There was a lot on his shoulders.

"Pretty beautiful sunset considering where we're going," Emily said as she walked up behind him.

"By the time the next sunset comes, the whole world will be different," Flynn said, smiling as she leaned against the railing beside him. "Hopefully for the better."

"I've seen so many new things over the past few weeks," Emily shook her head. "I don't know if I'll be able to see normal life the same."

"Well," Flynn replied. "Even if we win, life will be very different. Besides, we might still have the Revenant to worry about."

"At least we have one night to relax," Emily said. "Everything has been moving so fast I've barely been able to breathe."

"I would hardly call this relaxing," Flynn chuckled.

"You should really relax more," Emily said, turning around and putting her back against the railing so she could look at Flynn.

He finally looked up from the water and met her eyes. "I doubt Griffin is relaxing."

"He definitely won't be tomorrow morning," Emily remarked. Then she continued, "But it's bad to be tense before going into battle. At least that's what Bi told me."

"I'd rather be prepared than rested," Flynn replied.

"Hey Flynn!"

Flynn looked over his shoulder to see Cago approaching them.

"Sorry to interrupt you guys but they want us all below decks for the rest of the night in a few minutes," Cago said, walking up to the other side of Flynn. "They sent me up here to get you two."

"We'll be down soon," Emily assured him.

"Bi also told me not to leave without you," Cago said with a knowing smile. "Besides, I have something I want to show you."

"Well alright then," Emily said.

The three soldiers walked over to the door before making their way downstairs to their dorms. It comforted Flynn to see Cago smile. With everything going on, he assumed Cago would be the last person to be happy. It didn't take him too long to find out why.

They followed Cago into the bunk room that he and Flynn shared.

"What did you want to show us?" Flynn asked.

Cago held up a finger before suddenly vanishing from sight. Flynn spun toward a small radio as it suddenly began to play music. The overhead lights then turned off, leaving only a single lamp to light the room. Flynn spun around again to see the door open and close quickly.

"What-" Flynn was cut off when he heard Emily laughing. He turned to her. "Do you know what's going on?"

"When we were in Chicago I was super stressed after the events in Hawaii. I ranted to Genny for a while and..." She sighed and shook her head. "I guess Cago found out some of the things I told her."

"What things?" Flynn asked, concerned.

"It was silly," she said, dismissing the question. "I was super stressed at the time and-" She looked up, seeing the curious expression on Flynn's face. "I guess it wouldn't hurt to explain," she sighed again. "With all of this fighting and war I haven't gotten to spend any time with you. Even when we're together you always seem so tense and serious. I just wished I could have one night to... well, it's like I said, it's silly. I shouldn't even be considering my own feelings when the stakes are so high in this battle. People's lives were on the line-"

Flynn grabbed her hand and she looked up from the ground. "You're right," he said. "But now we have one night. Besides, Cago already set this up for us."

She smiled, stepping closer to him.

As they slowly danced to the radio's music, Flynn finally loosened up slightly. His mind drifted back to when they had gone to the dance together. That was the last time he had truly relaxed.

"After we win tomorrow," Emily asked. "Can we do this again?"

Flynn took a while to respond, enjoying the feeling of finally relaxing. "I'm sure we'll have plenty of time."

"What will you do?" Emily asked. "After we get back?"

"There will still be lots of things to take care of," Flynn pointed out. "Even with the Industry gone, the world will still need time to get used to treating us the same.

Besides, there are still a few other groups to worry about. Mr. Z spoke about the White Legions who-"

"Flynn." She placed her hand on his chest. "Relax, remember? We only have one night."

"Sorry," Flynn said, closing his eyes and taking a deep breath. When he opened them, Emily was inches away from his face.

"You might still need to keep your guard up," she said teasingly. "You never know when I could sneak up on you."

"I'm alright with that," he said quietly.

They both smiled as they continued to inch closer to each other. Flynn hated how his mind tried to stop him from being near her like this. He felt too vulnerable, too open to an attack. He felt like there were voices in his head telling him to get away, like hearing ghosts of his own mind.

"Voices of ghosts..." Flynn mumbled.

"What?" Emily backed up slightly, confused.

"I'm sorry Emily, but I need to go see Mr. Z," Flynn said urgently. "We messed up."

"He already knows we're coming," Flynn said quickly. He was standing in the middle of the counsel room where, with the help of Bi, he had managed to get in contact with Mr. Z, whose holographic form was now sitting in his chair.

"What do you mean?" Mr. Z asked.

"I lied about how we learned the location of the island," Flynn said apologetically. "Jakar was shot at the party so we had to find another way to get our information. We found a Red Army leader named Leech. Genny had to sacrifice herself for the information."

"I know Leech," Mr. Z assured him. "We used to work together, Flynn. He's on our side."

"Not anymore," Flynn said. "His voice, could you describe it to me?"

"I never heard him speak much," Mr. Z said. "He was pretty quiet and shy."

"Not the Leech we met," Flynn said. "His voice was gravelly and, although it was muffled behind his mask, it's unmistakable now. He shared the same voice as the gang member in the alleyway. The Revenant."

Mr. Z stared down at Flynn. "Are you sure?"

Flynn nodded. "A few minutes ago it was like... It was like I could hear the two voices in my head. Separately they sounded unfamiliar but hearing them together I am certain."

"An enemy like the Revenant *would* want both of his biggest enemies to fight," Bi pointed out. Flynn had nearly forgotten she was still here. "The weaker we are, the more power he has."

"What are we going to do?" Flynn asked.

"We don't have many options." Mr. Z shook his head. "A few hours ago, our farthest scout planes managed to get a view of the island. Even if they hadn't known we were coming before, they know now. I'll alert the others, but all we can do now is hope that they aren't able to amass all of their soldiers back to the island before we begin our attack." His holographic form disappeared.

"What we need now," Bi said, "Is a miracle."

INTERLUDE

21– Revival

Noise. That was all Diana could hear.

All around her, gunshots and yelling sounded in her ears, and Diana was scared out of her mind. Having only held a gun for the first time two weeks ago, being put out here in battle had her nearly paralyzed.

She stood with her back against a rock, the only form of comfort to her in the dense forest as the enemy troops marched toward her and the other members of Clan Duo who were all fighting for their lives against the dozens of robots and tanks.

Diana heard a noise to her right and turned to see an Enforcement soldier come into her vision around the edge of the rock. She jumped and fired blindly. She closed her eyes, waiting to die before blinking her eyes open in surprise as she saw the soldier on the ground, a small stream of smoke rising from its neck.

Gaining a little more confidence after defeating her very first robot, she peeked back around the rock. Marching right towards her were at least a dozen enemy soldiers, who raised their guns and fired as soon as she came into view.

She quickly jumped behind the rock, scrambling for an idea of what to do but nothing came. Even her short two weeks of training were absolutely forgotten.

She looked around. Every friendly soldier she saw was currently fighting, just as overwhelmed as she was. There wasn't anyone to help her.

That's when she heard a noise. A soft rumbling coming from the ground. She looked forward and saw a disturbance in the ground. A line of turned-up dirt that moved towards her. The underground disturbance, however, did not stop at Diana but instead went past her.

Diana looked back around the rock as the line of turned-up dirt reached her enemies. A humanoid figure then sprung up from the dirt, slashing with dual knives at the robots, shredding most of them into pieces before she even hit the ground, and finishing up the rest quickly after.

She then sprung into the air, landing lightly next to Diana behind the rock. She extended her palm. "My name is Cara."

She blinked. "Diana."

Cara nodded. "Nice to meet you, soldier. You seem pretty new to this."

Diana nodded a little too vigorously.

"Follow me," Cara said. She pulled her around the side of the rock and out into the densely wooded canyon. Even though it was midday, the forest was still so thick with trees and foliage that Diana could not see far. She wondered how Cara even knew where she was going.

Diana followed her through the canyon, which Diana noticed was probably made by a river due to its sharp curves.

Now is not a time to remember your geography class! her mind screamed at her.

Cara's head perked up, and she held up a hand to stop Diana.

"What?" Diana asked.

"Shh," Cara said, looking around for a second. She cursed. "Stingrays. We need to get behind cover."

Cara led her to a tall, stone pillar that connected to the canyon wall and they pressed their backs against it.

A beam of blue energy blazed through the forest, blasting through trees like they were made of smoke. From around the side of the pillar, Diana could hear the footsteps of Enforcement soldiers.

Cara turned to her. "Stay here."

She crept toward the edge, lashing out quickly as the first soldier came into view, cutting down the small squad.

She turned back to Diana and beckoned to her. "Come on!"

Diana was about to follow before the sound resonated through the canyon once again and she watched with wide eyes as the Stingray's beam hit Cara, whose body vaporized instantly, leaving nothing but a few floating ashes.

Diana screamed and backed closer to the canyon wall.

She heard more footsteps but this time she didn't even know where to go. Everything seemed so hopeless that, despite her best efforts to stop herself, she sat down and cried.

Darkness. That was all Darius could see.

He had been sitting on a hard wooden chair for the past few hours now, a gag in his mouth and a blindfold over his eyes. He had heard a few voices downstairs a couple of minutes ago, the first thing he had heard all night, and now footsteps coming up the stairs into the attic.

He heard the door open and felt the blindfold and gag get pulled off.

289

Through the dim light of the single window in the safehouse's dusty attic he could see the black silhouette of a man. He wore a black suit, tie and shirt, along with a simple black face mask and black fedora.

"Leech?" Darius asked. "What am I doing here?"

Leech leaned in close, his voice coming through the thin, unmoving slot in his mask. "Why did he send them here?"

"Who?" Darius asked.

"The Don! Father Abraham!" Leech said. "Why would he send them to your house?"

Darius assumed he spoke of the voices he had heard downstairs. "I couldn't tell you."

Darius saw a flash of movement and felt a fist hit him squarely in the face, throwing his head to the side.

When his sight came back he saw Leech's mask only inches away from his face. "Your father is dead, and in his final words he sends Vrazda's most wanted soldiers to your doorstep. Why?"

Darius drew a few deep breaths but said nothing.

"Why?" Leech yelled.

Darius jerked his head forward into Leech's, who stumbled backward toward the wall.

"You're part of the Red Army, Leech!" Darius exclaimed. "Why are you doing this? You were my friend!"

Leech looked up at Darius, and he saw that a piece of the mask was now broken off, exposing his left eye. The eye of the Revenant.

"Not anymore, Darius. Not anymore."

"Power. That is all humans will ever want."

Dr. Griffin stood with his arms folded, looking through the pane of glass that stood in the wall before him. "It doesn't matter who you are, or where you came from. Power will corrupt you."

On the other side of the glass, Shark stood in the middle of the floor in the dark room, the wires that were connected to his robotic form glowing bright red as energy flowed through them.

"Not even do I find myself exempt from the hunger of power, so as I finish off every last Ironborn I will fulfill my goal with killing myself."

The energy from Shark flowed through the cords and into the ground, where it traveled to the small, egg-shaped pods. As the energy reached them, the gaps in their hexagonal surface glowed for a moment before unfolding, growing outwards rapidly. The cords pulsed with extra energy as the pods expanded and the beings took form. Each one stood with a gun in hand, taking their places around Shark, their five sets of eyes glowing blood red with power.

"I've become ready for death. With the battle coming at dawn, I would suggest you do the same."

"Nothing. That's all we ever get out here."

Lieutenant Cooper turned around. "Will you quit complaining? We can do a game of foosball when you're done, just run the northside thermal scans."

"Foosball? You think that will help?" Alvey sighed. "The most important battle of the war is going on right now and the two of us are sitting here doing nothing."

"Hey, look at the bright side," Cooper said. "Out of everyone in Clan Xion, the two of us were the ones left behind. That makes us special!"

"Or not wanted," Alvey grumbled.

Cooper shrugged. "Think of it whatever way you like." He turned back to his computer and was so startled that he had to blink a few times to make sure he was seeing straight. "Hey Alvey?"

"Yeah?" he asked lazily.

"I've got something."

"Yeah right," Alvey said. "Very funny."

"No, I'm not joking," Cooper said. "Look!"

Alvey turned around and looked at Cooper's screen. He then hopped out of his seat and ran over to the computer. "What is it?" he asked curiously.

"Not sure," Cooper said. "Looks human though."

Alvey watched the thermal scanner data for a second. "It's coming to the door!"

They both stared as the red mark came closer to the tower. As it neared, they changed their view to the front door camera, where a soldier was shown crawling toward the front door.

Alvey's brow furrowed. "Is that... Cercies?"

A soft thud was heard as the soldier hit the door and stopped moving. They sat for a moment before Cooper turned to Alvey. "Well don't just sit there, let's go help him!"

They stood up and walked to the front door. Alvey typed in the code and it opened with a hiss. They then carried Cercies inside, laying him down on the ground before Cooper closed the door. He walked over to where Alvey knelt by the body. "He's unconscious, and needs food. Looks like he's been walking for days."

"Well if he walked the whole way back from his target, he probably hasn't eaten."

"Hey, check this out," Alvey pulled a piece of cloth out of Cercies' jacket. "This is a pilot's badge."

"Not just any pilot's badge," Cooper said, studying it with awe. "This is Lieutenant Axe's. The best pilot in the IPA."

Alvey looked at the badge. "Does that mean he's... dead?"

Cooper looked at the ground. "I imagine so."

Cercies suddenly gasped awake, gripping onto Alvey's arm like his life depended on it. "The rendezvous!" he said in a raspy whisper. "The rendezvous..."

Cooper knelt down. "Yes, this is the rendezvous point. You went on a mission and were supposed to fly back here."

Cercies' head flicked over to Cooper, his dazed eyes landing somewhere near the lieutenant's shoulder. "My mission?"

"Yes, your mission was to get a data chip," Cooper urged him on.

"The... the chip." Cercies arm flopped over to the inside of his jacket as if he was trying to grab something but his hand kept trembling so hard that he couldn't. His entire body seemed to be shaking.

Cooper opened his jacket and pulled out the thin data chip. He handed it to Alvey, who finally pried Cercies hands off of his arm. "Go scan this." Cooper ordered.

Alvey nodded and walked briskly toward the computer.

"The rendezvous!" Cercies yelled. "I must get... to the rendezvous..."

"Hey Cooper?" Alvey said. "I found something."

"The rendezvous..."

Cooper left Cercies' side and ran to where Alvey stood at his computer bay.

"This has some kind of coded message," Alvey said. "The computer is trying to decode it but for some reason it's not working."

"I can tell you." Cooper looked over to the source of the voice and was surprised to see Cercies sitting up. His eyes were still dazed but they had some consciousness in them. "I had to get back to the rendezvous point to warn them."

"To warn them of what?" Cooper asked.

"The Red Stone project. The final battle," Cercies said, shaking his head as he looked at the ground. "It's a trap."

PART III

BATTLE OVER CADMORE INDUSTRIES

22- Scorpion

Flynn watched as the final Enforcement boat sank under the water, having been blasted into pieces by the entirety of the IPA's fleet. As the highest point of the boat passed under the surface of the water, Cadmore Industries headquarters came into full view.

"So that's our target," Ryan said from behind Flynn. The others in his squad had been below decks getting ready during the first phase of the attack, but not Flynn. He wanted to be the first one to see their enemy.

"I still don't understand why we couldn't just drop a giant bomb on them," Ryan remarked.

"Because they have technology protecting against that type of attack, genius," Flynn heard Zane say. By the sound of it, the two were a few feet behind Flynn, getting some final things prepared for the mission. He kept staring at the island.

Everyone seemed a bit more on edge after hearing the news last night, but especially Flynn. For his team, surprise was their best ally. Their group would still be undetectable, but just the idea that Dr. Griffin knew the attack was coming would give him more time to think through a better defense, removing most of the IPA's element of surprise. Which meant even more of the weight was now on Flynn's shoulders.

"I don't like it," Cago said as he walked up beside Flynn. Flynn finally drew his gaze away from the island to look at his friend. "How were we able to take out their fleet so easily?" Cago asked.

"Apparently their largest fleet of boats got destroyed in a battle a little over a year ago," Flynn explained. "Once the Ironborn sank their largest ship, the *Leviathan*, most of the supporting Enforcement ships fell quickly. After this, Cadmore Industries stopped trying to push their front on the water, which is the biggest reason the IPA's boats haven't been of much use up until now."

Cago shook his head. "It still doesn't feel right."

"I agree," Flynn said. "But we don't have any other options."

Hearing the sound of shuffling footsteps, Flynn turned around to find a crowd of around a hundred soldiers walking toward him. Tarff, Emily and Blackeye stood at the front of the rookie army.

Flynn also saw that one of the IPA's airborne carriers had just landed in the center of the deck. The Iron

Knights, who were now exiting the vehicle, followed their leader over to the rest of the crowd.

Split extended a metal hand, and Flynn shook it. "Is everyone here?" Flynn asked.

Split nodded. "One hundred twenty-seven recruits, forty-one Iron Knights, plus your squad."

"Good." Flynn turned on his comm. "Bi, let me know when we're ready."

"You have about five minutes," Bi responded.

"Affirmative." Flynn turned back to the crowd that faced him. He paused for a moment, trying to think of something heroic to say. Taking a deep breath, he decided to remove his helmet.

"Soldiers!" he shouted, calling them to attention. "We have before us a mission of great importance! I know that not all of us seem ready. Many might be afraid, and for good reason. We are about to fight the most difficult battle of our lives. The battle to end the war that has plagued our existence for three years now. The survival of the Ironborn rests on our shoulders, and we are going to be fighting an uphill battle. We will be out gunned, outmanned, and out experienced. But it will be unexpected."

"As you are now under my direction, we have been given the name Scorpion Squad," Flynn continued. "The rest of the IPA is the body of our scorpion, but where the real danger lies is in the stinger. We are the small, yet powerful force that has the potential to bring down this base for good. We might not be the best, but they'll never see us coming."

A cannon blast from one of the destroyers signaled the start of the main attack, and a war cry sounded up from the soldiers.

"Load the boats!" Flynn called before re-covering his face with his mask.

"You really think we have a chance at this?" Cago asked.

"I'm not sure," Flynn said as he watched his small army board the two submarines that hung from the side of the aircraft carrier. "But if we never fight, we would have to continue living our lives in fear. It's a simple choice. Freedom or death."

Admiral Navari watched as the submarines dropped off of the side of the aircraft carrier, the stealth boats hitting the water before quickly disappearing.

Navari had been the grand admiral of the IPA's naval fleet for the entirety of the war. He currently stood in the bridge of the *Trident*, the largest of the IPA's vessels, giving out commands and starting each phase of the attack.

"Both strike teams are away, sir," the officer beside him stated. "As are the siege boats."

"Good," Navari said. "Begin Phase Two."

"Launching aircraft!" one of the naval officers shouted.

"Aircraft from the *Eclipse* and *Vanguard* are beginning their launch sequence," another officer confirmed.

The admiral watched as all fifty fighter planes took off from the *Trident*'s deck, followed by a squadron of bombers and a few larger aircraft.

"The siege boats full of soldiers are nearly at shore," another officer reported.

"Call to the destroyers," Navari told the officer beside him. "Tell them to start the barrage."

A cascade of attacks began to rain toward the base, as if a thousand flaming arrows were flying through the sky.

"Why aren't they shooting back?" Admiral Navari mumbled.

"Maybe we outrange them," his side officer suggested.

"With the Industry's technology?" The admiral shook his head. "I highly doubt it." He turned to one of the officers in the bay beneath him. "Send probes down into the water."

"Why, sir?" the officer beside him asked.

"I've got a bad feeling that Dr. Griffin knows something we don't," Navari stated.

"Sir!" the officer that had sent the probes called out. "Positive readings!"

"Already?" Navari was shocked. "What is it?"

"I-," The officer paused. "I'm not sure, sir. Our probes' range are reading out at a level surface about eighty feet down. It's like they've hit the bottom of the ocean."

"Impossible," Navari said. "At this distance, the ocean floor would be nearly-"

"Sir!" a different officer shouted. "We have what seems to be a submarine rising from our starboard side!"

Navari stepped down from the small balcony he stood on, walking briskly past the rows of officers and technicians so that he could watch out the side of the bridge's main window.

A column of water blasted up from the surface, a metal spire quickly following behind. Admiral Navari watched in shock as the metal structure continued to rise out of the water, quickly passing the height of the *Trident*'s bridge and still continuing to rise. The tall metal tower was followed by the gigantic deck of a massive battleship. Clan Neo's aircraft carrier, the *Eclipse*, was unfortunate enough to be right underneath the gargantuan ship's deck as it rose up to the surface, causing the entire vessel to be broken in half, its flaming pieces falling down into the depths of the ocean.

"Impossible," Admiral Navari whispered as he looked up at the ship that he had seen sink into the ocean in battle more than a year ago. "The *Leviathan* is still alive."

The officer beside him seemed just as dumbstruck. "That's one heck of a submarine."

"We have an urgent message coming from the *Trident*."

Bi looked up to see Vizler, one of the four members of Troy's elite squad. He was speaking with Troy about a transmission they had just received.

"What does it say?" Troy asked. All of the other soldiers in the submarine turned their attention to Vizler as he relayed the message.

"'*Leviathan* has returned,'" he said. "'*Eclipse* and *Tempest* destroyed, requesting support.'"

All eyes turned to Mr. Z, who sat at the front of the vessel.

"Without the support of our navy, our ground attack could fail, and our forces in the air would be without direction," Mr. Z stated. "We must send aid."

Troy nodded. "I will go."

"The last time our armies fought the *Leviathan*, we lost hundreds of soldiers," Bi said. "The odds of you four taking it out by yourself is very low."

"All these years and you're still trying to protect me?" Troy asked.

"I would say the same for any other soldier," Bi said. "You four are our best, but you stand no chance alone."

"We won't be alone," Vulcan, the third soldier in Troy's elite guard, pointed out. "We still have five boats out there."

"Besides," Troy said. "We should be able to buy the rest of you more time."

Bi was silent as she watched the three soldiers, along with their fourth, Titan, walk toward the back of the submarine, where they were launched upward to the surface.

"Without Troy, our attack will be much more difficult," Mr. Z stated. "Captain Dax, you will take point."

Dax nodded before turning to converse with some of his soldiers. Bi looked around at the group with her in the submarine. Every clan captain except Troy was here, plus Captain Dax's elite squad, the Purifiers of Clan Xion and, of course, Mr. Z himself.

Despite her tactical skills, Bi felt out of place on a vessel with all of the best soldiers in the IPA. She knew that the only reason they wanted her here was as a communicator with Flynn.

As if on cue, Mr. Z turned his attention to her. "Where is the Scorpion Squad?"

"Flynn?" Bi asked through the comms.

"We've arrived at the cliffs," he responded. "Starting our ascent now."

Flynn took deep breaths as he scaled the sheer rock face on the south side of the island. He and the rest of his soldiers had been dropped off of the side of the *Trident* in two submarines, which were now down in the water a hundred feet beneath him, making their way back towards the aircraft carrier.

All one hundred and fifty troops climbed the rocky cliff beside him, using their suits to traverse the difficult climb. The more elite strike team would be running toward the base on foot from the other side of the island but, since they were more detectable, climbing this cliff was not an option considering they would be target practice for any

Enforcement soldiers that would try and shoot down at them. Which left Flynn's group to get inside the hard way, using nothing but the added strength of their suits to climb up the cliff face. This also caused many of the rookies to fall behind early, as the feat proved difficult for them.

"How are you holding up?" Flynn asked Tarff, who climbed beside him.

"I'm alright," he replied. "With my strength, the climb isn't really that difficult. It's the height that bothers me."

"Well, we're nearly there," Flynn encouraged him.

Flynn had already given out the instructions to his unit on the submarine. As soon as they reached the top of the cliff, they would make a beeline for the base, trying to avoid being spotted as best as they could. Once inside, they would use their thermal scanners to search for any living people in the facility. From there they would split into teams, until somebody found Dr. Griffin. Nobody knew what powers the crazed technician had or how heavily guarded he would be, but they had to hope that with surprise on their side, they would be able to take him out.

Either that, or Flynn would get word from Bi that her group, the elite strike team, had taken out Griffin on their side of the base. Whichever came first.

Flynn felt a sense of pride that his sergeant had been chosen to be in the elite strike team, but at the same time, he worried for her. Although she was a tactical genius, and her combat skills were proficient enough for a normal mission, they were hardly on par with the likes of Dax and Troy. Despite this, Flynn knew she was smart enough to be able to keep herself alive, even if she wasn't the best fighter they had.

Before long, Flynn had made it to the top of the cliff. Being the first ones to make it, he and Tarff helped a few soldiers over the edge before they began running toward the base.

At first, the top of the building was visible, but it quickly passed out of view as he entered the treeline. The sounds of war filled the air as he ran. Gunfire and explosions came from the front of the island. A flaming Enforcement helicopter could be seen momentarily as it fell from the sky, crashing somewhere beneath the treetops in the distance.

"Get ready boys," Flynn said over the comms. "They will know we're here soon."

Flynn heard heavy footsteps as the Iron Knight who was completely surrounded in a mech suit lumbered behind him.

"Everyone is past the cliff now, general," one of the soldiers reported over the comms.

"Affirmative." Flynn contacted Bi, "Are you inside yet?"

"We've entered the base," Bi confirmed. "Now that we have drawn the soldiers away, you should be free to start your attack."

The noise of battle got louder as Flynn's army arrived at the south side of the base. As soon as Flynn exited the treeline, he looked up at the roof of the base, where four Enforcement soldiers were stationed. They were quickly shot down by a pack of IPA troops.

Flynn stopped in the middle of the small clearing that stood between the forest and the base, looking at the large metal door that blocked their entry.

"Split," Flynn said. "You mentioned you have a way to get inside?"

"Hammerhead," Split spoke to one of his soldiers. "Go to work."

One of the Iron Knights lumbered out of the forest and charged toward the door. In place of his hands were two giant hammers that he slowly cranked backward as he ran before springing forward the instant before he made contact with the door. The impact threw the soldier onto his back but the door had been completely blasted inward, destroying a few Enforcement robots as it was launched inside.

Flynn turned back to his comms. "Scorpion strike team is inside."

Bi ran as fast as she could toward the Enforcement compound in the distance. She had never considered herself a slow runner, but when running alongside some of the other people in the strike team, she fell behind quickly. Some of the regular soldiers like the Purifiers and Captain Pris were back with her, but Dax and the rest of his giant soldiers were far ahead already.

Once they got close enough to the compound, gunfire from soldiers and artillery on top of the base began to rain down on them, the bullets tearing through the trees.

Captain Pris stopped running, jumping incredibly high into the air before quickly scaling up the viney branches of a tree, sliding into a small perch at the top.

Bi continued to run, seeing Enforcement soldiers collapse out of view as they got shot from hundreds of feet away by Pris.

As the attacks from the top of the base began to diminish, however, the hum of planes began to fill the air. Bi glanced up for a moment to see a squadron of Enforcement planes diving toward them, guns blazing. The gunfire came down like rain, narrowly missing the group around Bi.

The squadron of planes flew back up into the sky before banking back around and going for the group of soldiers that was further ahead. As they dove down again, two of the planes flew too low, entering the range of handheld guns. They had no chance to fly back up as hundreds of bullets ripped them apart.

The attacks from the sky continued still, although now much more cautious. The next phase of defense began on the ground.

Bi was surprised as she caught up with the faster group of soldiers, who were now fighting against a small army of Enforcement soldiers.

"We're nearing the base," Mr. Z announced from the head of the group. "These enemies are all that stand in our way."

Bi drew her two pistols, firing into the trees as more robots appeared in every direction. The Purifiers, who had been running right behind her, detached the massive flamethrowers off of their backs and began to spew flame at the swarm of enemies.

As Bi continued to shoot, her brain began to analyze the robot's attack pattern. Most of them were running straight toward the group of Ironborn, only getting a few shots off before dying. It was like they were only-

"Slowing us down," Bi said over the comms. "That's their goal."

"Gadget, Hardware," Captain Dax commanded in response. "Get to the door and blast it open."

Bi glanced over momentarily to see the two giant men charge toward the facility, passing out of sight through the trees.

The rest of the soldiers continued to fight, but slowly made their way closer to the compound as they did. Another volley of gunfire rained down as the squadron of planes flew overhead. A few moments later, two more were torn out of the sky. With the way the broken pieces of aircraft arced through the sky as they fell to the ground, Bi guessed that they had been shot down by a larger cannon on the water.

"We're receiving word from the *Trident*," Mr. Z said. "One more battleship has been destroyed, but they've sent a second one away from the fight against the *Leviathan* to help overlook the battle on the island. Reports say that siege boats are working efficiently. We have clearance to start our strike into the base."

A burst of extra energy surged through the group as the base came into view. The door was gone, replaced by a jagged hole.

Gadget and Hardware were awaiting them inside, having just set up their enhanced scanner. Now that they were inside, the plan was pretty similar to the Scorpion Squad's. The strike team split into three groups of six. The Purifiers and Captains Neo and Duo were in one. Gadget, Hardware, Crusher, and Blade from Dax's elite squad were in the second team, along with Captains Xion and Pris, who had caught up with them right as they reached the base.

This left Bi in the main strike team, which was supposed to include the elite squad of Clan Troy, along with Annox and Bulsen of Clan Dax, Captain Dax himself, Captain Vilo and, of course, Mr. Z.

The three teams spread out, the first two groups splitting off to the sides of the base as Bi's group went straight toward the center.

"Scorpius," Bi said over comms. "We're inside."

Flynn watched as Zane and Ryan set up an enhanced thermal scanner in the entrance to the base. Flynn had already sent most of the rookies off in their designated groups to go hunt down the heat signatures that their helmet's built-in scanners could find, but now they would be able to get a connected view of the rest of the base.

"Done." Ryan stood up from where he had been kneeling, allowing Zane to operate the machine.

Flynn looked around at the soldiers he had left. Him, Cago, the twins, Blackeye, Tarff and Split, along with twenty of the new soldiers and ten Iron Knights. Whenever a group found Dr. Griffin, this group would go and help them. The hope was that this squad, being the largest, would be the initial one to find him, leaving the least amount of room for failure.

"I've got readings," Zane said. "Nine more lifeforms on this half of the base." He looked up at Flynn. "Five of them are moving together."

Flynn looked at the map that was being transmitted to the inside of his helmet from the machine. "I see them." He turned to the rest of his soldiers. "We will go after the group of five first."

Five of the new soldiers stayed behind to guard the enhanced thermal scanner while the rest of the group moved out.

Flynn led the group down the main hallway that went deep into the base before turning and running up a set of stairs. The inside of the base looked similar to most Enforcement outposts Flynn had seen, except much darker. Typically the passageways in an enemy base would be made with light gray steel, but here at the headquarters, it was all a shiny black. It felt almost like they were surrounded by shadow, a clean, metal house of horrors.

Thanks to the elite squad, Flynn's group had made it nearly halfway to their target before coming across any Enforcement troops. It wasn't until Flynn ran around a corner and his protective suit was pummeled with a barrage of gunfire that the group stopped running.

Flynn got a quick glance at the wall of enemies down the hall before he dove out of sight on the other side of the passage. He looked across the entrance to the hallway, where the rest of his squad stood, awaiting instruction. One of the more eager rookies was unfortunate enough to run out into the line of fire with Flynn. Apparently the enemy decided to target him, because his body lay motionless on the floor, the Enforcement soldiers continuing to shoot at him until they could confirm he was dead.

After the gunfire stopped, the sound of metal footsteps began echoing down the hall as the wall of Enforcement robots sent a few troops to go hunt Flynn down.

"They don't know that the rest of you are here," Flynn said over comms. "Ryan, get all of the heavy weapons soldiers ready. Once these soldiers get here, I can take care of them, but I need you to take out the rest at the end of the hallway while they're focused on me."

Ryan replied with a simple nod as he readied his hand-held gatling gun.

Flynn listened to the footsteps of the robots getting closer, waiting until they neared the corner before jumping out and drawing his hiveblade off of his back.

"Now!" He heard Ryan yell. Five IPA soldiers stepped out from behind the wall, firing their various heavy weapons down the hallway at the group of Enforcement soldiers who had their guns trained on Flynn.

Flynn quickly grabbed his matka, throwing it powerfully at the nearest soldier before leaping toward the next, thrusting his hiveblade through the robot's chest. He then used his powers to pull his mataka back to him, cutting through a third Enforcement soldier in the process. He slashed to the side, cutting down a fourth before turning to the final one, who collapsed to the ground before Flynn could do anything.

With the immediate threat gone, Flynn looked over to Ryan who, having already eliminated the robots at the end of the hall, was pointing his gun at where the fifth enemy had been standing.

"You're welcome," Ryan said as the squad made their way down the passage that was now littered with smoking robot bodies.

Flynn looked at the map on his helmet, which was showing only negative reports coming from all of the squads he had sent out. Each one was represented by a small red X, indicating that the thermal reading had only been a human officer. All they needed was one green mark.

Flynn led the group up another flight of stairs and down another hall, where they were met with an intersection.

"Which way, sir?" Split asked Flynn.

Flynn looked at his map, then at the four passageways around them. Before he could make a decision, however, he felt a bullet hit his helmet, knocking him to the side.

The IPA soldiers returned fire as a squad of Enforcement troops began to run toward them from one of the passageways.

More robots began to come from every direction, even appearing down the hallway Flynn's group had just come from.

"Defenses!" Flynn commanded.

Two of the Iron Knights, along with Tarff, set down the large metal barriers they had been carrying, setting up a small ring of protection.

"We're surrounded," Split said to Flynn. "They must have known we'd be vulnerable here and waited for us to arrive."

Flynn glanced around at the soldiers around him who were firing out through small gaps in the protective wall. Flynn decided to draw his own gun, firing at any soldiers he could while discussing the battle with Split.

"With these barriers in place, our forces should be able to hold a position here-" Flynn fired again, destroying another enemy. "But we need to get a squad of soldiers out somehow."

An Enforcement soldier with a jetpack zoomed down, landing in the center of the IPA's protective ring and drew two swords that crackled with electricity.

Split wasted no time as two long, slightly curved blades quickly appeared in his metal hands as if they had been shot out of his sleeves.

The robot was clearly no match for its opponent as Split easily cut him into pieces, his sword-fighting skills enhanced by both the power of his mechanical hands and their ability to rotate freely, allowing Split's blades to spin like a blender.

Two more jet troopers attempted to fly into the ring but Split jumped into the air, twisting sideways and flipping so his blades cut both of the robots clean in half.

"Only one of these passageways leads to our target," Flynn said over the sound of the hallway.

"Me and two of my Knights can come with you and your squad," Split suggested, his two katanas collapsing back down into the metal part of his forearms. "With our combined forces, we could easily lead a charge down any one of these hallways."

"The question is," Flynn said as he continued to fire at the oncoming robots, "Which one?"

Andrew stood inside the cramped siege boat alongside a hundred other soldiers, taking deep breaths as he watched the small map inside his helmet. He watched as the small glowing icons showed their boat quickly moving away from the aircraft carriers, getting closer to the island. With how fast they were moving, he guessed it would only take another minute for them to arrive at the beach.

"Hey Bolter," Broadside said from beside him.

Andrew turned to address his friend.

"Remember that time we stormed an Enforcement base last summer?" Broadside asked.

"The time when the Purifiers saved our lives?" Andrew asked.

Broadside nodded. "Today those guys are in there." He gestured his head toward the front of the boat, which was pointing in the direction of the island. "Which means we'll be saving them."

Andrew smiled. "How the tables have turned."
"I'm glad the rest of our squad is on a different boat," Broadside said.

"Why?"

"I don't want anyone making any bets on this battle," he replied.

"Oh," Andrew's smile faded. He still tried to lighten the mood. "I'm sure we'll win."

"I don't know," Broadside said. "You heard our briefing. As the ground troops, our only job is to draw out the enemy. If the teams inside fail, their army is much stronger than ours. Without them, we all die."

Andrew thought for a moment. "Their success or failure is not up to us, but we can still help. Once they realize that some of us are inside, their forces will be divided. The stronger we are, the more troops they'll have to send to us."

"Which puts us in even more danger," Broadside pointed out.

It pained Andrew to see his friend who was always so upbeat be so down on himself. "It puts them in more danger," Andrew countered. "With you out there on the battlefield, I'd be much more worried for the sake of our enemies."

Broadside chuckled, patting Andrew on the shoulder. "Thanks."

Looking at his map, Andrew could see that they were nearly at the shore.

"Soldiers," a voice said over the comms in all of their helmets. "Remember, our goal is to draw as many enemies as we can away from the base. Our scouting drones have discovered three watch towers on this side of the island, your new objective is to find one and destroy it. With all three gone, they will have no choice but to send the full force of their army out to us. Be prepared."

Andrew drew his gun, watching as Broadside drew a weapon easily twice the size of his. "We got this," Andrew whispered to himself.

The boat shook violently as it hit the shore, but the soldiers inside stayed steady, their eyes locked on the large door in front of them.

"Door dropping," a voice said over the comms. "Begin siege."

The large metal door at the front of the siege boat dropped, turning into a ramp as the Ironborn warriors ran out of the vehicle, guns blazing as they entered the shallow water.

Andrew looked at the large beach in front of him, that stretched up a few dozen feet before turning into a thick jungle. From where he was standing, he saw the top of two of the outposts they had been instructed to destroy.

With his gun readied, Andrew began to fire into the trees, where a solid wall of metal robots emerged, marching down the beach toward the IPA soldiers.

Looking side to side, Andrew could see that nearly all of the IPA's siege boats had now landed. There had to be at least twenty, each one with around one hundred soldiers. Against the lines of Enforcement robots that were emerging from the trees, they seemed like miniscule numbers, but so far Andrew could only see one dead Ironborn floating in the water, and the first wall of robots was already being diminished.

"Osprey away," a voice said over the comms.

As Andrew continued to shoot at the oncoming waves of enemies, a group of flying Ironborn soared overhead, using their powers of flight along with various other abilities to attack the further back lines of Enforcement.

At the front of the Osprey siege team was a soldier with giant flaming wings like a phoenix that Andrew recognized from stories he had heard as an Ironborn named Havoc. He watched as Havoc shot a column of flame down into the trees, lighting the forest on fire.

Before long, the first groups of soldiers made it onto dry land, where they began running up the beach at a much faster speed. The melee-specialized troops from Clans Dax and Duo ran to the front, some crushing enemies with brute force whilst others came in and out of view, becoming invisible to stealthily take out the robots one by one.

"Launching planes," a voice over the intercom said. A surge of encouragement spread through the troops on the beach. They wouldn't be alone for much longer.

23- Elusive Demise

Cadmore Industries Island
The Atlantic Ocean, U.S.A.
9:00 a.m.
Flynn

As soon as Vulcan made it to the side of the *Leviathan*, he began to climb, using his suit's magnetic abilities to scale the metal hull. His older brother, Captain Troy, climbed beside him. Titan, who was the largest and strongest Ironborn on record, simply grew to his full size, reaching up out of the water and grabbing onto the edge of the massive boat. Vizler, who was by far the smallest of the four soldiers, simply flew out of the water with his powers, readying his gatling gun.

As planned, Vizler, Vulcan and Troy paused right before coming up onto the deck, waiting for Titan to distract the majority of the gunfire. Despite the size of the boat, it tipped as Titan pulled himself up on the deck. The giant Ironborn distracted most of the Enforcement soldiers' attention, but their bullets did nothing to the towering man as he raised his massive warhammer into the air and brought it down on the deck, destroying the boat's main cannon and significantly damaging the hull.

Having gotten their cue, Troy and Vulcan pulled themselves onto the deck, Troy drawing two golden swords and the younger brother drawing one sword and a gun.

They wasted no time, instantly cutting down the nearest dozen soldiers in less than a second. Troy slashed through soldiers as if they were made of mist, his powers causing each and every one to turn to dust on contact. Vulcan's powers were similar, causing every bullet that came near him to vanish into black mist.

"Remember our objective," Troy reminded the group.

Vulcan looked up at the bridge of the *Leviathan*. A boat of this size would need a plethora of human officers, along with a captain. Killing him was their main goal.

As Troy and Vulcan quickly made their way across the deck, Vizler flew up over the edge, giving them support fire from the sky.

The entire boat shook as Titan's hammer pummeled into the hull again. Before he could swing his hammer a third time however, a metal hand burst out of the surface of the water. Considering that Titan had been the one to nearly destroy the *Leviathan* last time, Troy guessed that Cadmore Industries would have found a way to prevent him from doing it again. He was right.

326

A massive version of a juggernaut emerged from the water, tackling Titan off of the side of the ship. The pair of giants fell into the water, disappearing from view.

With the largest threat gone, the boat's cannons turned their attention back to the IPA fleet, and the soldiers on the boat began to focus on the three remaining Ironborn.

As Vulcan and Troy neared the large door at the bottom of the tower, they were met with a full squad of juggernauts. To any regular IPA soldier, this would hardly have been an even fight, but this time the juggernauts would have to fight Ironborn their own size. They were hopelessly outmatched.

Troy leapt toward them, cutting through two before they could even react. The third robot grabbed his forearms, stopping the golden swords when they were mere inches away from turning him into a pile of dust. A second juggernaut tackled him from the side, slamming his body into the deck.

Vulcan targeted the final robot, shooting its head three times as he charged the juggernaut. The large robot managed to hit one shot before Vulcan got to him, but the bullet didn't do any significant damage. Vulcan swung his sword, which got stuck halfway through the robot's abdomen.

The juggernaut punched Vulcan on his right jaw before going for a second jab, which Vulcan caught before kicking the robot in the chest, tearing its left arm from its body. As the juggernaut fell backward, Vulcan pulled his sword back out of its abdomen before quickly swinging again, disconnecting the robot's head from its shoulders.

He then turned to help Troy, but his older brother was in no need of help, as always. He had already destroyed both of his opponents and was now fighting a third that had come from around the corner.

Vizler landed on the deck beside Vulcan, quickly going to work on the door's control panel, decoding every bit of its security and opening the door in seconds.

As soon as the door was open, the three soldiers ran inside. They were met by a short hallway that led to an elevator shaft. Troy pried the elevator doors apart with his bare hands, revealing the expected. The elevator was gone.

The attempt to stop the three soldiers was fruitless, however, as Troy and Vulcan simply shot grappling bolts out of small launchers built into the forearm of their suits. The bolts pierced the top of the elevator shaft and the two soldiers began to slowly rise toward the bridge. Vizler flew past them, getting to the top before disappearing from view.

The buzz of a thousand wings filled the air, and Vulcan looked down to see a giant swarm of bug-like robots flying upward toward them.

Vulcan looked at his brother as if to say, *Is this their idea of a trap?*

Having dealt with threats like this hundreds of times in the past, it took no verbal communication for Vulcan to pull an electric charge from his belt, which he watched fall down the shaft for a few meters before Troy shot it with the pistol from his belt. The electric charge sent out a burst of electricity that traveled quickly through the swarm of closely-packed robots, shaking each one and frying its circuits.

The two brothers kept rising, quickly making it to the top, where the doors had already been blasted open for them by Vizler.

They ran out onto the bridge, which was already littered with dead bodies as Vizler's gun tore through anything that stood in his path.

Ignoring the main group of officers, Vulcan and Troy ran up to the back section of the bridge, where the captain, surrounded by eight guards, was surprisingly still not running away.

Vulcan ignored the guards and shot straight for the captain's head, but right before the bullet hit its target, the captain disappeared, turning into a dark mist and flying past the two soldiers.

Troy chased after the Ironborn captain as Vulcan faced the eight guards. He had only fought against this elite

329

type of Enforcement a few times, yet he didn't hesitate as he charged toward them, attacking with both gun and sword.

The elite guards seemed to be quicker than most of the Industry's robots, as well as more coordinated. One was able to block Vulcan's sword with a blade of its own, allowing the others to attack where he was now defenseless on his right side.

One soldier collapsed to the ground as he shot it with his gun but a second one leapt forward, knocking the gun out of his right hand. The other remaining soldiers tried to shoot at him but, unlike regular robots, quickly gave up after realizing their bullets were simply turning to dust.

Right as Vulcan managed to cut down the enemy that had blocked his initial attack with his sword, the remaining six guards charged together, catching him off-guard. He stabbed his sword through one enemy and bashed a second one into the wall, but the other four now found him an easy target and knocked him to the ground.

One soldier stabbed him with an electric prod, trying to keep him down. Pushing through the pain, Vulcan grabbed the robot, ripping him in half before using the two pieces of its body to bash in the heads of two more enemies. He then kicked the last opponent to the floor before stomping it into the ground, its metal frame crunching.

Vulcan quickly grabbed his weapons before turning back to Troy. The clan captain was standing in the center of the bridge, looking around as the apparition-like form of the captain flew around the room. The Ironborn would stay in mist form for a few seconds before becoming material to fire his gun, after which he would again turn back into a ghost.

Unlike a normal soldier, who would be constantly trying to shoot the ghost captain, Troy simply watched, studying his enemy. Vulcan watched as the ghost appeared, fired, and disappeared again. He moved around the room swiftly, seemingly with no pattern, but Vulcan knew Troy had him figured out. The ghost fired again, before disappearing for the last time. When he paused to reappear again, Troy had already shot him directly in the forehead, the bullet passing through his skull as his body became material. Because of the speed he was moving at before getting shot, his now material body went flying, slamming into one of the metal control panels before crumpling to the ground.

"With their captain dead, they won't have many options," Vizler said to Troy. "What is their next move?"

Before Troy could speak, the hum of an Enforcement bomber flying overhead filled the room. The three soldiers could do nothing as they realized the Industry's plan. Draw in the most powerful soldiers to the same place before taking them all out with one strike.

The bomber overhead dropped its payload, the first explosive causing the ceiling to collapse in, allowing the rest of the attacks to blow the bridge into smithereens.

"Found it," Zane said to Flynn over the sounds of explosions and gunfire. "The fastest way to our target is through the east tunnel." He pointed toward the designated path.

Flynn looked toward one of the Iron Knights. "Ranger, you'll be in charge of holding this position with the rest of the soldiers that we leave here."

Ranger nodded in response before turning back to shoot at the enemy.

Flynn turned back to the group of soldiers that was going with him. Tarff, Blackeye, Emily, Cago, the twins, Split, two Iron Knights, and four of the more experienced recruits.

Split gave the orders to one of his Knights, and they moved two of the metal barriers out of the way, exposing a hallway swarming with robots. The new, smaller strike team stood on either side of the gap inside the barrier, waiting for Flynn's signal.

Matchstick, who was one of the Knights going with them, loaded a missile into the rocket launcher that was part of one of his arms. Flynn motioned his head toward the gap in the barrier.

Matchstick nodded before spinning around the corner of the wall and firing his missile before ducking back out of view. Flynn waited until the missile landed before giving the signal.

"Go!" he said, and the group of soldiers ran out from behind the walls toward the now discombobulated line of Enforcement robots.

Dozer, the Knight whose entire body was surrounded by a mech suit, ran at the front alongside Tarff. The two soldiers crushed everything in their path until the rest of the group made it to the end of the hall, where Zane directed them to turn left.

Groups of Enforcement soldiers tried to follow them from the other three hallways, but the soldiers still defending the center of the hallway shot them down, allowing all fourteen soldiers to make it around the corner without getting shot.

"Target is two stories above us," Zane reported as they ran. "He seems to be going toward the roof."

Flynn felt his instincts heighten. If Dr. Griffin simply left the island, the scanners would no longer be able to locate his DNA signal, and all they would need to do was find the control room to turn off the army. Griffin would have been a fool to run away, and Flynn knew he was no fool. Something else was going on.

"Stay sharp," Flynn said. "He'll be expecting us."

After making it up the next two flights of stairs with little resistance, Zane reported that they were only two hundred feet from their target.

The group rounded another corner, where they were met with the final blockade. Down the hall was a wall of Enforcement soldiers like usual, but directly in front of them was a juggernaut.

Before anyone could react, the juggernaut grabbed one of the recruits and threw him into the wall, his body crumpling into a heap on the floor. Dozer and Tarff tackled the juggernaut to the side as the rest of the group ran past.

Flynn took a deep breath, channeling his focus. He then grabbed his mataka and threw it toward the blockade, sending a wave of energy with it. As the shield tore a robot in half, the wave of energy threw many of the surrounding soldiers into the air and broke a hole in the blockade.

"Cago, Matchstick," Flynn instructed. "You and the recruits stay here. We will go after Griffin."

The five soldiers broke off from the rest of the group, engaging in battle against the remaining enemies from the blockade.

Flynn and the others ran past, not wanting to risk letting Dr. Griffin get away. As they ran around the corner, their target came into view.

A platoon of Enforcement soldiers, four human officers and, in the middle of it all, Dr. Griffin.

Andrew ran into the trees, grateful to finally be off of the sandy beach. He could see his target in the jungle in front of him, the outpost's metal roof poking up through the treetops.

Broadside marched beside him, gunning down twice as many enemies as his smaller comrade. A few stealth robots dropped down from the trees around the two soldiers, so they stood back to back, gunning down the robots that were now coming from every direction.

Three large planes flew overhead, and Andrew felt an extra burst of morale. Out of the two outer planes dropped a few dozen land vehicles like the IPA's Landers and tanks, along with a few of the most powerful infantry units the IPA had including the Anu'manu'taki squad, also known as the giants of Clan Dax.

As the vehicles slowly parachuted down to the ground, the giants simply jumped out of the planes, landing roughly on the forest floor.

It was the middle of the three carrier planes however, that was of the most interest to Andrew. Inside was a brand new addition to the IPA's army, a fully intelligent robotic soldier named Proxy. Apparently the robot was the new leader of the IPA's Ironbots, and could transfer from one machine to another, making him nearly unkillable.

"Any soldiers that are near the center outpost," a voice said over the comms, "Charge it now!"

Andrew and Broadside managed to kill the remaining stealth robots, so they began running again. Dozens of other soldiers ran through the trees beside them, all charging toward the outpost.

A giant metal crate landed in the forest in front of the Ironborn. As Andrew ran past it, he saw that it was full of Ironbots who were quickly joining the fight alongside the rest of the IPA infantry. Dozens of other crates were landing all over the forest, adding greatly to the IPA's forces. Despite this, however, they were still greatly outnumbered, and their biggest threat was about to attack.

The main group of Ironborn was only a few hundred feet from the outpost when the first Stingray fired, its light red plasma ray incinerating a dozen Ironborn at once.

More Stingray blasts began piercing through the forest as the first Ironborn reached the middle outpost. As Andrew and Broadside entered the clearing, a massive battle was taking place. Dozens of Enforcement squads were combating against the IPA's forces in both close and long-ranged combat. Two juggernauts also lumbered through the battlefield, gunning down soldiers.

Two of the flying Ironborn from the Osprey squad attempted to make an attack at the top of the outpost but were both shot down by some of the heavier artillery that sat atop the building. Out in the distance, two more Osprey along with their leader, Havoc, were attacking the line of Stingray tanks, drawing their fire away from the ground troops.

Andrew used both of his pistols to shoot down an enemy robot, but he felt like he was taking more damage than he was giving out. With the two juggernauts in the mix, the IPA soldiers were not gaining any ground.

A group of Ironbots came charging out of the forest, and Andrew couldn't help but watch in awe at their coordination. They ran directly for the juggernaut, two sets of four robots grabbing onto its giant legs as the other five seamlessly made themselves into a tower, holding each other up in a pyramid shape so that the highest soldier was at eye level with the enemy robot.

The juggernaut swung at the highest Ironbot, throwing it to the ground, but one of the other robots leapt forward instead, planting a bomb with exact precision in the exposed mesh of wires near the back of the juggernaut's head.

337

The explosion decapitated the beast of a robot and, to Andrew's surprise, the Ironbots walked up to where he was standing. One of them began speaking to Broadside.

"The other three battalion leaders for this siege group have fallen," the robot stated. "My system says that you are now the highest ranking soldier in this sector, lieutenant."

The speaking Ironbot collapsed as a bullet pierced through its metal skull. A second robot began speaking in its place seamlessly.

"My name is Proxy," he said. "How can I be of assistance?"

The remaining Ironbots made a small protective circle around the two soldiers.

"We should have a Ram arriving soon," Broadside said to Proxy. "We need to clear a path for it to get to the building."

The robot nodded and the Ironbots spread out, attacking the Enforcement soldiers in a direct line, stirring up a divide through the battle. Andrew and Broadside followed close behind as more Ironborn and robotic allies continued to flood in from the forest, clearing a route through the battlefield.

The Ram itself, which was a fast-moving tank that had a thick metal spike on the front, came speeding through into the clearing, heading straight toward the side of the outpost.

The second juggernaut, noticing the oncoming threat, began running toward the Ram. As Andrew looked from the tank to the robot, he realized that the juggernaut would be able to intercept the Ram long before it reached its target. Apparently some of the other Ironborn realized this as well, as they turned all of their attention to the juggernaut.

One Ironborn extended out her hands, and two thick tree roots sprung out of the ground, tripping the large robot. The juggernaut stumbled, falling to the earth. Before it could get up, the Ram ran straight into the juggernaut's side, dragging it across the clearing before crushing its body between the hull of the Ram and the metal wall of the building.

As soon as there was a hole in the wall, the Ironborn poured inside, running around the now dead body of the juggernaut and making their way up the tower. Proxy and the Ironbots ran inside as well, Andrew and Broadside following close behind.

Just before they could get in, two more juggernauts lumbered out of the jungle and began to execute all of the Ironborn that were still outside of the outpost.

"We can't let them get inside, or our forces will die," Broadside instructed the soldiers around him. "We need to hold our ground."

Diamonds flew beside the carrier ship as it dropped down vehicles and troops to the island below. He looked at the other three planes that flew with him, two on either side of the larger vehicle.

"The carrier has dropped all of its cargo," Monk, Diamonds's co-pilot, said to him. "The elite strike team is asking for assistance."

Diamonds turned on his comm so that he was speaking to the other eight pilots in his squad. "Carrier TI-4, you are cleared to go back to the *Trident*. Hornets, come with me."

The large carrier banked to the left, turning around and making its way back to the aircraft carrier as the four Hornet jets made a diamond formation with Diamonds's ship at the front.

Using two of his arms to steer, Diamonds used his other two to flip a couple of switches in his cockpit, switching from the plane's wide-range scanner to the more precise, directional one.

"Target acquired," Diamonds said as the enemy appeared on the scanner. "Two squadrons of Enforcement Shredders."

"I see them," Monk confirmed.

"Hearts, Spades, you bank left," Diamonds instructed. "Clubs, you and I will dive straight."

The two Hornets tilted their wings, arcing around to the left as instructed.

"You ready?" Diamonds asked his co-pilot.

The sound of Monk casually chewing his gum came back in response. "I always am."

Diamonds shook his head. Even in the biggest battle of their lives, Monk was as laid back as ever. "Well, hopefully *they* won't be."

"Closing in," Clubs reported. "We'll be within range in four seconds."

"Affirmative," Diamonds said. "Ready guns."

"Guns standing by," Lindsey, Club's co-pilot reported.

Diamonds took a breath. "Engage."

The two fighter jets tipped downward suddenly, guns blazing as they soared downward toward their enemy.

Luckily, the Enforcement's planes seemed preoccupied with troops on the ground.

Monk, being the gunner co-pilot for the pair of Hornets, shot down three of the ten enemy planes in their first run while Clubs only managed to get one.

Lindsey, who was the tactical co-pilot, continued to relay them information as they banked upward, preparing for another run. "Four Shredders are following us, the other two are turning around for another ground strike."

"Hearts, Spades," Diamonds instructed. "Engage."

The two Hornets finished their left-bound arc, managing to take out two more enemy planes from the side, where they were completely defenseless.

The remaining two planes that were following, however, were now lined up perfectly with the first two Hornets.

"Evasive maneuvers!" Diamonds shouted as gunfire began to zip past the window of his cockpit. He tipped the nose of his jet back while also turning right, leveling his plane out so it was again parallel with the ground.

"They're firing missiles!" Lindsey reported. "Launch flares!"

Diamonds used one of his lower arms to press a button to the left of him, causing flares to spray out of the back of the jet.

"We have a malfunction!" Clubs said in a panicked tone. "Our flares aren't-" The noise was cut off by the sound of an explosion as both Clubs and Lindsey's lines went dead.

Diamonds cursed, flipping his plane around. Instead of waiting for the next strike, he engaged, targeting the Shredder that had shot down Clubs.

The enemy plane, thinking it had a few seconds to restabilize, didn't immediately try to dodge an attack. Diamonds used this as an opportunity to fire a missile.

Enforcement planes had programming that knew how long it took a targeting system to lock on, so Diamonds instead decided to fire it manually. Using his two lower arms to aim the shot, he fired.

The missile aimed true, blasting the Shredder out of the sky.

"Sir," Chatwin, Hearts's tactical co-pilot said. "Three more Shredders coming from the east."

"Hornets, regroup," Diamonds said.

The three jet planes remade their formation without Clubs, banking in a circle before addressing the new group of enemy planes. Diamonds looked down at his radar, where, to his shock, he saw four dots instead of just three. He had forgotten about the last jet from the original squadron.

The Shredder blasted bullets through the top of Spade's jet, killing his gunner co-pilot Mekka.

"Spades, Hearts," Diamonds said. "Take out the newcomers, I'll deal with this one."

Pulling back from the other two Hornets, Diamonds flew up to the same level as the attacking plane, where Monk quickly took it out, its burning pieces falling out of the sky.

"Spades, are you going to be alright?" Diamonds asked.

"I've lost Mekka," he replied. "But I don't think they damaged me enough to- " The right engine of Spades's plane sputtered suddenly before exploding, blowing the plane into pieces.

Luckily Spades had managed to destroy one of the oncoming planes before dying, leaving only two for Diamonds and Hearts.

"The two planes that we left down by the forest are pulling up," Chatwin reported. As he said this, the two planes below them got shot out of the air, taken out by some of the long-ranged cannons on one of the IPA's battleships.

"Not anymore," Monk remarked.

"Only two left, pick your target," Diamonds said. "Let's put them in the dirt."

"I've got one in my sights," Hearts reported.

Diamonds looked down at his radar, locating the other plane. He realized too late that it was already directly behind him.

He cursed as bullets tore through the top of his jet. He pulled away as quickly as he could, but the Shredder stayed close behind.

"Target down," Hearts said.

"I've got one on my tail," Diamonds replied. "Monk, can you get a shot?"

No response came.

"Monk?" Diamonds looked back to see the bloodied body of his best friend slumped against the glass canopy of the backseat.

"They have anti-aircraft locked on us," Chatwin reported.

"I only need a few seconds to lock on," Hearts replied. "I've almost got him."

The three jets chased each other through the sky in a line, weaving through the air like a snake.

"Target locking," Hearts said. "Fi-"

His comm went silent as the anti-aircraft gun from the ground landed a spray of bullets directly through his plane.

Diamonds looked out his window to see the flaming plane plummet toward the ground. "Just me and you," he said shakily, looking at the small green dot on his radar.

Despite his best attempts, Diamonds couldn't get the enemy jet off of his tail. Every time the Shredder had the chance, it would land a few more shots on his plane, and he knew its integrity wouldn't hold up for much longer. Without Monk to return fire back at the enemy, he was doomed.

A loud bang alerted Diamonds that he had lost one of his engines, and he had to fight just to keep his plane in the air. He looked down at his belt, where he had two explosive charges.

Taking a deep breath, Diamonds made sure the plane was level before pulling the lever on the side of his seat, ejecting him from the plane.

Even though he had already been moving at the same speed as the vehicle behind him, he barely managed to magnetically attach himself to the Shredder without getting his arms torn off. Crawling toward the back of the plane, Diamonds used his two lower arms to set the explosives near the engine. He crawled back to the front of the plane.

Enforcement planes had no pilots, as they flew themselves, so the program flying the plane could do nothing as he blew up both engines.

As the Shredder plummeted toward the ground, Diamonds removed his helmet, looking out to the sky one last time as a tear for his fallen brothers rolled down the side of his face.

The jet then crashed into the top of the Enforcement compound, killing the final member of the Black Aces.

The hallway shook as if an explosive had just hit the roof above them as Bi ran deeper into the factory. They had already found multiple human targets on their way through the metal maze of a building, but none of them were Griffin. The base itself was made to be difficult to navigate, as it had long, straight passageways, completely void of any cover from incoming gunfire. Luckily, with Captain Dax and his two elite guards Bulsen and Annox leading the way, gunfire didn't slow them down much.

The group of soldiers burst down another door, which led them into what looked like a testing facility. It was full of computers and control panels, all of which were shut down permanently, just like every other one they had found so far.

Besides finding Dr. Griffin, the strike teams were also supposed to find the control room that could shut down the army once his DNA signature went offline. If Bi could find a working computer, she might be able to locate that room.

Bi watched as Dax shot the human Enforcement officer who was trying to get out from the other side of the room.

"Another negative," Dax said. "Let's keep moving."

As they continued down the hallway that was littered with destroyed Enforcement robots, Bi looked at the small map inside her helmet. More than half of the heat signatures had already been eliminated, all coming back negative. Just as they had initially guessed, Griffin was near the center of the base, where it would take longer to reach him.

The strike team cleared two more rooms before finally entering another testing facility. Unlike the first room, this one had a small observation room on the upper left side, where an Enforcement officer was currently using a computer. Dax shot through the glass observation window, killing the officer.

"There's your computer, sergeant," Dax said. "Let's see what you can do."

Bi quickly climbed the stairs to the observation room. She quickly began scanning through the layout of the base on the computer, lining up the passageways with the less accurate map in her helmet.

"I found it!" she reported. After memorizing the location, she made her way back down to the rest of the group.

"I found the control room," Bi said. "Third floor, hallway 8B, third door on the left. Right near the center of the base."

"Would you look at that," Dax remarked. "You did something useful."

"I found something else too," she said to Mr. Z, ignoring the comment. "Dr. Griffin's chambers. The two rooms are in the same hall."

Dax huffed before exiting the room, the group following close behind as they made their way toward the designated location.

"I can see the rooms on my thermal scanner," Vilo reported as they got closer. "Only one lifeform."

"We have him now," Dax said.

As they sprinted up a flight of stairs and turned a corner, the group was met with an Enforcement blockade. The dozens of robots, even with two juggernauts on their side, stood no chance against Dax's elite.

Bulsen and Annox each fought a juggernaut by themselves as the rest of the group gunned down the regular Enforcement guards defending the end of the passageway.

Bi shot with her dual pistols, her focus as keen as ever as she landed every shot. The enemy soldiers were diminishing slowly, but they fell quickly once Bulsen managed to defeat his juggernaut, which he threw down the hall. The metal giant crashed through the blockade, sending metal pieces flying through the air.

Annox pounded his opponent into the wall as if he was boxing, denting every piece of the juggernaut's armor before drawing his gun and shooting it in the head.

Bi ran past the now scattered blockade, quickly opening the door on her left. She shot the two Enforcement soldiers that awaited her inside first before killing the human officer. Looking around, she could tell that it was the right room.

She walked out into the hallway. "We have our switch. Now we just need to unlock it."

The others gathered near the door directly across the hall from the control room. They hesitated for a moment, not knowing what dangers might await them inside.

Finally Dax decided he wasn't going to be a coward and kicked down the door. It flew inward with a loud crash, revealing a solid white room.

Bi readied her pistols, expecting a fight. But there was no Enforcement to shoot. Just a single old man.

He stood in the middle of the room, leaning on a cane. The room itself looked like the inside of an insane asylum, with white padded walls, and nothing but a sink and a simple white bed. Bi realized that this was where he lived. Only a man so crazy that he wanted to kill his own species would have to lock himself inside of his own asylum.

Dr. Griffin looked unfazed as Dax raised a massive gun toward his head. Dax decided not to waste any time, pulling the trigger before Griffin could even move.

Due to the heavy caliber of Dax's gun and the lack of armor on Dr. Griffin's body, the old man was torn in half, everything above his waist turning into a red stain on the floor as the lower half of his body collapsed to the ground.

Bi took a deep breath, staring at where the man had been standing. They had done it. After years of fighting, after hundreds of soldiers had died, they had finally won.

"Captain Dax has eliminated the target," Bi reported over comms to Flynn's group. "Griffin is dead."

Flynn used his powers to propel himself down the hallway, where he began to cut down the Enforcement guards surrounding the group of officers.

With the help of Split, everyone except for Dr. Griffin was dead in a matter of seconds. The crazed man began to back away but Flynn froze him in place with his powers.

Griffin seemed to struggle for a moment as Split walked up to him, using his blades to chop off both of the doctor's arms at the elbows. The old man's eyes grew wide but his jaw was being held in place, not allowing him to scream.

"Like how that feels?" Split asked venomously.

Blackeye seemed to decide it was best just to kill him as she fired her sniper rifle, hitting Griffin right between the eyes.

"Make sure he's dead," Flynn said as Split stepped back from the body.

Blackeye stepped forward, walking up to the old man's body. She turned back and nodded at Flynn, who breathed a sigh of relief.

He reached over to press a button on his wrist so he could speak to Bi, but her voice came through first.

"Captain Dax has eliminated the target," she said. "Griffin is dead."

Split and Blackeye looked at Flynn, who glanced down at the dead body on the floor.

"Could you repeat that?" Flynn asked shakily.

"Griffin is dead," Bi repeated.

Before Flynn could reply, the dead body of Dr. Griffin exploded, filling the hallway with flame.

24- Griffin

"Scorpius, do you copy?" Bi asked. No response came.

"Comms are down," Vilo said. "The *Trident* isn't responding."

Bi left the asylum room and walked across the hallway to the control room. She worked for a few moments before locating the command switch. She typed in the code to turn it off, but she was confronted with a red message.

Key not eliminated.

"He's still alive," Bi breathed.

"Are you out of your mind?" Dax asked from the doorway. "How on earth could he still be alive?"

The lights in the hallway shut off suddenly, replaced by red emergency lights. The group moved back out into the hall, where the sound of metal footsteps echoed their way.

354

The six soldiers watched as Shark walked around the corner, followed by the other four members of the Blood Squad.

"You didn't think it'd be that easy, did you?" Shark mocked. "If so, then your ignorance has brought you death." The robot drew his sword, pointing it down the hall at the group of soldiers.

The rest of the Blood Squad charged as the Ironborn opened fire. The bullets did very little to the Blood Squad robots.

As the two groups collided, everyone chose their targets. Annox and Bulsen targeted Bull, Mr. Z and Vilo focused on Wolf, and Dax confronted Shark.

Bi first shot toward Hawk, who was still shooting from the end of the hall, but the robot dodged to the side, using his metallic wings to spin out of the way. Bi fired again, but before she could see if the shot landed, she was thrown to the ground by an unseen force.

Bi felt the weight of Fox lighten momentarily and, assuming he was trying to stab her with his knife, she rolled to the side, dodging the attack.

She then stumbled to her feet, trying to listen for footsteps over the sound of the battle. A small scraping sound alerted Bi to Fox lunging toward her, so she sidestepped out of the way before shooting at where she estimated the robot's metal body had landed on the ground.

Bi glanced at the others for only a moment, but managed to see Bull grab Bulsen by the shoulders before pulling the Ironborn's face into its knee. Bulsen collapsed to the ground, dead.

Annox, who had used his powers to turn his body into solid steel, used this as an opportunity to attack from behind, tearing a few pieces off of the robot's back and tackling it to the ground.

Bi dodged to the side again as Fox jumped toward her. She spun, shooting the invisible robot again. It flashed into view for a moment when the bullet struck its body before vanishing again.

When Fox lunged again, Bi used what she had learned from the first two attacks to know his trajectory, allowing her to grab the robot by the neck. She then slammed Fox against the wall, firing at its head after he became visible.

The robot kicked, landing a hit in the center of Bi's chest. She stumbled back, losing sight of him. She looked around, preparing for a different attack this time. Unlike most Enforcement soldiers, the Blood Squad could learn and adapt. Bi felt confident that Fox wouldn't attempt the same fruitless attack four times in a row.

As she listened for any indication as to where the robot was, she was met with silence. She waited, yet no attack came.

Her attention was then suddenly pulled across the hall as Vilo was attacked from behind by an invisible force, knocking her to the ground.

Bi shot at the unseen creature, landing four solid hits before it finally stopped stabbing Vilo.

Fox only managed to get a few feet away before it was crushed by Annox, who accidentally stepped on the robot.

Bi ran over to Vilo, who had many stab wounds in her abdomen, her suit having been already weakened by Wolf, who was now fighting sword against sword with Mr. Z.

"Are you alright?" Bi asked.

Vilo shook her head. "I'm losing blood quickly." She coughed harshly. "Not even my own healing powers are helping much." She pulled the bloodied clan captain's badge off of her uniform, handing it to Bi before speaking her last words. "Lead them well."

Bi grabbed the hand of her captain as Vilo let out her last breath. Bi reverently placed the badge in her utility belt.

Looking up at the battle, it was clear who was winning. Dax and Annox were holding their own, and Mr. Z seemed to be able to fend off Wolf's attacks, his red cape waving as he dodged the robot's moves, expertly predicting each one before it was made.

Despite this, it was a downhill battle. The Ironborn would get worn out eventually, and Hawk was still providing cover fire from the end of the hall.

"To anyone that can hear us," Bi said. "We need help."

Flynn rose unsteadily to his feet, looking around at the damage that the explosion had done. He quickly ran to Emily, grateful to find that, although her helmet was destroyed, she was alright.

Split also stood up, having been far enough away from the blast to survive with minimal injury.

Blackeye, on the other hand, had been right beside the body.

She sat against the wall clutching her chest, surrounded by a puddle of blood. Her helmet had also been shattered by the explosion, exposing a face with soft skin, blonde hair, and two completely white, blind eyes.

Emily ran to her side. "Blackeye!"

358

"I'll be alright," Blackeye replied.

"Are you sure?" Flynn asked.

"Yes," she confirmed. "Although I'm not sure if I can move from this position without causing more blood loss."

"Scorpius," Split interjected. "There is one more lifeform on the map."

Flynn looked at the map inside his helmet to see that Split was right. All of the other lifeforms had come back negative, but now that they were this deep in the base, the final one had appeared.

"Emily," Flynn instructed, kneeling down by her side. "You stay here with Blackeye. Split and I are going to hunt down Griffin."

Emily looked at him, "That's too dangerous."

"Don't worry about me." Flynn replied.

Before Flynn could stand up, Emily grabbed his wrist, pressing a button that caused his helmet to collapse down into his suit. She held his gaze for a moment before pulling him into a kiss. She then pressed the button again, closing his helmet. "Go." She said.

Flynn and Split ran down the hall toward the dot on their map.

"Good idea leaving her." Split remarked, "She wastes too much time."

Flynn regretted having to leave her behind, but someone needed to watch over Blackeye, and bringing her to fight Griffin would put her into even more danger.

As he ran, Flynn tried to dissect what he had just seen. How could Dax have killed Dr. Griffin if he was right there? Could one of them have been a robot? Flynn had no way to know for sure.

The two soldiers quickly found the door that led to their target, which Split opened, leading to the largest room in the entire base.

Giant machines and conveyor belts were stacked from the floor all the way to the ceiling, which looked to be as tall as the compound itself.

"The factory," Flynn said.

"So this is where all of those horrid beasts came from," Split said in disgust.

They made their way through the abandoned factory, which looked like it had been out of use since David Cadmore's death. Without him, making the robots was impossible, even if the factory assembled most of the robots all by itself.

After entering the factory, the thermal scanner in Flynn's helmet suddenly stopped working, but the lifeform hadn't moved since they discovered it, and Flynn still knew precisely where it had been on his map.

As the two soldiers neared their target, Flynn pulled out his gun. A few dull yellow lights still hung from the ceiling, giving the whole room a shadowy atmosphere.

Flynn and Split paused as they were about to reach their enemy, standing behind a large metal shelf. If the map was still correct, Dr. Griffin would be right on the other side.

Spinning around the corner of the shelf, Flynn was greeted by the same eerie face that he had seen a bullet hole in only a few minutes ago.

"Hello Scorpius," Dr. Griffin said.

Flynn pulled the trigger, firing a barrage of bullets into the old man.

Griffin collapsed just as he had before, lying dead on the ground.

"Now that's just mean," Griffin's voice echoed through the factory. Split and Flynn looked around for a moment before seeing him standing on a conveyor belt a few dozen feet above them. Flynn shot at Griffin as well, who fell to the floor with a crunch.

"Wasn't killing me once enough?" Dr. Griffin asked, another form of him appearing across the floor. Split shot him this time, but the voice kept speaking, continuing seamlessly from one body to the next.

"I wonder sometimes if anything is enough for some people," another Griffin said before getting shot down.

"That's the problem with humanity," Griffin continued, reappearing yet again. "They can never have enough." Split shot that one as well.

"The more power they get, the more they want," the doctor said. "They can never have enough."

The floor was slowly beginning to be littered with dead bodies, making the already eerie factory even creepier.

"That is why the Ironborn are such a large threat," Griffin said. "Their thirst for power is stronger than anyone-" He was cut off mid-sentence this time as Split shot him in the jaw.

"-Else in the world," he continued elsewhere. "Sadly, I am the only one who seems to have the willpower to do anything about it."

"You're insane," Split spat, keeping his gun trained on his target but not firing.

"No," Griffin replied. "I'm the only one who isn't. You and all of the other Ironborn are just too blind to see it." Suddenly the lights began to flicker. "And that is why you must die."

The lights flickered again, turning off for only a moment before coming back on, but when they did, the entire factory was full of hundreds of bodies, each one an exact copy of Dr. Griffin.

Flynn shot at the hoard a few times before grabbing his hiveblade off of his back as the beings ran toward him. It was unnatural to see someone so old run so fast, and Flynn was caught off guard as one of the doctors' projections grabbed his hiveblade with surprisingly great strength.

Flynn shoved the man away, cutting him down before doing the same to a dozen other projections. They came from every direction, crawling out of pieces of machinery like rats running toward the scent of food.

Split and Flynn began to become surrounded by rings of corpses as the projections kept charging. They began picking up tools and other loose pieces of metal from around the factory, brandishing them like weapons as they charged toward the two Ironborn.

The sound of metal creaking caused Flynn to look up. He barely had enough time to react as he saw a giant metal pipe falling directly toward him. Using his powers to push the debris to the side, he caused it to land in the crowd of projections.

A loud bang shook the air as a second pipe hit the ground, crushing Split underneath its weight. Flynn was in shock for a moment after seeing his fellow soldier be killed, but he had to recover quickly as the projections kept up their attack relentlessly.

Flynn blocked an attack from a projection with a wrench before using his powers to throw a second one off of his back. A conveyor belt above Flynn's head began to break, and he had to jump out of the way to avoid getting crushed.

Landing on one of the conveyor belts, Flynn began to climb, fighting the projections as he tried to gain higher ground.

Stopping a few levels above the ground, Flynn was able to look around for a few moments as the stream of projections slowed. He stood in the middle of a conveyor belt, knocking off all of the enemies that were coming toward him from every direction.

"Come on, Flynn," he mumbled to himself. "Think outside the box."

As he used his powers to throw a projection through the air, Flynn noticed something. The projection never hit the ground.

After a few moments of using his hiveblade, Flynn tested his theory by throwing another projection. After getting far enough away from Flynn, the being simply vanished.

Piecing things together, Flynn began to understand things from Dr. Griffin's side. If the doctor had the ability to make cloned versions of himself, there must be a limit, otherwise he could've just fought the entire IPA army by himself. That must be why when Flynn threw a projection far enough away from himself, who Dr. Griffin's target, they would disappear, and he would make another one closer to him. He was simply being efficient, getting rid of any unneeded projections that weren't of use to him.

The conveyor belt began to shake and Flynn had no time to react as the piece of machinery fell to the ground.

Flynn had to roll to break his fall, and his hiveblade fumbled out of his grasp. The swarm of projections instantly began to attack, stabbing at him with sharp pieces of metal.

Despite the fact that they were only using physical strength, their sheer numbers began to weaken Flynn's suit. The Ironborn attempted to bash projections aside with his mataka, but he was always exposed from one side or another, and there was no way to escape.

Reaching out with his powers, Flynn made a sphere of energy around himself, using his abilities to hold back the enemies from all sides. He could feel his body aching, his suit only being able to help him so much.

Knowing he couldn't hold this position for much longer, Flynn tried to think, tried to find a way out. Before he could even begin to brainstorm, a familiar pain shot through his chest, emanating from where the Stingray blast had hit him.

The wall of energy dissipated and Flynn was once again swarmed with enemies. As his suit's integrity continued to diminish, Flynn saw the lives of thousands of Ironborn flashing before his eyes.

He saw a squad of soldiers fighting a downhill battle against two juggernauts. He saw a fleet of ships getting blown to pieces by the *Leviathan*. He saw a squadron of planes getting shot out of the sky. He saw Bi and the clan captains slowly getting killed off against the Blood Squad, the new recruits that he was supposed to lead to victory trying to hold off enemies from every side, Cago and the twins trying to stop wave after wave of Enforcement soldiers from getting to the rest of the group. And finally, he saw Emily, who was trying to keep Blackeye alive, praying that Split and Flynn would find a way to end this battle.

His entire species was relying on him, and he could do nothing.

As the swarm continued to pummel him to death, Flynn began to focus less on fighting and more on thinking. A voice rang out in his mind. It was the voice of Bi.

"To truly know your enemy is to gain victory."

As Flynn was curled up on the ground, he racked his mind, trying to think like Dr. Griffin. As he did, an idea came to his mind.

A person who can create projections of himself would only be able to truly die one way. The source. Therefore, Dr. Griffin would naturally want to keep himself more protected.

With the use of his powers, Flynn could sense the bodies of the projections around him, just as he could sense any object when he tried to move it. As his mind scanned the multitude of enemies, Flynn noticed an anomaly in the chaotic pattern. An area where there was a higher density of projections, right near the far wall of the factory.

With the last bit of energy he had left, Flynn desperately pushed the nearest projections away before quickly leaping through the air toward the dense pocket of projections, shredding through them with one final push of motivation.

As he cut down dozens of projections, Flynn found what he was searching for. He saw something in the eyes of one of his enemies, something he hadn't seen in any other. Fear.

Flynn targeted that version of Dr. Griffin, attacking him with his hiveblade. Unlike the projections, the real doctor stumbled backward to dodge the attack.

Flynn lunged toward the doctor, kicking him squarely in the stomach. As the crazed man fell, sliding on the ground before hitting his head against the metal wall, the projections flickered out of existence.

The real Dr. Griffin drew a pistol out from inside his lab coat, firing all six shots at Flynn as the Ironborn slowly walked toward him.

Flynn watched his suit's integrity drop to zero on the last shot. One more bullet, and the doctor might've had a chance. But he didn't know that.

"My death is not the end," Dr. Griffin said. "Humans always need more. Their thirst for power will tear them apart."

"I need to let you know something, doctor," Flynn said, standing above where the lunatic lay helpless on the ground. "We're not humans. We're Ironborn."

With that, he dove his hiveblade downward through the crazed man's stomach, piercing his heart before removing the blood-stained blade.

25- Missing

The Bakery, Sacramento
California, U.S.A.
5:30 p.m.
Flynn

Flynn looked at himself in the mirror, trying to read his own eyes. Watching split die had taken a toll on his mind, just like losing any other friend to the war. Just like Genny's death had.

Thanks to her, most of his wounds had healed, excluding a scar that ran over his left eye and, of course, the scar from the stingray blast. That giant, spider-like scar had nearly killed him in his fight against Griffin and was spreading further, the purple veins now nearly reaching the sides of his chest.

Flynn thought about his friends, who were down stairs right now, preparing to eat dinner. They were finally happy and, although the world was still getting used to it, free. He couldn't tell them about this weakness, especially not Emily. He would take care of himself.

"Hey Flynn!" Cago called up from downstairs. "Bi is here!"

Turning on the faucet, Flynn rinsed his face in the cold water for a moment, taking a deep breath before throwing back on his shirt and heading downstairs. Bi had informed him that she had an announcement regarding the future of their squad, but hadn't let on as to what it was. He was about to find out.

Flynn walked down the stairs and out into the main room of the bakery, where the rest of the group was waiting for him, talking and laughing around the table. Even Blackeye, who had recently come back from the IPA's infirmary, would say the occasional remark, her face now maskless.

As he sat down beside Emily, they all began to eat, enjoying the meal that Tarff had prepared for them, which was amazing, as always.

"You should have seen Zane and Ryan when Blackeye first showed up," Emily remarked to Flynn beneath the noise of the other conversations, "They were practically tripping over each other to try and help her."

Flynn smiled and looked over at the twins, who were deep in conversation with the girl, "I've never seen them so invested in a conversation before." He then turned his attention back to Emily, "Her injuries have improved a lot since two weeks ago."

Emily nodded in agreement as she finished taking a sip from her drink, "When you and Split left me in the hallway, I thought for a second that she wasn't going to make it, but the girl is tough."

"Sorry for leaving you there." Flynn apologized.

"Don't be." She replied, placing a hand on his arm, "You did what was best."

The conversations quieted as Bi stood up at the end of the table.

"I know that you are all curious about the announcement I hinted at before coming here this evening." Bi began, "And I also know that you are all wondering what the future looks like for us."

Everyone seated at the table looked at each other nervously, knowing that this could be their last time together.

"This morning, the IPA sent out a casualty list." Bi continued, "Five hundred soldiers dead. Nearly a third of our organization." Bi took down at the table in a moment of silence before adding, "Along with one Clan Captain. Vilo. She died in my arms during the mission."

Flynn's curiosity grew. "With Vilo gone..." He said.

"I have been personally elected by her to take the mantle." She held up a metal medallion. Excited chatter began but was quickly shut down as Bi held up her hands to quiet them, "Which also means that someone must take my place."

All eyes turned to Flynn.

"Lieutenant?" Bi inquired.

"I would gladly accept the role." Flynn replied.

"Does that mean our group is staying together?" Zane asked.

Bi nodded, gaining a cheer from the entire squad. "Beyond that," Bi said to Zane, "The council was impressed with the skills you displayed during your escape from the Sacramento Enforcement prison, and suggested that you take Flynn's old job as Lieutenant."

Zane's eyes grew wide. "You're kidding."

Bi smiled and shook her head, "Unless Flynn rejects the recommendation."

"It makes the most sense to me." Flynn replied.

Zane turned to his twin brother, who was already glaring.

"Don't even start." Ryan said.

"Now," Bi said, bringing everyone's attention back, "With the fall of Cadmore Industries behind us, this group will need a new objective. The IPA has assigned the Scorpion Squad," She glanced over at Flynn as she said the name, "To be an Insurgent Task Force. The insurgent-hunting squad's have the job of hunting down rogue Ironborn, almost like a policing system to make sure that both our species and humans are safe." Bi pulled out a small letter from her pocket, reading a few lines off of the bottom, "The Scorpion Insurgent Task Force will be stationed at warehouse W7 in Sacramento California and will include the eight following soldiers. Flynn Sterling, sargent, Zane Marrius, lieutenant, Ryan Marrius, Cago Jones, Tarff'Antu'Loga Anu'Manu'Taki, Brooklyn Erickson," Blackeye shied back into her chair slightly, "Emily Sharp, and Proxy."

"Nice to know that they included me as a soldier." Proxy said from the ceiling speakers, causing everyone to jump. "Considering I helped more than most of the other Ironborn in the final fight."

Sometimes Flynn forgot that he had installed the robot into the bakery's computer system.

"Although this is the last meal we will have as a squad," Bi concluded, "I will be watching over you all from

372

my new station in Florida, where I will be researching the continuously growing cases of disappearing Ironborn, as well as all new reports on the Revenant and other larger threats. Our leaders will be working with a group of human ambassadors in a Human-Ironborn combined counsel to create peace and equality for all beings. This freedom would be possible without all of you."

Another cheer went up from around the table as Bi sat down, giving her squad a proud, yet bittersweet smile as they finished their meal.

"Hey," Emily said as the other conversations began, "Remember what I asked you the night before the attack?"

"I do." Flynn replied.

"Well, you promised," She reminded him, "Sounds like you owe me a date."

Flynn pulled his leather jacket out of the closet, pulling it over his shoulders. He looked at his mataka and hiveblade, which hung on his wall, not having been used since the Battle over Cadmore Industries nearly a month ago. Even with the initial danger gone, Flynn still felt like he wanted them close.

The news had been blowing up recently as the world was still shocked from the Industry's fall, and Ironborn had begun to live more freely, using their powers out in the open. Flynn had actually used his own abilities for practical use a lot more recently, which he did again now to make the Lamborghini's keys fly off of his desk and into his hands. The Lamborghini that he had was gifted from Bi after taking her place as Sargent.

He felt the familiar excitement of being around Emily rise up inside of him. Tonight was finally the night that they could be together, uninterrupted, without a war constantly looming over them.

As Flynn exited his room and made his way downstairs, he passed the room that Zane was currently in, filing reports on some insurgent Ironborn and missing Ironborn cases. Ever since his new appointment to Lieutenant, Zane had redoubled his efforts to be helpful, and had also been making phone calls to talk with Blackeye on a regular basis. Blackeye herself had been given Bi's old personal apartment, which is where the two had lived for the few months that they had been removed from the IPA. Flynn didn't think he could ever get used to hearing her speak, but it was nice to finally get to know the face behind the mask.

"Hey Flynn," Cago said as he entered the main room of the bakery. "Do you mind if I spend the night at the warehouse? Me and Tarff wanted to do some training sessions."

"That's fine with me," Flynn replied. "You two can take the truck."

"Alright thanks." Cago replied, "Have fun with Emily."

"I will." Flynn said with a smile. He turned to walk out the door when he heard a voice calling his name.

"Flynn!" Zane said loudly as he came down the stairs.

Flynn turned to face his friend, "Does it need to happen now, Zane? I'm about to leave."

"I know, I know," Zane said as he made his way through the bakery's tables toward the front door, "But we have a problem."

Flynn saw the serious look on his face and paused, "What's wrong."

Zane made it to where Flynn was standing, "I was going through the missing file reports and I found something." He pulled a crumpled piece of paper out of his pocket and shoved it into Flynn's hand.

Flynn unraveled the list of reports and began reading the columns. The names of various Ironborn and their information were listed in rows down the page, nearly twenty new disappearances having been reported just this week. A stab of shock went through him as his eyes reached the bottom of the list. The most recent disappearance, reported only hours ago.

Emily Sharp

Epilogue

Unknown Location
Emily

Emily felt like she had been falling for hours when she finally hit solid ground. Her vision began to become less blurry and she stood up, trying to get a hold on where she was, on what had happened to her, but she couldn't remember anything.

As her vision unblurred, she saw that she was on a mountaintop covered with trees, but as she looked outward, things didn't look right. The world seemed too small and flat, as if there was an end to it only a few miles away.

And even stranger than that, she saw a large variety of different lands, ranging from volcanic lava lakes to frozen oceans to dry deserts.

And weirdest of all was him. A young man stood in front of her. He had dark skin, black hair, and was wearing street clothes and a hoodie.

"You must be new around here," he said. "Welcome to The Rift."

Acknowledgements

This book was honestly so fun to write and edit, which is in large part thanks to the many people that helped me with it along the way. I want to thank my dad and my editor Faith who were my two largest contributors to making this all a reality, along with many friends who read through the manuscript or preordered a copy before it was even published. This book was honestly not even near the level it is now when I first wrote it, and that is because of all of you.

I also want to thank Brandon Mull who really got me into reading and writing with his amazing books and also kindle direct publishing that made this all possible for someone as young as I am.

Most importantly I want to thank you, the reader, for spending your time on this book. I love this series and all of the stories it tells, and I have always been very excited to be able to share it with all of you, whoever you might be. Remember to stand up for what you believe in, no matter what.

-Kyler Wright

ABOUT THE AUTHOR

Kyler Wright is a sixteen year old author who has always loved reading and first started writing books at the age of twelve. He finished Cadmore's List at the age of fourteen and is now on book four of what he plans to make into a five book series.

Kyler lives in central Utah with his two brothers, one sister, father, and pet gecko named Smawg. He has loved this story for a long time and is very excited to share it with all of you.

Flynn and our heroes will return in:

IRONBORN

THE RIFT